*Also by Caroline J Sinclair*

My Music, The Arch-rascals & Me
– The Memoirs of Ludwig van Beethoven

# My Music, My Drinking & Me

## The Memoirs of Jean Sibelius

Caroline J Sinclair

*MAK*Books

Published in Great Britain in 2015 by MAK Books
an imprint of MAK Publishing
www.mak-books.com

A CIP catalogue record for this book
is available from the British Library

ISBN 978 0 9527804 4 1

# Contents

Chapter 1: *Where It All Began*   9

Chapter 2: *To Helsinki*   14

Chapter 3: *Student Days*   20

Chapter 4: *Berlin*   28

Chapter 5: *Aino*   35

Chapter 6: *Marriage*   44

Chapter 7: *Tragedy*   51

Chapter 8: *New Acquaintances*   60

Chapter 9: *Music And Drinking*   68

Chapter 10: *Ainola*   75

Chapter 11: *A Sibelian Symphony*   83

Chapter 12: *A Meeting Of Musical Minds*   90

Chapter 13: *Two Russians And A Frenchman*   98

Chapter 14: *A Financial Crisis*   106

Chapter 15: *More Family Problems*   112

Chapter 16: *Aallottaret*   118

Chapter 17: *The Impossible Fifth*   124

Chapter 18: *Ups And Downs*   131

Chapter 19: *Indecision*   138

Chapter 20: *Pure, Cool Water*   144

Chapter 21: *Aino's Letter*   150

Chapter 22: *No One But A Norseman*   157

Chapter 23: *Isolation*   164

Chapter 24: *A Struggle*   169

Chapter 25: *Santeri*   176

Chapter 26: *War*   183

Chapter 27: *Old Age*   189

Chapter 28: *Cigars And More Cigars*   197

Chapter 29: *Uncertainty*   201

Chapter 30: *Worries*   206

Chapter 31: *An Undesirable Visitor*   210

Chapter 32: *Slowing Down*   215

Chapter 33: *The Twinflower*   224

Chapter 34: *Another Birthday*   229

Chapter 35: *A Long Hot Summer*   233

Postscript   238

Sibelius's music   241

About the author   243

Main sources   243

*Never write a single superfluous note;*
*for one has to live every note.*

– Jean Sibelius

# Acknowledgements

First and foremost, I am indebted to my editor, Dr Mary Harrap, for her encouragement, advice and painstaking editing of this book. Thank you, Mary, for going beyond the call of duty to help me realise my vision.

I would also like to express my appreciation to Captain Kari Niemi for giving me the benefit of his excellent knowledge of Finnish military history.

Unless otherwise stated, all translations from Finnish, Russian and French are my own, but I am indebted to Dr Claudia Wagner for her assistance with translations from German to English.

Grateful thanks, also, to all my friends for their continuing interest and support.

For Kathy
My beautiful and inspirational daughter

*Chapter 1*

# Where It All Began

My father[1] died when I was two years old. I grew up with the idea that he had been a bad man. Whenever my mother[2] spoke about him, it was with a detectable element of disapproval. She complained about how he had spent all his money on drinking, card-playing and buying all sorts of things that he did not need, instead of paying the rent. In addition to that, he had been left with his friends' debts for which he had been guarantor. So, when he died, his estate had to be declared bankrupt, and we had to move across the town to live with my maternal grandmother.

There was always heaviness and oppressiveness in the atmosphere when my mother spoke of the debts – 'over 4,500 marks, two year's wages! That is all that he left us!' She said that she was a parson's daughter, and it was unseemly that she should have had to live with a man of such character.

But I was rather confused; for my father was a respected doctor who helped people and, surely, this made him a good man. It is as if I have a memory of him, a happy one, of me sitting on his knee, and there was a smell of a cigar. However, my mother reiterated time and time again that he was not a man whom I should look up to; consequently, her view of my father became my own, and I began to look down on him as much as she did. My sister, Linda, who was two years older than me, disapproved of him as well, as did my brother, Christian, who was born after my father died.

I cannot remember clearly what happened to us after my father passed away, but I have a vague recollection of us moving around a lot to live at various different addresses in Hämeenlinna, and there was a whole host of other relatives gradually coming into the picture, mostly women. I also remember spending the summers at

---

[1] Christian Gustaf Sibelius (1821-1868), Ph.D, a physician.
[2] Maria Charlotta Sibelius (née Borg) (1841-1897).

my paternal grandmother's house in Loviisa, going in the sauna, swimming for hours in the lake and picking blueberries and mushrooms in the forest. And occasionally, my father's brother Pehr came from Turku to visit us.

Pehr was a stern-looking man, but that was deceptive; he was great fun to be with, and very good with children, so we always looked forward to his visits. I firmly believe that it was he who, through example, influenced the way that I would one day behave with my own children.

When I was seven, I was sent to a Swedish primary school and, around the same time, my Aunt Julia, my mother's sister, began to give me piano lessons. Although I was very keen on music, I did not like the lessons; for I had to play what was asked of me and not what *I* wanted to play. And the school was not to my liking, either. This meant that I was always in trouble for not concentrating during the lessons. Quite often, I would spend my time writing little phrases of music in my exercise books, instead of listening to the teacher. Or I simply sat there making up little tunes in my head.

My teacher was fighting a losing battle with the likes of me, I am afraid; I spoke Swedish and so I could not understand at all why I had to waste my time in school 'learning' it. And I could not see the point in having to learn other boring subjects, either. Music was the only thing that interested me.

However, my mother had other ideas and, when I took home my first school report, she had plenty to say to me about it.

"Janne, you should be thoroughly ashamed of yourself, bringing home a report like this! I sincerely hope that this is not a sign of things to come! What would your father have said about this?"

I wondered why she had brought my father into it, considering how much she despised him, and I thought that if I had explained to my Uncle Pehr about my interest in music, *he* would have understood.

"Well, Janne, what have you got to say for yourself?"

"…"

"Nothing? Listen, Janne, you *must* try harder! You must stop daydreaming and take your lessons seriously if you are to make something of yourself."

It was the same scenario with Aunt Julia, except that she was worse than my mother, if that was possible. It was not that I did not want to learn the piano, it was just that I did not want to learn it *her* way; *her* way was boring, full of all sorts of restrictive exercises, whereas *I* wanted to play proper music.

"Janne," she said, "you will never learn to play the piano properly if you do not do your exercises! Why is it that you always think that you can completely forget what I have said and play whatever you like?"

"…"

"Well? Answer me!"

"The exercises are boring."

"Boring, indeed! Perhaps I have to give you something to remind you that you are not here to do whatever you like!" And she hit me on my knuckles with a knitting needle, which made me even less inclined to do what she wanted.

So, I just sat there and did what I was told. But when the lesson had finished, on the way out, at the door, I shouted, "Boring! And I don't like the piano!" and I ran out.

Not liking the piano was not entirely true, but I said it to rile her. I liked playing the piano, but not learning it, particularly with her. What I really wanted was to learn to play the violin. However, I was stuck with my aunt, and I felt that she was one more woman who did not understand me. Therefore, I took my vengeance by not practising. And I took my vengeance on her one step further; one day, when another of her pupils arrived for his weekly lesson, I gave him the benefit of my advice, such as it was.

Ville was a boy around my own age and, like many Finnish children, his hair was so blond that it was almost white. When he knocked at the door, I went to answer it.

"Huh, it's you. I have heard you play," I said to him. "You are not good. I wouldn't bother … c-c-coming. You, you will never learn to play."

He did not say anything, but gave me the customary Finnish response; he simply stood and stared at me. And, when he had stared at me sufficiently, he turned and walked away.

Of course, his mother contacted my aunt and related Ville's story, and then I was in trouble.

"Janne, what do you think you were doing? Whatever has got into you? I can tell you this: *that* boy will be much more of a musician than you will ever be! *He*, at least, does his homework! It is high time that *you* did that, too!"

Needless to say, I received the usual punishment of a rap on the knuckles – only this time it was a lot harder – and I then decided that my mother and her sister were both horrible and that when I grew up, I would never marry a woman who knitted!

But if Swedish primary school and piano lessons were bad, they were nothing in comparison to the ordeal of having to transfer to a Finnish primary school two years later! This was so that I would learn Finnish and be able to apply for a place in high school that, in Hämeenlinna, was a Finnish one. And I began to wonder, at that stage, how on earth I was going to survive so many years at school and I certainly did my very best to avoid going there. However, my attempts at staying away were largely unsuccessful as my mother could see past my imaginative pretexts.

For instance, I remember one particular winter's morning in my first year at the new school. I was snuggled up in a warm bed and wanted to stay there, but my mother insisted that I got up, with the usual entreaty.

"Janne, get up now! Your porridge is on the table and it will get cold if you do not come quickly!"

I hated cold porridge. So, I was forced to get up, but I was determined to find a good enough reason not to go to school.

"It is really dark outside, mother! An elk might come and get me."

"Nonsense, Janne! Other children are not afraid of elks!"

"A, a bear, then. A bear will attack me! It's not worth the risk of me getting attacked by a bear. Just for the sake of go-going to school. It might come behind me and eat me up! Then, then you would say, 'I should not have forced my son to go to school in the dark. Now *this* has happened to him!'"

"I will say no such thing! There are no bears round here! If there were, we would surely have heard about it by now. Now, come on, eat up your porridge and stop all this nonsense!"

"But, but it's cruelty to children. No children should be sent out in the dark! Especially, when the temperature is at least, at least a *hundred* degrees below freezing. Huh, having to trudge through the snow just to ... get to school. *And* it'll be dark when we're coming home!"

"Well, Janne, children's education in Finland[1] will not cease on account of what the weather is like and whether it is dark or not. Now, do hurry up! See, Linda and Christian are already ready to go!"

"Does the school really need three Sibelius children –"

"I am glad you can count! The school *does* need three Sibelius children, and your first lesson is at 8 o'clock!"

So, the battle was lost for that day, and I was sent off to school with not so much as a kiss goodbye, and I missed my Uncle Pehr.

It goes without saying that my progress at school continued to be very poor, despite the fact that I fell in love with my young teacher, Lucina Hagman[2], and vowed to myself that I would marry her when I grew up! So, it was the same old story with the school reports as before, except that I started to do very well in natural science. That was probably for the reason that it involved collecting flowers and plants during the school summer holiday, which I liked to do. Therefore, I spent hours roaming in the forests and meadows, searching for plants of different forms, colours and textures.

Already, at that age, I was drawn to nature, establishing my life-long love of it; the forests, lakes and meadows, the changes of the four seasons, wind, rain and sunshine, the colours, smells and sounds. I am glad that I learned to appreciate nature; for all my life, it has provided me with so much – a source of wonder, beauty and tranquillity. To me, like to most Finns, Finnish nature is a big part of my identity. That is why I could never have lived anywhere in the world but in Finland; for its nature is so dear to me. It would have been the end of my music if I had ever had to live elsewhere, although I was always aware that there was little chance of me becoming a composer of worldwide renown unless I at least made the effort to travel abroad in order to promote my music.

But, to return to my schooldays, although I was good at natural

---

[1] In Finnish: Suomi. At the time, it was the Grand Duchy of Finland, an autonomous part of the Russian Empire.

[2] Lucina Hagman (1853-1946) became a headmistress and founder of several schools, pioneer of the women's movement and one of the first female Members of Parliament. Among the issues that she campaigned for in the parliament were the right of married women to control their property, women's access to civil service posts, equal pay and the rights of illegitimate children.

sciences, I ended up having to repeat the fifth year – much to the horror of my mother. However, perhaps to bribe me into putting a bit more effort into my schoolwork, she called upon Gustaf Levander to teach me to play the violin. I loved the violin; for, unlike the piano, it could sing. And when Uncle Pehr, who owned several musical instruments, gave me my own violin, I was in seventh heaven.

I immediately started dreaming of becoming a virtuoso who would bring audiences to their feet, but it was just a pipe dream and nothing ever came of it. Nevertheless, I did, later, form a trio with my brother, who played the cello, and my sister, who played the piano, and we worked our way through a vast repertoire of Beethoven, Mozart and Haydn, before turning our attention to music by Mendelssohn and Schubert, and finally finding Tchaikovsky and Grieg. I wrote a fair number of compositions at that time, too, for the three of us to play.

This music-making also spurred me on to take school a little more seriously at that point; I wanted to study music properly at university and I knew that that would be impossible if I did not pass the final school exams. Therefore, I applied myself to studying the subjects that I hated in order to be able to follow my dream.

*Chapter 2*

# To Helsinki

My mother's mind was made up: "I think that we should move and go to live in Helsinki. There will be much better opportunities there. If you are to go and study in Helsinki, we need to find accommodation there. Aunt Evelina is going to come with us and she will do some dressmaking to earn us some extra income. Now, Janne, what do you intend to study?"

I thought it was obvious what I should study, but I knew that my mother would find a way of convincing me that some other subject, other than music, would be more appropriate.

"I know what you are thinking," she continued, "but you really should think of studying something like law or medicine to ensure that you have a *secure* job with a *regular* income. Music will not provide you with that."

"But – er – I am, I am *not* – cut out to be a … doctor. And you – um – *know* what I want to study."

"Well, law, then. That is a respectable profession."

"Er … I will think about it."

"We all love music, Janne, but it is more of a pastime than a profession, you must realise that."

I thought about it, for all of two minutes, and I knew, beyond all doubt, that I did *not* want to be a lawyer, but I had to satisfy my mother somehow or I would never be able to get what *I* wanted.

"I suppose that I could study … law *and* music."

And so it was decided that, in the autumn of 1885, I would enrol to study law at the Imperial[1] and music at the Music Institute[2]. But to me it meant music only; for I had absolutely no intention of wasting my time reading law books, although I did not tell my mother that, of course.

It was when I was at university that I was introduced to alcohol. All through my childhood and teenage years I had learned that alcohol was something horrible and despicable – those who consumed it were despicable people. I would never drink alcohol. I had seen some boys of my age have a drink in the woods, and then slur their speech and fall over. I never wanted to be like them.

But, at the university, when we students got together, often someone brought a bottle of alcohol with them. Naturally, I refused a drink. I also told the others about the perils of drinking, but in vain. However, at the same time, there was a degree of fascination on my part. *That* was the dangerous drink, and my friends drank it. They said that they felt really happy, and I felt an outsider. So, I started to wonder that if they all had it, could it really be that perilous. Perhaps I could just have a little taste, perhaps not; I knew that my mother would be angry if I did.

But the day came when I felt that my mother did not need to

[1] The Imperial Alexander University in Finland, now known as the University of Helsinki.

[2] The Imperial's music faculty. In 1939, it was renamed the Sibelius Academy.

know, and my curiosity got the better of me. I had my first taste of alcohol; it was *viina*[1]. And it tasted foul and burned my mouth, but being part of the group felt good. The next time, we mixed the *viina* with cranberry juice, and the taste was palatable. When I started to feel its effects, I was positively surprised; the feeling of not quite being in control of your movements was exciting, and so was the change in my personality. I was always a bit quiet and had difficulties in finding the right words and expressions, but when under the influence of alcohol, I became much more extrovert and felt that the words were flying out of my mouth. Very soon, I was looking forward to our drinking evenings at somebody's lodgings or in a bar. And eventually, I started to lead the real student life, which meant wild parties that sometimes lasted for days – when vast amounts of alcohol were consumed. For some reason, I suffered a lot less after-effects than some of my fellow students did.

Alcohol made me feel happy. It was not that I was unhappy as such, but I did suffer, intermittently, from a sort of melancholy, which I attributed to a certain self-doubt in my make up. Owing to the fact that I had not been a very bright pupil at school, even my grandmother had often called me 'Slapdash Janne', and those words still echoed in my mind. So I found myself thinking that perhaps I was incapable of doing anything well and that I was destined to be a failure. But now, after a few drinks, I felt that I could accomplish anything.

Mitrofan Vasiliev[2], my tutor for my principle subject, the violin, was a tall, slim, dark-haired man of Russian extraction who had a moustache and whiskers and the darkest eyes that I had ever seen. When I met him for the first time at the institute, I was taken with his kindly face and effusive manner, and I thought that

---

[1] A Finnish clear, non-flavoured spirit made of grain, potatoes or wood cellulose, although nowadays it refers to all spirits. The most famous brands today: Koskenkorva and Finlandia Vodka.

[2] Mitrofan Vasiliev, a Russian violinist. Very little is known about him. It has been suggested that he was born at the end of the 1850s and is said to have studied in St. Petersburg and to have been a member of an imperial string quartet.

he would be an excellent teacher.

He said that he was from Smolensk, but had studied in St. Petersburg, and he told us that his violin was an authentic Stradivarius given to him by a Polish baron. He really was a very lively character with unbounded energy, and I liked him enormously, but I was less enthusiastic about the amount of time that he said I should practise every day, which was four whole hours! It seemed excessive to me.

"You are a genius," he said, "but even a genius must practise! Do you want to be a good violin player? In that case, the only way to accomplish that is to practise, practise, practise! I cannot emphasize that enough. That is the way, and the *only* way. There is *no* other way. Dedication and practise! It is not enough to play *well*; you must strive for *perfection*!"

"But four hours a day –"

"It is very little! How much do you sleep? Eight hours, shall we say?"

"Sometimes more, sometimes less."

"Depending on how much carousing you have done the night before?"

"Well, yes, but –"

"So, if we allow eight hours for sleeping and if we allot four hours for violin practise, that means that you still have twelve more hours in the day for other activities. So you see, four hours practise is actually very little!"

I was impressed by his argument, but I still doubted that I would be able to live up to his expectations.

"You are a talented student, Jean Sibelius, and you must not let your talent go to waste! It must be seized, harnessed and allowed to develop so that you are ready to conquer the world with it!"

Yes, I was now 'Jean' Sibelius; for I had adopted the French version of my name, following the example of a seafaring uncle who had done the same. I was hoping that the new name would make me more sophisticated.

However, I must tell you more about Vasiliev. He was a charming man and, in the course of our lessons, I learned a lot of German; for Vasiliev taught in German. He was obliged to do so as we did not speak Russian, and he did not speak Finnish or Swedish. However, like all people who are forced to speak a language that is not their own, he would occasionally use the odd word in his native language, in his case, things like 'tak', 'nu' and 'syechas'[1] and, when I played particularly well, he would repeat the word 'molodyets'[2] with great enthusiasm and much gesticulating.

Naturally, being Russian, he was very keen on Russian music – as, indeed, was I – and sometimes, when the lesson was over, he would begin to talk about 'the great Tchaikovsky', whose works were to have a significant influence on my own music.

I much preferred Vasiliev to Martin Wegelius[3], the founder of the institute, who was my tutor in music theory and composition. Wegelius was pleasant in his own way, but he was far too pedantic for my liking, and it was 'stick to the rules' all the way with him. A 'methodical approach' was one of his favourite sayings, and he was quite firm in his disapproval of 'flights of fancy' in our compositions, saying that they were inexcusable.

Many of the things that he taught were unnecessary, in my opinion, and, as for his temper, well, it was well known! If you did not stick rigidly to the syllabus, he would get into a terrible rage, and I am sure that his voice could then be heard all the way to Helsinki railway station!

Naturally, I could never have openly disagreed with him, on anything. In Finland, a province of the Tsarist Russian Empire, people had no voice; they had learned that any questioning of authority figures could lead to serious trouble, and it was best just to accept what the authorities decreed. Had I spoken my mind, I would have forfeited my right to study at the university, and who knows what would have happened to me then.

So, when Wegelius spoke about Wagner, as he often did, we students kept our opinions to ourselves and merely nodded politely. However, to my mind, he was obsessed with Wagner, and I did not share his passion. Neither did I agree with his point-blank refusal to have any music by Brahms played at any of the concerts at the institute. I thought that this was rather petty and I have never been impressed by pettiness of any sort. But, at that

---

[1] The Russian words for 'so', 'well' and 'how', respectively.

[2] A word much used by Russians to express approval and praise, meaning 'well done', 'bravo' or 'good man/boy/girl/woman'.

[3] Martin Wegelius (1846-1906), a Finnish composer and musicologist who studied in Leipzig, Vienna and Munich. He wrote some orchestral works and a large number of chamber and vocal works.

time, most music lovers affiliated themselves with either Wagner or Brahms, the two separate camps being extremely antagonistic towards each other, and that was the way things were.

Still, at the end of the first year, I had managed to earn Wegelius's approval – he made a particular mention of my good ear and my excellent sight-reading skills – even though I had only done the minimum amount of work, writing my own compositions, instead. It goes without saying that I did not show them to Wegelius. When I think about it, already at that time, I wanted to go my own way. That is probably why, when I later had pupils of my own to teach, I insisted that they should not be too strongly influenced by me; they should follow their own instincts about composition, and their original and unique voice, as far as that was possible, should be heard.

Armas Järnefelt[1] was a bit scared of Wegelius, as well. I got friendly with Armas in 1887, and we got on so well that we remained lifelong friends after that. He was a student of piano and theory and he, too, was from a Swedish-speaking family.

The two of us often used to get together and discuss topical issues. One, which was raging at the time, was the infernal language strife[2] – albeit we talked in hush tones, lest the walls had ears.

The Fennoman movement[3] was gathering momentum and becoming more and more vociferous in its demands, which, if they had been implemented, would have meant that all the university courses would have been conducted in the Finnish language.

---

[1] Armas Järnefelt (1869-1958), a Finnish composer and conductor, the first to conduct Richard Wagner's operas in Finland.

[2] This conflict was about what status Swedish, the main language of public administration, courts and higher education, and Finnish, that was spoken, at the time, by 85% of the population, would have in cultural, political, educational and other national arenas. Remnants of this conflict still remain in present-day Finland; there is strong resentment to the compulsory learning of Swedish in all Finnish schools, since approximately only 5% of the population are Swedish speakers.

[3] The Fennoman movement aimed to raise the Finnish language and Finnish culture to the position of a national language and culture. A significant proportion of Fennomans actually came from the Swedish-speaking upper classes who learned and promoted the Finnish language and also fennicized their names.

"Er ... to be honest," I said to Armas one day, "I do not want to get in-in-involved with the language question. In my opinion, why, why should either language, or culture, be ... dominant? Over the other. Surely, the two cultures, they should be able to, to exist side by side, um ... without all this arguing about it."

"But we *are* living in Finland," he said, "and I suppose that the Fennomans have a point. Besides, the country has been under the rule of, first, Sweden, and, now, Russia, and people are starting to clamour for *Finnish* identity, and that means having Finnish, instead of Swedish, as the first official language. After all, most people in Finland are Finnish speakers."

"So ... where do *you* stand, then?" I asked Armas.

"Well, in my family, we speak Finnish and Russian. Indeed, my father is a true Fennoman, and my mother is a patron of Finnish culture. Therefore, I am inclined to support the Fennomans."

"But things like this can lead to civil war –"

"God help us, I hope not! That would disastrous for Finland and would not solve anything."

*Chapter 3*

# Student Days

Ferruccio Busoni[1] came to the institute as a piano tutor from Empoli in Tuscany, and his full name was Ferruccio Dante Michelangelo Busoni! His mother was half-German, and so he taught us in German. It was surprising how young he was – he was five months younger than I was! – but he was very worldly, and astonishingly astute and articulate for a man of his age.

In the very first tutorial, Busoni made clear to us his three main aesthetic beliefs: essence, oneness and what he called 'Klassizitat'.

"By essence, I mean music that is free from prescriptive labels.

---

[1] Ferruccio Dante Michelangelo Benvenuto Busoni (1866-1924), an Italian composer, pianist, editor and writer. He was also a piano and composition teacher, and a conductor.

By oneness, I mean music that is free of prescriptive devices, and by Klassizitat, I mean the mastery and the sifting of all the gains of previous experiments in music and their inclusion in strong and beautiful forms. Music should distil the essence of the music of the past to make something new."

This exposition of his ideas made an immediate impression on me. Even though I did not fully understand it, looking back, I believe that what he said was to have a considerable influence on my compositional methods.

It was probably owing to his age that we began to meet up socially, and I really enjoyed his company. He was gay and full of life, whereas Finns tended to be quite reticent and stiff and behave with the utmost correctness, as if they were in fear of some kind of reprisal for bad behaviour – but such was life under a Tsarist regime.

Anyhow, feeling a bit isolated in the 'backwater', which was how Busoni described Helsinki, he formed a social circle of his own – made up of students – and Armas and I were part of it, along with Adolf Paul[1] and Armas's brother Eero[2]. Busoni had a huge dog – that looked like a St. Bernard – called Lesko, and so he came up with the idea of calling our little clique 'The Leskovites', after his dog.

Our parties were extremely lively affairs; for Busoni's sharp wit and lively repartee were infective. I have to say that we had an enormous amount of fun, especially when we had had a few drinks – as we often did. Busoni used to say that he was astonished by the fact that we had no student orchestra, but what could one expect, he said, when Helsinki was 'so lagging behind other nations in terms of its musical development'.

One evening, he was telling us about how he had studied in Leipzig with Carl Reinecke, who himself was a former pupil of both Felix Mendelssohn and Robert Schumann.

"It is my opinion that Schumann was not much of a composer. It is a blessing that he was confined to a lunatic asylum when he

---

[1] Adolf Paul (1863-1943), a Swedish writer of novels and plays. His work was highly controversial, the critics of the time considering some of his novels as obscene because of their violent and sexual content.

[2] Erik (Eero) Nikolai Järnefelt (1863-1937), a Finnish realist painter. His most famous painting is *The Wage Slaves*, portraying malnourished country folk burning brushwood.

was, so that he did not assault the world any longer with such works as *Carnaval*! That was appalling, to say the least! He was clearly on a par with Schubert, who was also an amateur, albeit a slightly more gifted one!"

"So ... who *is*, in your opinion, a, a great composer?" I asked.

"Oh, Mendelssohn! Mendelssohn was an even greater child prodigy than Mozart, although few people realize it. Imagine, he wrote the overture to *A Midsummer Night's Dream* when he was only seventeen years old! That was pure *genius*! Anyone who can write a piece of *that* quality at *that* age is a genius!"

"Ah, well, in that case, it is, it is too late for *me* to become a genius!"

"Oh no, Jean, you undoubtedly have the makings of a genius! And I would not say so if I did not mean it! Play something for us!"

"I do not know –"

"Something of your own. Yes, one of your own compositions!"

"Well – I – perhaps – a little something that ... I wrote recently."

I watched Busoni out of the corner of my eye as I played the piece and I saw his grey eyes light up. When I had finished, he threw his hands into the air, saying: "Wonderful, wonderful! I think it is *you* who can teach *me* a thing or two! Such feeling, such originality!"

Such effusive praise I had never received from anybody, and I wondered whether it was the drink making him prone to exaggeration or whether he really did see something in my music.

"So ... you, you think that it is ... good?" I asked him.

"But of course! Piano technique is one thing, but true creativity and talent – that is quite another thing! Yes, quite another thing!"

"Here, here!" My friends seemed to agree with him.

"Perhaps, you could play now. And show us how a maestro plays." I said, attempting to hide my embarrassment.

"All right," he said, wrapping the tails of his coat around him, "I shall play you a piece by the great Liszt. I met him, you know, in Vienna, when I was very young. He was the most *amazing* pianist I had ever seen! So charismatic and energetic! And the way his fingers went over the keys – it was pure poetry! I wish that you could have witnessed it! Oh, what a showman he was, but he could play like the devil! And I met Brahms, too!"

"He who is not to be heard!" said Armas.

Busoni was puzzled. "Not to be heard? What do you mean?"

"Wegelius does not care for Brahms and he will not even allow his music to be played at the institute."

"But why ever not?"

"To him, Wagner is God, and so Brahms has been given the boot!"

"Then *he* should be given the other boot!"

Busoni was playing while this conversation was going on, but it did not seem to distract him, and neither did his hair, which he had to push back now and again with his left hand.

"This was a lesser known piece by Liszt, but by no means inferior to the more popular pieces. Take note, it is always worth exploring a composer's lesser-known pieces; for there are many gems to be found! Now, I will play you something of my own, and then we shall have another glass of wine."

Busoni played with such verve and passion that we were entranced. If Liszt played with flair, so did Busoni, and I felt a degree of envy; I knew that I would never reach his level of competence. On the other hand, did I need to? What I really wanted to do was to compose, and I did not like to be in front of people anyway, so others could just as well be the performers of my music.

When Busoni had finished playing, he said: "Let us toast the great Liszt!"

This we did, many times over, and it is fair to say that we all became quite drunk, whereupon the conversation drifted from music to girls.

"There is quite a pretty girl in Vilnius's violin group," said Armas.

"And how would *you* know?" said Eero.

"I have seen her!"

"What does she look like, then?"

"Dark hair, plaited on the top of her head. Dark eyebrows. Her clothes are too dark, though."

"Have you noticed her, Jean?"

"Er, no."

There were quite a few girls at the institute, but I had not approached any of them in a romantic sense for the simple reason that none of them appealed to me, in that way. Besides, I was too concerned at that time with solving the dilemma of whether I had what it took to be a composer, or whether I should just throw it all in and live the life of an idiot – for which I had ample credentials. It was still hard to get rid of the idea that I was a good-for-nothing dreamer, despite the praise heaped on me by Vasiliev and Busoni.

Nevertheless, I continued composing and finished quite a number of pieces for the piano and violin, but I did not know whether they had any particular merit. However, Herman Csillag, who by that time had taken over Vasiliev's post as violin tutor, said that I had 'a gift for melody', and Busoni so enthused over a Suite for string trio that I began to think that perhaps I might have a future as a composer.

Indeed, in 1889, I saw my first work in print: the song *Serenad,* which was a poem by Runeberg[1] whom I had, in fact, met when I was a young boy. *Serenad* appeared in a collection of Finnish songs, and this gave me a taste of what it would be like to be a real composer. And when Kajanus[2] had been heard to remark that there was little point in anyone else composing anything now that I had made my mark (!), I started to feel that perhaps I had found my vocation.

"Mother likes to meet budding musicians, and we have talked about you so often that she said that it was time to invite you to visit. She wants see you in the flesh," said Armas.

Thus began my acquaintance with the Järnefelt household, which was to yield much more than admiration for my music,

---

[1] Johan Ludvig Runeberg (1804-1877), the national poet of Finland and Sibelius's own personal favourite. He wrote, in Swedish, poems about Finnish rural life. His most famous work is *Fänrik Ståls sägner* ('The Tales of Ensign Stål*, in Finnish: *Vänrikki Stoolin tarinat*) about the Finnish War of 1808-9, emphasising the common humanity of all soldiers in the conflict, but lauding the heroism of the Finns.

[2] Robert Kajanus (1856-1933), a Finnish conductor and composer who championed Finnish national music. In 1882, he founded the first permanent orchestra in Finland, the orchestra of the Helsinki Philharmonic Society (now known as the Helsinki Philharmonic Orchestra).

although I did not know it then.

My first visit to the Järnefelts made me feel a little nervous as I had not had many dealings with other people's parents and I did not know quite what to expect. I was also wary on account of the Järnefelts' position in society; from what Armas and Eero had told me, their father was Lieutenant-General August Aleksander Järnefelt and their mother, Elisabeth, was from a noble family in St. Petersburg.

Nevertheless, despite my reservations, I tidied myself up, bought some flowers to take for Mrs Järnefelt – as is the custom when visiting – and hoped that I would make a favourable impression.

After I had been introduced to the Järnefelts, Mrs Järnefelt offered me coffee and *pulla*[1], which I accepted politely. However, I detected an element of reserve on their part that made me feel slightly uneasy. And, besides, I had got used to the relaxed and informal gatherings with my friends at Busoni's.

It did not help that Mrs Järnefelt asked me about my law studies; she had broached a subject that I was not keen to discuss. I surmised that Armas must have mentioned that I had enrolled to study law, as well as music, and so she had decided to question me about it.

"I am – afraid that – er – I gave up my law studies. At the end of the first year," I told her, somewhat ashamedly.

She raised her eyebrows. "And why was that, pray?"

"I do not – want to – be a lawyer."

Lieutenant-General Järnefelt looked at me intently and muttered, "Hmm, not a lawyer …"

I felt very embarrassed and I looked at Armas, hoping that he would rescue me.

He took the hint. "You know, Jean is something of a composer already! Ask him to play you something. Actually, play them a section from the Suite in A minor!"

He then addressed his mother, saying, "Busoni, our piano tutor, said that it was an astonishing piece for a student to have written, and he was right! It is for a string trio, but Jean can play some of it to you on the piano."

---

[1] A mildly sweet Finnish bun or dessert bread, flavoured with crushed cardamom or cinnamon.

I was grateful to Armas for steering the conversation away from my futile law studies, but I wondered whether my piano playing was enough to redeem myself in the eyes of his parents.

"There may be – some wrong – notes," I said, "but I shall try …"

Fortunately, I played faultlessly, and Mrs Järnefelt, at least, seemed delighted.

"Your piano tutor", she said, "was right. You are a very talented young man!"

The afternoon progressed quite smoothly after that, but I was still worried about what sort of impression I had made. However, the next time I saw Armas after the visit, he assured me that his mother had liked me very much.

"What! In spite of me, um … failing to do my law exam?"

"She thought that the whole thing was very amusing! Besides, law does not interest her; she is far too tied up in the arts to be bothered about that!"

"Ah, well, that *is* a relief! At least, she … seemed to like my music."

"Indeed, she did, very much. And my father thought you were absolutely charming!"

"Really? Then I suppose – I mean – does it – mean that I will be invited again?"

"You are already invited!"

And so, as time went on, my visits to the Järnefelts became ever more frequent, and I discovered that Mrs Järnefelt was actually quite jolly when I got to know her better. She confided to me that she was a close friend of Juhani Aho[1], who was a budding writer at the time, and that she was endeavouring to help him find a style of writing that would be his own. And I, being all of twenty-two, was in awe of this, since I knew nothing about writing books and, indeed, was not that good at linguistic expression, to say the least.

That is true even today. I think that there are expressive

---

[1] Juhani Aho (born Johannes Brofeldt) (1861-1921), a journalist and writer of novels and short stories who moved from realism to neoromanticism. He was one of the founders of the Finnish language *Päivälehti,* the predecessor of the biggest subscription newspaper in Finland and the Nordic countries today – *Helsingin Sanomat ('The Helsinki News').* It has been suggested that his relationship with Mrs Jarnefelt was not purely platonic.

limitations in all language systems and I have found language particularly difficult as a means of expressing myself. As a child, I did not concern myself with how I expressed myself but, when I grew up, I became concerned that what I said might be misinterpreted or would sound silly. If I have to, I can write something, provided I have time to work on it and revise it and get it right, but I find speaking very difficult. And people have commented that, although my music is fluent and flowing, they are surprised by how hesitant my speech is. But I never seem to be able to find the right words; none of them seem to convey the meaning of what I want to say. I dread having to speak in public, so I suppose that I let my music speak for me.

But even musical language has not allowed me to express adequately my own visions of things in all their nuances. Sometimes, when I have been composing, I have found myself thinking that if only the score could be realized in a different way – not as notes on paper – but how else could it have been written?

However, as I was saying, I visited the Järnefelts regularly, sometimes accompanied by my brother Christian and, on one occasion, the ladies of the house even staged a little pantomime to the accompaniment of Armas and me on the piano. I say 'ladies of the house'; for Armas and Eero had two sisters, Elli and Aino.

Aino was the prettiest girl that I had ever seen in my entire life, and I fell in love with her instantly. I knew from the very first moment that I laid eyes on her that she was the girl that I would like to marry. She was pretty, yes, pretty, with dark hair in a long plait, and such a sweet face.

I remember, I was playing the piano and then stopped – I had played a wrong note. I looked up and caught Aino looking at me, but she immediately turned her head away. I thought to myself, I would kiss you now but, if I did, I most probably would not ever see you again!

I think that Armas and Eero realized quite quickly that I had feelings for Aino. Our friendship continued as before, but I noticed, from certain remarks that they made, that they were not going to encourage me to court her. On the contrary, protective of their younger sister, they said that she was too young for suitors and not interested in them.

"Aino is our father's favourite," emphasised Armas, "and he wants to keep her at home."

So, being unsure of myself and not wanting to spoil my friendship with Armas and Eero, I made excuses not to visit the Järnefelts for a while and I pursued another girl. However, I could not get Aino out of my mind.

*Chapter 4*

# Berlin

When I graduated from the institute in 1889, Busoni and Wegelius each had their own ideas about my future. Busoni was of the opinion that I should study in Russia under Rimsky-Korsakov, whereas Wegelius insisted that I should go to Berlin.

I was obliged to follow my tutors' recommendations but, as they could not agree on what the next step for me should be, I left them to their wrangling and, in the meantime, I composed two pieces of music – one for strings and the other for cello and piano.

Eventually, it was Wegelius who got his way – he was, after all, the director of the Institute – and, in September 1889, I set sail for Berlin, having secured a scholarship of 2,000 Finnish marks.

The money was most welcome; for my financial situation at this time was far from good. Indeed, I had begged for money from my relatives on more than one occasion. And when I had turned to my mother, she had lost no time in telling me that I was exactly like my father; he had 'squandered' his money, too, and he had had to borrow money for his graduation fees, which she hoped would not prove to be the case with me. Then she had lectured me, long and hard, on the perils of drink and warned me that I would always be in debt if I became a drunkard, like my father.

I had mixed feelings about leaving Finland. On the one hand, I was curious and excited about what was awaiting me in Berlin but, on the other hand, I felt extremely downhearted; for I was leaving Aino behind and I had not even had the courage to tell her how I felt about her.

Part of me said that I was not a suitable husband for her in any case. I was not from an aristocratic family, and so her parents were unlikely to consent to their daughter becoming my wife, however much they liked me. However, another part of me was angry for being such a coward.

It did not help that Eero and Juhani Aho were travelling with me; I could hardly talk to them, especially Juhani, about my reluctance to be parted from Aino. I was particularly disturbed by Juhani's presence on board. I suspected that he was a rival for Aino's affections – the way he looked at her had not escaped my notice – and, what is more, I thought that he had a better chance with her than I did since he was her mother's protégée.

In the circumstances, I would have preferred to travel alone. However, Eero and Juhani were going to Paris and they had decided that it would be a good idea for us all to travel together on the same ship. Eero was going to continue his art studies at the Academie Julian, while Juhani was intending to write a novella set in Paris, having obtained a Finnish government bursary to do so.

Unfortunately, on the day we set sail, Aino was standing on the dockside with her parents, and I did not know what to do, so I pretended that I had not noticed her.

I had noticed her, however, and she appeared to be very upset, but I told myself that she wept for she would not see her brother for a long time. I did hope, though, that her sadness had, in part, something to do with me.

From the moment that I arrived in Berlin, I realized that I had stepped into a completely different world, and it was only then that I understood why Busoni had described Helsinki as 'a backwater'. It was, quite literally, as if I had come from a wilderness to civilisation.

On my very first evening in the German capital, I was taken to the Kroll opera by Werner Söderhjelm[1], who had come to meet me when I arrived. Wegelius had requested Söderhjelm to keep an eye on me whilst I was in Berlin, and he very kindly took me to

---

[1] Werner Söderhjelm (1859-1931), a Swedish-Finnish diplomat, translator and literary historian.

see a magnificent performance of Mozart's *Don Giovanni* with the Portuguese baritone, Francisco d'Andrade in the title role. What a way to be introduced to the cultural life of Germany!

My teacher in Berlin was Albert Becker[1], a professor of counterpoint at the Akademie der Kunste, where we had our lessons. Becker, I thought, had the air of a composer of days gone by. He was a kindly looking man with a long beard and spectacles, albeit his kind face hid a personality that was made of steel.

He was a man who spoke his mind: "You have wasted your time with Wegelius, but we will soon put that right! What you need is a thorough grounding in counterpoint and the technical niceties of composition! Let us be clear, from the very start, that you cannot expect to be a good composer unless you have a thorough grasp of the fundamental elements of composition!"

I was never interested in the formal approach to composition, but, as I was to learn, this was what he demanded. However, it did not in any way change my way of thinking; I still thought that it was boring not to be able to do anything else but study counterpoint.

Another thing that annoyed me was his constant criticism. One day, for example, I showed him a piece of music that I thought was quite creative, but I could see that he was in total shock.

"But you have used alternating major and minor forms in the same triad!" he shouted. "And, as for the second theme of the finale, that is the work of an amateur!"

I thought that Becker was a real wig from head to foot – and I wrote to Wegelius to tell him so. However, Wegelius lost no time in writing back to me to say that the composer of the magnificent Mass in B minor was no such thing, and that I should take seriously what he had to say.

And then Becker introduced a new obsession – fugues. These I found as boring as studying counterpoint. At the same time, Wegelius was expecting me to send him some music to illustrate to him what I had learned under Becker. So, I had to write and tell him that I had nothing to send him; for everything else was forbidden, except the study of Bach's fugues and motets.

Just before Christmas, Wegelius came to Berlin to visit me, but

---

[1] Albert Ernst Anton Becker (1834-1899), a German composer and conductor of the Romantic period.

not before calling on Becker first. When he entered my apartment, I was sitting on my bed with a glass of wine, not expecting anything good to come out of his visit.

"So, how is Jean?"

"Er ... thank you for asking, but, um ... do you need to ask? I am sure that Becker has told you what, what a hopeless case I am."

"Is that what you think?"

"Yes! Is it not obvious?"

"In fact, he has told me that you are a charming young man and decidedly very gifted."

"Indeed? But he has done nothing but cri-cri-criticize me – from the moment that I arrived here."

"You cannot expect constant praise from the likes of a man like him! And you are here to learn, which, by necessity, will involve criticism if you are to learn well."

"But ... I am not sure that I should be here –"

"Nonsense! And that drink will not help you any!"

"Er ... well ..."

"But you must understand that all this hard work will be worth it in the end. And, besides, surely you are left with some spare time to enjoy all that Berlin can offer."

"Well, I have managed to go to a few concerts. I went to hear Dvořák's symphony in D minor."

"Wonderful!"

"And I heard Beethoven's *Eroica*. And, before that, *The Ruins of Athens. And* the Ninth."

"Even more wonderful! You see, had you been in Helsinki, you would not have had such delights!"

"No ... no, I would not. In fact, I, um ... made notes in my book at the Beethoven concerts."

"Excellent, excellent!"

"And I went to see Wagner's *Tannhäuser*. It was very ... powerful!"

"Ah, you have finally been privileged to enjoy the wonder that is Wagner! It is a pity that I did not see it myself. I should like to have done so."

"I saw *The Master Singers*, as well."

"Another magnificent masterpiece! You are spoiled here in Berlin, Jean. You are spoiled. Such wonderful opportunities!"

"Yes … but I am homesick."

"Of course, you are! That is to be expected. But you will overcome it and, after all, this year will see you in good stead for the future. Becker is an excellent teacher, and you will not have such a wonderful opportunity again, so you must make the most of your studies. But let us go out somewhere to eat, and you can tell me everything about what you have been doing here for the past few months."

Wegelius did his best to encourage me and asked me to send him any new compositions, but, after he had left Berlin, I still felt extremely downhearted, not only about my studies, but about my entire situation. In Finland, at least, people had praised my talent, such as it was, but here I felt like a good-for-nothing. Furthermore, my confidence was eroded even further by Richard Strauss. I went to a performance of his tone poem *Don Juan* and, after it was over, I left the concert hall in very low spirits – Strauss was only a year and a half older than me, but he was already writing astonishing music and conducting it with such aplomb and confidence. That was something that I would never be capable of.

And so, I took refuge in drink. Indeed, there was no shortage of drinking places in Berlin, and they and I became very well acquainted. I frequented them with some friends – musicians – that I had made since my arrival in Germany, who were from Norway and Denmark, and we consoled ourselves in our homesickness by talking of all the things that we missed from our respective countries. Our favourite haunt, as I recall, was the Augustinerbrau on the Berlinerstrasse, where we spent many a riotous evening.

I felt better after a few drinks and, in a state of intoxication, I even thought that I might still have it in me to write decent music but, when the effects of the drink wore off, I went back to feeling sorry for myself, not to mention wondering how I would survive financially.

Söderhjelm took it upon himself to reprimand me on more than one occasion, and this was one of them: "The way you are living, it will get you nowhere! Wegelius would not be at all happy if he knew!"

"Money is mere trash!" I told him, with all the petulance of youth. I did not need him telling me what to do or how to live.

Nevertheless, I wondered how I was going to survive; for if I continued spending at the present rate, I would soon be destitute. Hence, reluctantly, I wrote home, begging for money.

Christian did send me a few hundred Finnish marks that he said had been raised by selling personal family items, but he warned me that I was living quite beyond my means, and that they could not afford to send me money indefinitely. He also reminded me that he knew how much my lessons with Becker cost per month, and insisted that I should have been able to live quite adequately on what was left over from my scholarship money. Furthermore, he commented on the fact that other students managed to live on far less than the amount that I had.

His admonitions only served to demoralize me even further, and I continued to drown my sorrows in drink. But then Busoni arrived in Berlin, and that lifted my spirits.

"I am going to Leipzig with Adolf Paul! He is coming to Berlin to meet me," he told me excitedly. "*You* should come with us!"

I might have preferred it if there had been just the two of us, Busoni and me, but I had no choice in the matter.

"Er ... I must admit that it would be good to ... get away from Berlin – even, even for a short while. You see, sometimes, I feel so down-hearted."

"You absolutely *must* come with us; I am going to play Sinding[1]'s Piano Quintet in E minor with the Brodsky Quartet!"

"All right! And that calls for a new top hat!"

Leipzig turned out to be just what I needed; we all dressed up and went out every evening and had a riotous time. And, indeed, I put my new top hat to good use. However, I wore it in rainy weather, so, by the time I returned to Berlin, it was no good to me, and I gave it to a carriage driver.

Two months later, I saw Adolf again. I was standing on Potsdamerstrasse, looking at some concert posters – I remember that I was wearing a new chequered suit – and he suddenly appeared out of nowhere.

"Ah, so you have not died of dysentery, then?" I said to him. "What a disappointment!"

"Hah! Nice to see you, too!"

"But, now that you are here, I will give you the pleasure of, of

---

[1] Christian August Sinding (1856-1941), a Norwegian composer known for his lyrical works for piano. He is often compared to Edvard Grieg and regarded as his successor.

hearing what I have written of my ... new piano quintet!"

For want of any better company, I was prepared to make merry even with Adolf, so we bought a bottle of wine and went to my apartment.

"Here, pour us both a drink," I said, "and have a cigar!"

I lit one myself, sat down at the piano and started to play, but then something seemed to stop me.

Adolf looked puzzled.

"*Perkele*[1]! It is ... hopeless," I said. "I will never be able to finish this!"

"But you are the most talented one amongst us. Of course, you can finish it!"

I was surprised that Adolf saw me as talented and I instantly regretted my sarcastic way of greeting him on Potsdamerstrasse. He had clearly noticed that I was downhearted, and his encouragement was sincere. He was, I decided, worthy of my friendship, and I ought to be kinder towards him in the future.

"Well ... perhaps, if you think so. I might try to complete it."

"That is more like it! You need to be more determined."

"Mmm ... you are right. Thank you, Adolf. W-without your encouragement, I would have, er ... given up."

So, thanks to him, I did finish the Quintet and I sent it to Wegelius, but I doubted whether he would regard it very favourably, especially as I myself thought that it was rubbish.

I was quite correct in my prediction – Wegelius was not very impressed and he especially did not like the fourth movement. In fact, he wrote to me: 'Originality does not consist of all our curious whims and fancies.'

I then thought that I should have known better than to send it to him in the first place; he had always been severely critical of my work, and nothing I ever wrote satisfied him.

As for Busoni, even he disappointed me in his response. He did not like the second movement, he said, although he

---

[1] The name of the chief Finnish pagan god who was demonised by Christianity. Used as a common interjection, although less offensive than many other swearwords in Finland, it is unique in its seriousness and high potency, and is regarded as one of the most energising words in the Finnish language. It has even found its way to other Nordic countries and beyond.

maintained that the first movement was 'wunderschön[1]'.

Therefore, of the five movements, only two of them saw the light of day when Busoni played them at a concert at the institute. I had written five movements, but he thought that only two of them were of any merit!

Adolf, to give him his credit, did play it at a concert in Turku, but, even then, the finale was left out.

## Chapter 5
# Aino

Albert Becker's last instructions to me, before I left Berlin, were like those of a father to his son. He told me to try to be a man and to remember my responsibilities – I think that he meant that I had a responsibility to myself to behave sensibly and to make the best use of the musical education that I had received. He also said that I should not imagine being anything other than what I was, and he instructed me to work intelligently.

With these words as my mental sustenance, I journeyed back to Finland, and it was an enormous relief to be back in my homeland. I had missed the sights and smells of my native country, and I had missed my family even more. The rigorous lessons with Becker had completely exhausted me, not to mention the constant drinking parties. That is why I went to my Aunt Evelina's house in Loviisa to rest and recover.

There I enjoyed all the Finnish food that I had missed whilst in Berlin – *viili*[2], *ruisleipä*[3], *piimä*[4] and, of course, *pulla* – and I walked in the forest and breathed in the scent of the pine trees. Being back in Finland felt really wonderful.

---

[1] Wonderful, beautiful.

[2] A type of yoghurt in the Nordic countries with a gelatinous texture.

[3] Rye bread.

[4] Sour milk.

After I had had the chance to wind down, I started to reflect on my time in Berlin. I acknowledged Becker's good intentions regarding my musical education, but felt that perhaps my studies in Berlin might have been a waste of time. Whatever Wegelius had said, I still believed that Becker did not rate me very highly. The only person who understood me was Kajanus; he knew that an artist like me had to find their own way, which was something that Becker did not comprehend.

I was astonished, therefore, when I later learned that Becker had written a long testimonial for my application for a continued State scholarship, as I did not expect that he would do so, and I was duly awarded 2,000 Finnish marks, which was a lot of money in those days.

The thought of such a large sum of money made me feel quite exhilarated. But what was even more uplifting about this sudden change in my money situation was that it made me feel more confident about asking Aino to marry me. Surely, she would not turn me down now that I was far from penniless.

I had thought a lot about her whilst I was in Loviisa, as I had in Berlin, realizing that absence had only served to make my feelings for her stronger than before. How I longed to tell her that I loved her and that I wanted to marry her. And, one month later, in Helsinki, that is exactly what I did.

"Aino," I said, "you – you know how – I … feel. So … er … marry me!"

I did not know how to talk to women, and, admittedly, it was not a very romantic proposal.

"Do you love me, Janne?" she asked.

"Er, love you? But of course I do!"

"Then I will marry you!"

"So … are we, are we engaged …?"

"Yes, I believe that we are!"

The next day, Aino travelled to Vaasa, where her family was now residing, and I returned to Loviisa, where I mused on our secret engagement and attempted to write some music, albeit that was difficult for I kept thinking of Aino all the time! All I wanted was to be with her, but that was not possible until we were married, which was a long time in the future. Besides, I still needed to study abroad in preparation for my future life as a composer, and I had set my sights on Vienna.

I had explained to Aino that Vienna was the musical capital of Europe and that, as such, it had the best to offer me in terms of a musical education. I did not like the idea of leaving her behind in Finland, but I assured her that I would write to her as often as I could while I was away and that I would return within a few months.

When I said all this, she clung to me tightly, as if she did not want to let me out of her sight. However, she told me that she understood and she gave me her blessing.

So, I travelled to Vienna in the October of 1890. I liked Vienna, but it was a very expensive city, and I knew that the scholarship money would not last very long. That is why I was forced to start playing the violin in order to earn more money.

Hence, I joined the Conservatoire orchestra as a violin player, and it did prove quite useful to me; for the other members of the orchestra showed me the potential, and also the limits, of their instruments. This was to be of great benefit to me as a composer.

Some of them also showed me how much they could drink when we went to the bars together. However, I will not dwell on that now, but suffice it to say that I had spent a considerable amount of money by the time I met any of my tutors for the first time, which was about a month after my arrival in Vienna.

The reason for the delay in the start of my studies was that nothing had been arranged before I left Finland. Busoni had written a letter of introduction to Johannes Brahms, but, for some reason that he did not disclose, Brahms was not interested in taking on a pupil, and so I had to seek help elsewhere.

Wegelius suggested Karl Goldmark[1]. Therefore, one morning, I simply arrived at his apartment and knocked on the door. It was quite a while before the door opened, slowly, and a man who was only half-dressed peered at me, yawned, and asked me what I wanted.

I told him my name and briefly stated my business, wondering if I had called at an inappropriate time, but he made a sign for me to enter, apologizing for his untidy appearance and reassuring me that he was glad to see me.

"You can sit here," he said, pointing to an armchair, "and you

---

[1] Karl Goldmark, also known as Carl Goldmark (born Károly Goldmark) (1830-1915), a Hungarian composer, music journalist and co-founder of the Vienna Wagner Society.

can tell me all about yourself."

"Well ... there is – not much – to tell. I studied at the Helsinki Music Institute. I had violin tuition there – and piano tuition. And then I completed – um – a year's study in Berlin."

"That sounds very good. And who were your tutors in Berlin?"

"Albert Becker."

"I see. And what did you learn?"

I was startled by this question and thrown off balance for a moment or two, but I attempted to answer it in a way that would impress him.

"Er ... well – I learned – about counterpoint," I said. "And, and I also learned that – that I needed – a thorough grounding in, in the basics of composition."

"Excellent! It is always admirable if one can acknowledge one's deficiencies and set about gaining the knowledge one needs. Yes, I think I will be able to help you. Forgive me, by the way, that I am not fully dressed – I am afraid that I had rather a late night last night and, I confess, I was still sleeping when you knocked at the door. Let me think ... what about us we meeting the day after tomorrow and, in the meantime, I will prepare some exercises for you."

"Thank you for ... agreeing to help me. Brahms turned me down."

As soon as I had said this, I thought, *Perkele*! I felt that I should not have mentioned Brahms, or that he had refused to be my tutor; for then Goldmark might have thought that he was my second choice and Brahms had turned me down for a good reason.

"Is that so? I am afraid that he *is* rather a difficult character, so it does not surprise me. However, he *is* a gifted composer, that much must be acknowledged. You know, those who admire Wagner despise Brahms, and Brahms's devotees dislike Wagner intensely. Personally, I think that all the antagonism is rather silly, and I would never take sides – why should I? They are both excellent composers!"

This last comment made me warm to Goldmark, and I began to feel more at ease and to enjoy listening to him talk.

"So, you play the piano and the violin. I play the violin myself. I was a violinist at the Music Academy in Sopron, in Hungary, but then I was sent here to Vienna by my father, and I have been here ever since. I have earned a living by playing the violin at the Carltheater and at the Theater in der Josefstad."

He then rose and said that what must I be thinking when he had not even offered me a cup of coffee, and that he would go and make some.

While he was gone, I rummaged in my pocket and took out a folded-up piece of paper on which I had written out the notation for a Quartet in B flat. Considering how friendly Goldmark was being towards me – in spite of my disturbing his sleep – I thought that he might like to take a look at it and, hopefully, give me his opinion on it.

When he came back with the coffee, I showed it to him, but, to my surprise and disappointment, he declined to look at it in detail, which made me feel uneasy. However, we continued to converse quite affably and, after a while, I took my leave. I did not wish to outstay my welcome on this occasion.

I did not know what to think after that meeting. At least, he had invited me in to talk and had agreed to give me tuition, but his reluctance to edit my score preyed on my mind, and I thought that it was rather odd that he had not wished even to see what I had – or had not – accomplished.

In fact, in the end, it turned out that Goldmark was of limited use to me. He advised me to study the scores of other composers, but he did not seem to be able to offer me the instruction that I needed. No wonder, then, that he had not wanted to study my Quartet at our first meeting. So, regretfully, for I did like him, I had to enrol at the Conservatoire and study under Robert Fuchs[1], as well.

However, I did receive one very valuable piece of advice from Goldmark, concerning self-criticism.

We had just finished our lesson for the day, when he suddenly turned to me and said: "You know, one can never be too critical of one's own work. The first version that we write of a piece is only the beginning of its gestation; after that begins the real work of putting right all that is wrong!"

"Have you ever ... discarded a piece altogether?" I asked him.

---

[1] Robert Fuchs (1847-1927), an Austrian composer and music teacher whose piano trios were much admired by Johannes Brahms. His best-known works were his five serenades, hence, Fuchs acquired the nickname of 'Serenaden-Fuchs' ('Serenading Fox').

"Indeed, I have! I have written no less than three orchestral overtures, which I have subsequently destroyed. Sometimes, a work is beyond repair and is not worth attempting to resurrect."

"Ah, I shall remember that."

"It does not in any way mean that you are a bad composer, rather that you are a conscientious one."

It was a relief to me to know that my tutor did not think ill of me if I made a few mistakes now and again, and I began to feel a little more confident. Unfortunately, however, my good mood was shattered on Christmas Eve, when, feeling homesick and missing Aino, I decided to distract myself by reading, out of curiosity, Juhani Aho's novella – the one he had written in Paris.

I wished afterwards that I had left it unread. The writing was effective, indeed, but what that writing was about, that was what disturbed me and angered me to the utmost degree.

My suspicions regarding his interest in Aino were gloriously confirmed; not only did I recognize his depiction of Aino, but I was forced to read his very explicit description of how much he desired her.

I began to wonder whether she had encouraged his folly, but I decided that that could not possibly have been the case; for Aino was not that kind of girl. Then I considered whether I should challenge him to a duel but, of course, I knew I would do no such thing.

Instead, I tore up the book and decided that I would resume my reading of *Kalevala*[1], instead, and have a drink. In fact, I ended up drinking myself into oblivion.

A few days later, I auditioned to be a violinist in the Vienna Philharmonic Orchestra, but I was not accepted. The reason for this was that I suffered from stage fright. This became blatantly obvious to them as soon as I started to play, and so they considered that I was not a suitable candidate for the post.

After that, everything seemed to go from bad to worse.

Goldmark was no longer as friendly towards me as he had been before; he had formed the opinion that I was pursuing his young niece. This was not actually the case. It was *she* who pursued me; I had noticed that she always seemed to be there when I presented myself for a lesson with her uncle – and for

---

[1] The Finnish national epic.

what possible reason except to make eyes at me.

Then Fuchs decided that he was not happy with an overture that I had written and, instead of instructing me as to the best possible way of improving it, he simply stated that it was 'barbaric'.

Remembering Goldmark's advice about self-criticism, I attempted to rewrite it and I subsequently sent it to Kajanus, telling him that it was doubtful that I would live much longer; for I was so unhappy. But, then, being unhappy, I wrote to him again and asked him not to perform it anywhere.

By this time, not only was I unhappy, but I was sick, as well. However, I did not dare to mention it in any letters to Aino for fear that she would have asked me the cause of my illness, and this I could not possibly have told her. Were she to have known, I was quite sure that she would have called off our engagement and would have wanted nothing more to do with me; I had venereal disease.

What I told her later was that I had been in hospital and had had a kidney stone removed, but that I was quite all right, and she had no earthly cause for concern.

Had she known, also, of my precarious financial situation – the hospital refused to discharge me until the bill had been paid, and I could not pay it through lack of sufficient funds – that would have been the last straw.

I was forced to write to Christian, knowing how difficult it would be for him to raise money for me – although I had no other option – and when he finally succeeded in sending the money, I paid the bill and went to Berlin where I drowned my sorrows with my old friends.

This meant, of course, that when I returned to Finland, I did not have the warm welcome from my family that I would have wished for.

"It is shameful, Janne: *again* we have had to sell the very clothes off our backs in order to pay your debts! Will you *never* learn? You *must* take more responsibility! We cannot finance your extravagant lifestyle for ever!" This was my mother speaking.

"I know. I –"

"And with the little money we manage to get together for you, you buy cigars! It really is time that you earned your own living for none of us can help you for ever. *I* cannot help you, and *Christian* cannot help you! *You* do not look after your money. So, why should *he* be burdened?"

I attempted to appease her by suggesting that I could give violin lessons, but she looked at me with her eyebrows raised as if to say, 'And how much do you expect to earn from doing that?' However, I did give some lessons in Loviisa – for there was little else I could do to get money – and I was able to pay of some of my old debts, at least.

But if my family seemed against me, that was nothing compared to the humiliation that I suffered when my 'friend' Adolf had his book published. He had clearly based one of the characters – a man called Sillen – on me, but he had made him into a womaniser, which I was not.

I had never particularly liked Adolf that much and I liked him even less after he had done this to me. I was not a womaniser, therefore, I did not understand why he had made Sillen into one. Perhaps his intention to cause me trouble was deliberate, I do not know, but cause me trouble it did: Aino was furious.

"I cannot believe it, Janne! This is the worst possible thing that could happen to me! This character, Sillen, is clearly you, is he not? And he has all those women! Huh, what have you been up to? Janne, have you betrayed me? I should have guessed, you staying so long in Vienna! And on the top of everything else, now it has been made public for everyone to read about!"

"No – Aino – I did not know! I had no idea – that, that he was, um, pla-planning to – write a book, and put *me* in it! Of course, I would have en-endeavoured to ... stop him – if I had known!"

"Yes, well, you did not stop him, and now, no doubt, everyone is laughing at me! What are they saying behind my back?"

I assured her that the contents of Adolph's book bore no relation to reality, and told her how sorry I was about the book.

"I am – I am not a – womaniser! Aino, believe me! I – er – only strayed once ... or twice. But it did not mean anything! It was ... that I was so lonely –"

"And just when my family has become used to the idea of us marrying!"

"But – but how – are they ... to *know* ? That Sillen was based on me? Unless, unless you *tell* them."

"And what else have you not told me? I am sure that there

must be something!"

"There is *nothing* else! I assure you!" I told her, feeling more and more desperate.

She looked at me indignantly, and I was not certain that she believed me but, eventually, I could see that she was beginning to calm down.

"You must promise me, Janne, that there will be no more indiscretions! I simply cannot bear it!"

"No, Aino. You have my word."

"Very well ... we shall speak no more about it."

I cannot put into words how relieved I was that Aino had not broken off our engagement, which, by that time, was not a secret anymore – even Armas and Eero had come round to the idea.

"I do love you, Aino! I have, I have *never* loved anyone else. And, and I *never* will! You must believe me!"

"I do believe you, but I am afraid; for you have the power to hurt me so!"

"I promise. I will *never* hurt you again."

Aino clung to me, and, in that moment, I resolved to make her worthy of me. I decided that I would concentrate on my work and make something of myself, so that she would be proud of me.

This turned out to be not just a short-lived intention made under emotional pressure. Indeed, I composed the symphonic poem, *Kullervo*[1], based on *Kalevala*, and I surprised even myself by the determination that rose up inside me to write it. It was the longest score that I had ever worked on, lasting a good seventy minutes. Furthermore, although it was based on Finnish folklore, and Paraske[2] had once sung to me, it was my own interpretation of *Kalevala*.

Kajanus, with whom I had established a closer friendship by this time, was quite enamoured by *Kullervo*, whereas Wegelius definitely was not. Perhaps Wegelius's old rivalry with Kajanus played a role in his attitude, as well as his disapproval of me choosing as my subject matter something that was Finnish when

---

[1] Named after a character in the *Kalevala* who is sold into slavery.

[2] Larin Paraske (née Paraskeva Nikitina) (1834-1904), the most notable rune singer of Finnish-Karelian poetry. Her 32,000 lines of epic and lyrical poetry, proverbs, riddles and lamentations is the largest amount of oral material in *Kalevala* metre that has been collected and written down from one person.

*he* vigorously upheld the Svecoman[1] position. However, as I have said before, I have never seen any reason why the Finnish and Swedish cultures could not coexist in Finland without the petty wrangling, so I did not pay too much attention to Wegelius's opinion.

Nevertheless, I was disturbed by the fact that the critics put undue emphasis on the Finnishness of the piece – there were many other aspects of the music that they could have written about. But such were the critics; they seldom assessed things correctly.

<br>

<br>

*Chapter 6*
# Marriage

My dear Aino and I were married on the 10ᵗʰ of June 1892 at Tottesund Manor, in Maksamaa, near Vaasa, which the Järnefelts had rented for the summer. While all Aino's family were present, unfortunately, my mother was unable to attend; for she was unwell at the time.

Aino looked very beautiful but, then, she always did. And I considered myself a very lucky young man, especially as she understood that, although marriage and children were important to me, I also needed to be free to pursue my art undisturbed.

After the ceremony, Aino's father was the first person to wish us well: "I hope that you will be very happy together." Then, taking me aside, he added, "Janne, make sure that you will look after her. I believe that you know how much my little Aino means to me."

"I do. And I will – look after her – er – to the – to the very

---

[1] The Svecoman movement arose in opposition to the Fennoman movement and Fennoman-inspired reforms. Svecomans, consisting of members of the Swedish-speaking 'elite', but also of uneducated farmers and fishermen, asserted that Swedish speakers represented a different, superior 'race' to the Finnish speakers.

best of my ability," I reassured him.

"She is still very young, and I would not like to worry."

"There is no – need – um – for the Lieutenant-General to … worry. She is – er – I *will* look after her."

Whether I managed to put his mind at rest or not, I do not know, but after the others had offered their congratulations in turn, there followed an impressive feast; for the Järnefelts had spared no expense in making our wedding day a memorable occasion for everyone. Indeed, I still remember the main course – veal in cream sauce, potatoes and peas. And there was music and dance. It was a magnificent day.

For our honeymoon, we went to North Karelia – this was made possible by a grant of 400 Finnish marks that I had received for my research into Finnish folk songs and *kantele*[1] playing. We stayed at Monola House near Lieksa and were lucky to find suitable accommodation, even though I had not booked anything in advance. But when you are young, you do not worry too much about such things.

When our honeymoon was over, Aino returned to stay with her relatives in Kuopio, and I continued further into Karelia where I heard many rune singers – I was particularly captivated by the ancient melodies sung by Shemeikka[2].

After my expedition, Aino and I stayed in Kuopio for a short while, before we returned to Helsinki. There we rented an apartment, and my brother, Christian, moved in as our lodger. This was not the ideal way to start married life – with a third person sharing the household – but financial pressures forced us into this situation. Aino, to her credit, was very accommodating, and Christian said that he would keep out of our way as much as possible.

Thus, we began our married life, and I set to applying for teaching posts both at the institute and the Orchestra School – which I secured – and to writing more music.

Unfortunately, after *Kullervo*, I was seen as a spokesman for Finnishness through my music. This was a position that I was extremely wary of; for I wished to remain neutral, outside of the

---

[1] A traditional plucked string instrument of the dulcimer and zither family native to Finland and Karelia.

[2] Pedri Shemeikka (1825-1915), known as the last great Finnish rune singer.

political squabbles. In fact, I was troubled by the folkloristic aspects of *Kullervo* in this respect, and I therefore withdrew it. I told people that I was planning to revise it, but that was not the case. I did write another tone-poem, but I was not satisfied with that, either, and I felt that I had to write something better.

Meanwhile, I had other things on my mind; Aino was pregnant with our first child.

"Oh think, Janne, we shall have a child of our very own!"

"Then I had better start earning some … money!"

"But you have your teaching posts."

"Yes, but, but that is not sufficient. Hmm, I could try to write something to sell. Perhaps I should write some … piano music. What do you think …?"

"Yes … why not, after all, you did study the piano. Oh, Janne, I am so happy! I can hardly wait for the baby to arrive – although it *is* difficult to imagine us as parents!"

Strangely, it seemed as though no sooner had she said this than the child was already with us. In the middle of March the following year, Aino gave birth to a daughter, and we called her Eva.

"Is she not the most adorable baby?" Aino used to say, unaware that I had other things on my mind and that I was getting more and more worried about our financial situation.

"You did not hear a word that I said, did you?"

"I am sorry, Aino dear, it is just that, um … this apartment, it is too e-e-expensive – even with Christian as a lodger. I think that we are … forced to move. Somewhere cheaper, away from the centre of Helsinki, into the outskirts."

"That does not matter, Janne, so long as we are all together. Ooh, look at her, she is so beautiful!"


"I cannot believe it, Janne! How could you? How could you waste what precious little money we have? What sort of a composer are you if you spend all your time in the bars, drinking and smoking? I hardly ever see you any more! And Eva hardly ever sees you! This is not the way that I envisaged our life would be. I thought that we would be so happy together. You are such a disappointment to me! I thought that you saw your friends to discuss music and art, but all you do is get drunk and then come home – when you feel like coming home, that is – smelling of alcohol and cigars. I am *so* disappointed in you that I do not know what to say!"

Neither did *I* know what to say to *her*; everything that she had said was true, and I had nothing in the way of defence.

"It seems to me that you prefer to spend your time with your friends rather than staying at home with Eva and me! And what sort of friends are they when they have no qualms about leading you to neglect your family? Huh, and I am disgusted by the fact that my own brother is one of them."

Responsibilities. Someone else had talked to me about my responsibilities, apart from my mother: Becker, in Berlin. And now his words came back to haunt me.

Aino continued her tirade and, finally, she announced: "I cannot stay here with you any longer! I am going home to my parents!"

What could I have done to prevent her from leaving? The answer was nothing – she had made up her mind. So there I was, alone, after only one year of marriage.

The friends of mine that she had referred to were Axel[1], Kajanus, Adolf and her brother Armas. Sometimes others joined us, including Oscar Merikanto[2], but those four were the main culprits. We called our group the 'Symposium' and we did talk about music and art, and we often performed music, but when we got together, more often than not, it served as an excuse to get drunk.

Over the years, exaggerated stories of our meetings have circulated. For example, there is one telling how Kajanus left a Symposium meeting and took a train to conduct in Viipuri[3]. When he returned two days later, we were still drinking at the same table

---

[1] Akseli Gallen-Kallela (born Axel Waldemar Gallén) (1865-1931), a Finnish painter best known for his illustrations of the *Kalevala*. He painted a portrait of Sibelius in 1894.

[2] Oscar Merikanto (1868-1924), a Finnish composer, pianist and organist. His compositions include operas and incidental music, as well as short works for solo instruments and voice, but he is best remembered for his popular songs, such as the evergreen *Kesäillan Valssi* ('*A Summer Night's Waltz*').

[3] Vyborg. At the time, it was Finland's second largest town, situated on the Karelian Isthmus, on the north coast of the Gulf of Finland.

in the same restaurant and had not noticed that he had been away, and I said to him: 'Stop pacing up and down! Sit down and drink like everybody else!'

But I do remember one memorable occasion when we had all consumed a few too many and we decided that it was important to telegraph Adolf's mentor, August Strindberg[1], to tell him that we were drinking Pommery. I cannot remember now whose idea it was, but we did it in any case, and Strindberg replied that it must be very boring in Finland!

However, Aino did come back eventually, and I promised to behave myself, and somehow or other we settled down – that is, until Axel had an exhibition of his paintings, and Aino heard about one particular painting called *The Problem*[2], which certainly lived up to its name. It was a remarkably good painting but, I am afraid, it depicted my friends and me in rather a bad light; in the picture, we were all drunk.

"Is there no end to the humiliation that you cause me?" Aino said. "It is just one thing after another! You promised to change, but I can see that you really had no such intention! I should not have believed you! Perhaps I should not have married you in the first place. Is this the kind of life that I am to lead henceforth, with my husband constantly causing me embarrassment?"

She continued, in tears, "Janne, please think of me for once and try to live a respectable life!"

I told her that I was sorry and I begged her not to leave me again, promising that I would change my ways: "In fact, I – have some new ideas – to work on. I would not be able to – bear it – if you – if you left me again! I, I cannot manage without you!"

Aino stayed. And it was true what I had told her; I planned to write an opera. However, a commission prevented me from doing so straightaway; namely, I was asked to write some music on Karelian subjects. I did honour the commission for the reason that it came from the students of Viipuri University who were planning

---

[1] Johan August Strindberg (1849-1912), a Swedish playwright, poet, novelist, essayist, painter, journalist and critic. His novel *Röda Rummet* ('*The Red Room*') is considered to be the first modern Swedish novel.

[2] This painting from 1894 depicts a meeting of the 'Symposium'. In the picture, Sibelius appears to be in a drunken stupor, as do Akseli Gallen-Kallela and Robert Kajanus. Oscar Merikanto is so drunk that he has collapsed onto the table.

to stage a series of tableaux, depicting the history of Karelia, to raise funds for education in eastern Finland – and besides, I have never been able to say no to people if they need help. However, I was not altogether pleased that the acclaim that my songs and orchestral pieces gained came for the perceived nationalist sentiment in them rather than for the music itself. I did not set out to compose from a nationalistic viewpoint. Indeed, I always wrote my music to reflect my feeling for the land itself and, if anything, I wished to distance myself from politics.

These pieces eventually constituted the *Karelia Suite* – when I had pruned down the original seven pieces into three – and this was the first work that I was proud of writing. I felt that it was fresh and original, and it had memorable melodies that people would like.

But my satisfaction in composing was short-lived; after the *Karelia Suite*, I did not manage to compose anything that was worth mentioning and, besides, I had money troubles, again. I gave lectures at the university for a short while but I did not earn much money from that. And, hardly had Aino and I become accustomed to having our first daughter, Eva, than Aino became pregnant again, and we soon had a second daughter, whom we called Ruth. This meant that I had to devote some of my time, at least, to Aino and the children, which, unfortunately, interfered with my work as a composer.

Nevertheless, I eventually got myself into the habit of working again and I began composing a new tone poem, based on the adventures of Lemminkäinen[1]. This was a step forward for me – in a sense, it heralded my future symphonic writing. However, just one day after it was premièred, Aino's father died, and Aino now commanded my attention more than my music did.

She was quite distraught, and it pained me to see her so distressed, especially when she had two children to look after who did not understand that their mother was grieving. They, too, were restless and cried more than usual. I believe that they sensed her sorrow.

"It must be difficult ... you were always your father's favourite ..."

As I have said previously, I have always found language

---

[1] A character in *Kalevala*. He was a handsome, arrogant ladies' man.

inadequate, especially in difficult situations such as this was; mere words are not enough. That is why, when August had been laid to rest, I often sat at the piano and played to Aino. I was then able to convey to her my sympathy and understanding in a way that I would not have been able to do with words.

It is entirely possible, on reflection, that much of what I was feeling, later, found its place in Lemminkäinen. But, once again, it was disappointing to me that it was seen as a political statement for the Finnish cause, rather than what it was; an exploration of Finnish character through folklore.

Furthermore, music critic Karl Flodin wrote a scathing review and suggested that the symphonic form might suit me better, and I began to think that he was right. I also thought that, if I wrote a symphony, I could distance myself from tangible themes and write music that was more abstract, albeit I could let it be inspired by Finnish nature. But did I have it in me to actually write a symphony?

However, I was not in a position to start a symphony at that time; I was soon busy with an application for the professorship at the institute, following Faltin's retirement. 1887 had seen a sharp rise in my debts, so I was eager to secure a steady income. And, to my relief, I received the professorship. But then, Kajanus, who I thought was my friend, appealed – he was one of the other candidates – saying that I should be free to compose. Consequently, *he* was offered the post, instead! However, I was given a consolation prize; a Tsar's 10-year grant, but it only represented half of a professor's salary.

"*Perkele!*" I said to Aino. "I wanted that professorship!"

"Of course you did. And you deserved it!"

"This is unbelievable! Kajanus, he has always supported me. And, and, and now he has done this! Huh! How, how clever of him … to say that I should be, um, free to compose! I am really angry that, that he should go against me … in this way. *And* behind my back!"

"I agree that going behind your back is disgusting! But … perhaps there is truth in what he says. You *are* a composer and not a teacher. And you communicate much better through music than with words."

"Well … but I do not trust Kajanus any more! It is a, a strange business."

"It certainly shows that you cannot always trust your friends."

"No ... it is a ... thoroughly strange business ..."

When I think about it, I always seemed to have unpleasant things to contend with, which distracted me from my composing. It was only a little over a year after Aino's father died that my mother passed away, as well, so we had two bereavements in a very short space of time.

I say 'bereavements', but, in fact, I was not very upset about my mother's death. I had very mixed feelings. She had never been a very affectionate person, which is why I loved Aino so much; for she was entirely different in that respect. Then there was the question of mother's resentment towards Aino for the very reason that she was different, which was why my mother moved to Tampere – to be further away from us. Why, then, should I grieve?

However, she *was* my mother and she had fed me, clothed me and looked after me in many other ways. Furthermore, whenever I smelled fresh rye bread, wherever I was, I always thought of her; her rye bread was the best in Finland.

First, Kajanus had betrayed me, and then my mother had died; so, it was little wonder that I needed a drink to help me cope with it all.

*Chapter 7*

# Tragedy

In 1898, I was once more in Berlin. Aino went with me for two months, but she returned to Finland in the April; she did not like leaving the children with relatives too long. After she had gone, I had the chance to meet up again with Busoni and Adolf Paul – by this time, I had forgiven Adolf for his contentious book.

Reunited with my friends and feeling better after I had confided in them about my recent troubles, I summoned up the courage to approach the German publishing house, Breitkopf &

Härtel[1], about my music, with Adolf as my moral support. We were going to offer them a suite of songs that I had written for Adolf's historical drama *Kung Kristian II*, a project that I had become involved with, although I was not keen on some of the rather violent and bloodthirsty elements in the story. The drama was set in the sixteenth century and was about the love of Kung Kristian II – ruler of Denmark, Sweden and Norway – for a Dutch commoner, Dyvecke. At the same time, Dyvecke was also loved by a Danish nobleman, who, unsuccessful in his pursuit of her, poisoned her, thus provoking the rage of the King, who had the nobleman killed.

I have to say that this drama was typical of Adolf, whose work was always controversial. However, it had met with considerable success, and I was quite pleased with the music that I had composed for it, which included a Nocturne, an Elegie scored for strings alone, a Musette to be danced by Dyvecke, a Serenade and a tempestuous Ballade to reflect the anger of the King.

However, when we arrived at the publishers' building, my confidence soon faded away.

"Ooh, I am not sure that, um, this was such a good idea," I said.

"Rubbish, it is an excellent idea, and you *will* secure a deal, I know it!"

"I wish that *I* could be so sure."

"Leave it to me!"

As we entered the office belonging to the head of the company, I saw the man himself, Oskar von Haase, seated at his desk, and behind him on the wall was an imposing, and disconcerting, portrait of Ludwig van Beethoven.

"They, they are not going to want my music – not after Beethoven," I whispered to Adolf.

"Shh, I will do the talking."

To his credit, Adolf spoke eloquently on my behalf and, without too much effort, he did persuade them to publish the *Kung Kristian II Suite*. He had shown how determined he was to help me, and for that I was most grateful.

"*I* could not have persuaded them to pub-publish anything. Most likely, I would have let them have my compositions, er …

---

[1] The world's oldest music publishing house, founded in 1719 in Leipzig, Germany.

for nothing!"

"In which case, Janne, you would have been very much out of pocket!"

"Yes, indeed! But, thankfully, you were here! Perhaps now, I can finally start, um ... working on the symphony!"

"Which you are more than adequately qualified to write, may I say."

"You, you are such a good friend! But ... regrettably, I must return to Finland; there is so much to distract me here."

It was true, there were many distractions and, when Axel arrived in Berlin a short while later and organized meetings of the Symposium again, we all reverted to drinking on a regular basis. So, I did not manage to leave Berlin, and my symphonic writing was abandoned before it had even begun.

It was not until June, therefore, when I returned to Finland, that I finally began writing sketches for my first symphony. But when I started, I worked so hard on it that I did not even have the time to attend Busoni's concerts in Helsinki at the end of September, which was very regrettable.

Considering what had happened in the last few years, I suppose that it was inevitable that it would have a bearing on my music. I had seldom been able to express in words, to anyone, what I had felt. So therefore, the first movement had a brooding atmosphere at the beginning, with the solo clarinet rising above the timpani pedal point. Also, feelings long forgotten and a certain nostalgia for past times found their way into the symphony, particularly in the melody for violins and cellos in the second movement. The final movement was not without its melancholia, either, despite dramatic statements made by the cymbals and drums.

The symphony did reflect other emotions, however. Aino gave birth to our third daughter, Kirsti Marjatta, whilst I was composing. The joy that we had from our new addition to our family possibly accounted for the lively Scherzo and for what I thought of as 'rabbits jumping' in the first movement. It could be said that it was the perennial idea of life and death existing side by side that was uppermost in my mind, and this idea found expression in my symphony.

As for the atmosphere of conflict that pervaded the symphony, I believe that this arose from the ambivalent emotions that I had regarding my mother's death. I was aware, though, that some people would think that it depicted my country rising up against Russian tyranny – subconsciously, perhaps it did, I do not know.

But one thing was sure; I had never, as far as I could recall, worked so consistently and determinedly on any piece of music before. So it was particularly unfortunate that it had to be put on hold; for I was obliged to write something in protest against Bobrikov's[1] Russification of Finland. Many important people, including Emile Zola, Anatole France and even Count Nikolai Tolstoy, had added their support to the protest by the young Fennomans and Swedish liberals, so it seemed to me that I could no longer remain impartial, although I would have wished to remain so.

"You *must* support the cause," Aino told me. Despite her multi-cultural background, she had always been pro-Finnish in her cultural politics.

"Well … I do not know. I am writing abstract music now, therefore, I am, er … above politics! Besides, I very much admire Tchaikovsky."

"But we cannot allow Finland to be dictated to by Russia, whatever you may think of Tchaikovsky! Soon we will all be expected to speak Russian, for Heaven's sake! It was not so bad before, when the government in St. Petersburg allowed cultural and ethnic differences amongst its peoples, but now … Janne, you *must* take a stance! I know that you do not like offending people, but we are talking about Russia! Half a million people have already signed the petition to Tsar Nicholas!"

If I did not wish to offend the Russians, I wished even less to offend my wife. "Yes … perhaps I have a duty to –"

"*Something* will be expected of you. You cannot stand on the sidelines for ever! You simply cannot!"

---

[1] Nikolai Ivanovich Bobrikov (1830-1904), a Russian soldier and politician, was appointed in 1898 by Tsar Nicholas II as the Governor-General of Finland. He was in charge of implementing the first campaign of Finland's forced Russification – to limit Finland's status as the Grand Duchy of Finland and ending its political autonomy and cultural identity – until his assassination in Helsinki. The two campaigns of Russification (1899-1905 and 1908-1917) are known as *sortokaudet/sortovuodet* ('oppression period/oppression years'), during which there was widespread resistance from the Finns, including petitions, strikes and, ultimately, active resistance.

Aino was right, of course. Therefore, I duly wrote a piece of music called *Song of the Athenians* – which was premièred in April 1899 alongside the symphony – describing the resistance of the Greeks to the invasion of the Heruli in the third century. It was received loudly and enthusiastically, but I could not help thinking of the irony of the situation: I had composed a song in defiance of Russia and yet, in my symphony, I had allowed myself to be influenced by two of Russia's greatest composers.

In truth, there was more than a hint of Tchaikovsky in it, especially in the second movement. Moreover, elements of his sixth symphony were recognisable in the fourth movement. In addition, I think that the first subject of the opening movement owed something to that in the first movement of Borodin's E-flat Major Symphony. However, influences from other composers are inevitable – even Beethoven did not completely find his own voice until he wrote his third symphony – so I considered that I had more than enough time ahead of me to find mine.

And, on the whole, I was pleased with the symphony at the time – it was only later that I considered it too emotional and too indulgent – and I was awarded a government grant of 2,500 Finnish Marks in recognition of my achievement.

The Russification policy was a hard pill to swallow; it declared that Russian laws took precedence over those in Finland. It also stated that all official communication was to be in Russian, and it disbanded the Finnish military, forcing its soldiers to serve in the Tsar's army, instead.

Moreover, once the policy was well and truly implemented, the freedom of the press no longer existed, and newspapers that offended the censor were closed down for months on end.

I felt that I was forced into a situation where I had to continue to take a stance against Russian tyranny. I did this by writing seven pieces of music, for a series of tableaux representing Finland's past, for a three-day festival in aid of the Press Pension Fund. Out of these, I later put together a concert suite of three pieces, which were published as *Scènes historiques* in 1911.

All'Overtura, which I wrote to accompany the first tableau of pagan Finland – it has the bard of the first cantos of *Kalevala*, old

Väinämöinen[1], singing of ancient memories, while the Maid of the North sits on the sky's collar-bone upon Heaven's arch, weaving cloths of gold and silver – was very evocative, and I particularly liked that one. But it was the last piece, called *Finland Awakes*, that really captured the mood of the time and, although I had not intended it to be so, it became the symbol of my country's fight for independence, and the hymn-like melody in it has now almost become the second national anthem. Ralph Vaughan Williams wrote to me, saying that it was 'highly significant not only for the music of Finland, but the whole of Europe' and that I had 'lit a candle that would never go out'.

I scored it mainly for the woodwind – two flutes, two oboes, two clarinets, two bassoons, four horns, three trumpets, three trombones and a tuba – to which I added also a timpani, bass drum, cymbals, a triangle and strings, and the whole work lasted approximately eight minutes. It was not, as was sometimes claimed, an amalgam of Finnish folksongs, but my own original composition. Indeed, if there were any similarities at all to other pieces of music, I would cite Beethoven's *Egmont* as the main subconscious influence.

The slow beginning of *Finland Awakes*, with snarling brass and thunderous timpani resembling the growling of a large dog that is threatening a much smaller one, I suppose, was an analogy in my mind with Finland's position at the mercy of the ruthless Russians.

However, this music was not, for me at least, wholly political: it embodied not only the strength and determination of the Finnish people, but it was set against the backdrop of the grandeur and beauty of the nature in Finland.

Of course, in Finland, it could not go under the title *Finland Awakes*, for political reasons, and so it was performed as 'Impromptu'.

To my mind, it was not one of my better compositions, which is why its popularity surprised me, but I soon had other things to think about; that year, tragedy struck my family again. The most terrible thing happened, the worst thing that can happen to anyone: we lost a child.

It all started when, one day, Kirsti, our little radiant Kirsti, who

---

[1] The heroic central character of *Kalevala*, a shaman with a magical power of song and music.

was only fifteen months old at the time, began to run a fever.

"She is so hot!" said Aino. "God help us! Do not let it be typhus!"

There was a typhus epidemic raging in southern Finland at the time, so naturally, Aino feared the worst.

"But babies do get fevers, don't they?"

"I think that this *is* typhus! Arvid's[1] child died from it, and now Kirsti has it, too!"

"It may *not* be –"

"But she has a rash, as well, and she is very drowsy!"

"Then we had better get the doctor!"

The doctor came immediately. "Is she coughing?" he asked.

Aino told him that she was. "*And* she has diarrhoea."

"I am sorry to have to say this, Mrs Sibelius, but I believe that she has typhus, and I am afraid that, unfortunately, there is little that we can do for her."

At these words, our world collapsed. Aino was crying, and I did not know what to do. Wondering how we were going to survive such a blow, I found myself thinking about Turgenev's book, *Fathers and Sons*, in which the hero, Bazarov, dissected a local peasant and then died after contracting typhus.

"But is there nothing …?" I asked.

"I am afraid not."

The doctor shook his head and looked at us sympathetically, whilst taking a step backwards. "For what it is worth, I am very sorry."

Kirsti died on the 13th of February 1900.

"I should have cared for her better," Aino said.

"No, Aino, you are *not* to blame."

Poor Aino, she would have needed someone to console her and support her in her grief, but I did not have the moral fibre to be that person. I was weak and helpless in the face of tragedy. All that I could do to cope was to have a drink and forget what was happening. So, while Aino openly poured out her grief, weeping continuously, I chose to withdraw into myself and to drink myself into oblivion.

I could not help it. I knew that I should be strong for Aino's sake, but I drank nonetheless. I could not bear the thought that I

---

[1] Arvid Järnefelt (1861-1932), Aino's brother, a writer, farmer and lay preacher.

would never again hold Kirsti on my lap and I would never again see her smile when I tickled her under the chin. Losing Kirsti was the worst thing that had ever happened to me, and I would have given the world for it to have been me who had died and not her. I wanted my daughter back and yet I knew that nothing and no one would bring her back.

Then, one day, in a rare moment of sobriety, I composed a fantasia for cello and piano into which I poured all my pent-up despair.

"I am so sorry, Aino," I said, as I sat at the piano, "it, it feels like this ..."

I had tears running down my face as I said these words, and Aino came over to comfort me. This made me weep even more; for her kindness and concern for me, in spite of her own grief, prompted all the emotion that I had kept inside me to be released.

Faced with the loss of Kirsti, I did not know how I was going to carry on. How did one carry on after the death of a much-loved child?

"It is hard, Janne, I know. But we must stay strong for the sake of Eva and Ruth."

"Yes ... we must ..."

But it was just a few months after Kirsti's death, I am ashamed to say, that I left Aino to cope on her own and I accompanied Kajanus on a trip to Europe with his Philharmonic Orchestra. Kajanus knew what I thought of him when the music professorship was awarded to him, instead of to me, and for a long time he had been trying to make amends. So I relented and agreed to go on this trip but, I suppose, the real reason for going with him was that it offered me a way of distracting myself from my sorrow over Kirsti's death. I felt bad about leaving Aino but I simply needed to go away, even in the company of Kajanus.

When we were in the harbour, waiting to board the ship for Europe, I caught sight of a young man who was very noticeable; he was wearing a bowler hat and he was constantly twitching his moustache. He headed towards members of our orchestra to give them flowers. He then approached me and gave me an envelope.

I opened it and noticed immediately that the note inside did not bear a signature, but had been signed 'X'. The contents were short and to the point: I should change the title of 'Impromptu' to *Finlandia*.

I looked up in surprise, but the young man had already gone.

Later, when I mentioned the incident to Kajanus, he was quite bemused. "Well, whoever he was, he had a damned good idea!" he said.

"If it *was* his idea!"

"Well, who else's would it have been?"

It *was* a good idea, though, I had to agree, and I kept it under my hat, resolving that I would give it some serious consideration later.

I was pleased to be on good terms with Kajanus, again. However, I was supposed to be assistant conductor, but he seemed to want to conduct at every concert, leaving me with virtually nothing to do. On the other hand, as I was still very shaken by Kirsti's death, I did not think that I was capable of conducting, anyway.

In spite of my bereavement, I tried to keep everybody's spirits up, evidently thinking that, by doing so, I would make myself feel better.

However, I did *not* feel any better and I grew homesick, and I told myself that I would never again leave Finland and that I would stay there for ever. Besides, the Germans and the French were not impressed with my symphony, which was far superior to *Finland Awakes,* which they *did* like, and this annoyed me. Actually, over the years, the success of *Finland Awakes* has irked me; I have felt that it has overshadowed everything else that I have done.

"They, they do not understand a-a-anything about music!" I said to Kajanus one evening after a particularly unsatisfactory concert. "And the Germans – huh! – they think that they are the, the *only* ones who can write music! And the French cigars, they are rubbish!"

## Chapter 8

# New Acquaintances

Axel Carpelan[1] was a very determined young man. It was he who had handed me the letter signed 'X' and, on my return from Europe, we met again, and he revealed his identity.

Sitting opposite me in Kappeli[2] on the South Esplanade, he talked, quickly, about himself whilst I drank my cold beer and studied him – not without a great deal of curiosity; for he was a stranger who had made up his mind to become acquainted with me, and this fascinated me.

He appeared to be quite cultured, certainly well read, and he told me that he would have wished to become a professional violinist, but for the fact that his family had been against it.

"I smashed my violin – I was so angry – and I threw it into the river!"

"Oh, dear!"

"I told my parents that I would not go to university."

"So … what happened?"

"I did go in the end."

He proceeded to tell me about his studies, and I listened, although I told myself that many people would not have done so; he certainly had the tendency to talk too much. However, something about Axel intrigued me. He was a bit of a dandy, with his polka-dot tie and his sideburns, not to mention the tufts of hair that formed something in the semblance of a beard in the middle of his chin, but I liked him and he was a pleasant

---

[1] Baron Carl Axel Frithiof Carpelan (1858-1919), the great uncle of the author Baron Bo Gustaf Bertelsson Carpelan (1926-2011) and the hero of the latter's award-winning novel, *Axel*.

[2] Founded in 1883, this restaurant was a fashionable meeting place for artists and musicians alike. It was particularly popular in the summertime because, already at that time, it had cooling equipment to keep beer cold. Live music concerts were also given on the outside bandstand. Kappeli is still open today.

distraction.

"I correspond with Viktor Rydberg[1]," he said.

"Indeed?"

"And I am acquainted with Axel Tamm[2]."

He suddenly became very effusive. "I would have many suggestions for you if you would be so kind as to allow me to put them forward. For instance, you should write a violin concerto! And a 'woods symphony'! And music to Shakespeare!"

I was impressed by his enthusiasm. "And, and where would I get the inspiration? For all these works."

"In Italy! You must go to Italy!"

I had never in my life met anyone like Carpelan – he was so forthright and self-confident – and I wondered why he was so resolute in his desire to advise me. At the same time, I also wondered why it was that I seemed to attract people like him and Adolf Paul. Surely, they should be looking after their own interests and not mine.

However, I could not help thinking that Carpelan had some very good ideas, and I liked his positive character.

"Hmm, yes … but I am afraid that, that I do not have the funds … to go to Italy. In fact, well, I have debts."

"But that is not a problem! *I* can raise funds for you!"

"Ah … er … how?"

He took off his spectacles, proceeded to clean them with a handkerchief and then said, "Fear not, I have ways and means!"

"Well, then, at the very least, I must, um, treat you to another beer!"

I did not take seriously his intention to raise the money – I thought it a whim on his part – but his interest in my music was sincere, and the more we conversed, the more I was taken with him. He was eccentric but very likeable.

To my astonishment, he was as good as his word and, indeed, he did provide me with 5,000 marks[3] for the trip to Italy.

So, in October 1900, Aino, Eva, Ruth and I set off. On the

---

[1] Abraham Viktor Rydberg (1828-1895), a Swedish writer and member of the Swedish Academy (1877-1895), known as 'Sweden's last Romantic'.

[2] Axel Tamm (1876-1954), a Swedish patron of the arts who gave Axel Carpelan an allowance.

[3] €22,600 in today's money.

way, I wanted to stop off in Berlin. Unfortunately, our stay there became prolonged – until January 1901 – and most of our money had gone. It went on the hotel, that admittedly was the most expensive, although Aino claims that it went on my restaurant bills. But after I managed to get guarantors in Finland for more bills of exchange, we were able to continue to Rapallo in Italy, where I intended to write a cycle of tone-poems suitable for Europeans.

We rented a villa, which had the most beautiful garden full of flowers, including highly scented roses and magnolia that I can still smell now. There were almond trees, also, and cacti and cypresses.

"You are very fortunate in having people willing to support you financially," said Aino, as we were walking in the garden one morning, "but it is a shame that you waste so much money on alcohol."

Her references to my drinking were becoming more and more frequent as the years went by. Of course, I knew that I was being selfish in using our money for my own ends but I could not help it; it was only when I had reached a certain level of inebriated assurance that I could write good music.

I chose to ignore Aino's comment and distracted her by talking about the weather.

"Is it, is it not marvellous, here in Italy, Aino? Think how cold it must be getting in Finland!"

"Oh yes, it is wonderful. If we were in Finland now, we would be wearing galoshes and overcoats!"

"Yes, we would! Imagine that! We really must make the, the most of our stay here."

"Yes, we must! It is good, Janne, that we have time to spend together – it is seldom that we do that nowadays. I know that I promised, when we married, to understand that you needed more in your life than me and the children, but even so –"

"Even so, I should spend more time with my family."

Indeed, Aino and I regularly wandered in the scent-laden forests and walked along the beach from Rapallo to Zoagli, often carrying the children on our backs. And I was relieved to be in a different environment and leave the troubles in Finland behind. I even managed to write a few sketches for the Second Symphony.

Carpelan wrote to us frequently, saying that he was with us in spirit. His letters caused us much amusement; for in them he warned us about all manner of unfortunate things that might affect our health, such as overripe fruit, the Neapolitan ice cream and the possibility of contracting malaria. And we thought that we could now add hypochondria to the list of his eccentricities.

"He is, um … out of the ordinary, for sure. I do not think that, that he has much money. And, yet, he arranges money for me – while he lives in, in some, in some lodgings. Somewhere in Tampere."

"So he lives alone, does he? Does he not have a wife?"

"That is another peculiar thing. No, he is not married. But … he told me that, er, he once courted an aristocratic lady."

"And was she not interested in him?"

"Apparently, she was not. He said that, er … he used to wait outside her house, for a mere glimpse of her, but she … sent him away!"

"But why?"

"I do not know. According to him, she just said, 'Get out of my sight, and preferably out of town!'"

"Oh dear, one cannot help feeling sorry for the poor man! But he *is* a little eccentric."

"Well … yes. But he has an in-in-intense *feeling* for music. Also, he seems well informed about the musical life, um … in other parts of Europe."

"He does?"

"Oh, yes. I think that, that he loses himself now in books and music. To, to console himself. You see, he would have wanted to become a violinist, but, er … it was his family, they were against it."

"That is a shame!"

"Yes, it is. Indeed."

"They were like your family!"

"Yes … we have that in common. But now he is giving me his wholehearted support. I expect that he would want me to, to write to him about, er … what I have been working on here – but I will not."

"You will not?"

"No. Compositions, you see, they are like butterflies; touch them once and their magic is gone."

"Ahh."

"So, I cannot write about my music … whilst I am composing

it. People will eventually hear it for themselves – one day."

But we did not only talk about music or people whom we knew: we talked about anything, be it larks and thrushes or the colour of the sky. It was not what we talked about, but that we had time to be together, sharing our experience. A long time had gone since I had seen Aino so happy. Our time in Rapallo was idyllic. But it was not to last very long; our daughter Ruth contracted typhus, and it was more than we could bear after the cruel fate dealt to Kirsti.

"Oh, Janne, what are we going to do? Whatever are we going to do?"

I did not know. But I did know that I could not tolerate the idea of losing another child to this awful disease and that I must leave Rapallo, before I had a nervous breakdown.

"But you cannot leave now, Janne! I cannot take care of Ruth on my own! She may even die!"

"And *I* will die, too, if I stay!"

"Your own daughter! Honestly, Janne, how can you be so selfish?"

"I *cannot* stay here – not after Kirsti!"

So, ignoring Aino's pleas for me to stay in Rapallo, I went to Rome and walked the streets there, thinking about Ruth and fearing the worst. I felt guilty but I knew that I would have been no help to Aino if I had stayed with her and that it was better that I had left. But I prayed with all my heart that Ruth would not die.

I was forced to write to Aino to ask her to send my hairbrush and some linen, and I apologised to her for my thoughtlessness and insincerity, saying that we ought to talk later. I also wrote to the children, saying that I was a changed man when surrounded by all the beauty in Rome and that I needed to gain respect in my own eyes and work hard at my music.

In the meantime, Aino succeeded in nursing Ruth back to health, but I knew that Aino was put out by my absence, which she called my 'thoughtless and thoroughly selfish behaviour'. Nevertheless, after two weeks in Rome, and with much trepidation, I returned to Rapallo.

My welcome was what was expected; Aino sulked for several days, and the atmosphere in the villa was really depressing. When she finally started speaking to me again, she told me that, in fact, Ruth had not had typhus at all but gastric fever. So, my cowardly running away was even more despicable.

"I – I – I know that, um, it, it, it was wrong of me – to leave you. But I had to. I went to, um, Palestrina masses – and prayed for Ruth. I felt it deeply – after Kirsti. But you must forgive me, Aino. Otherwise ..."

And she did forgive me, again. She looked at me almost with pity in her eyes and she put her hand on the top of mine. Her capacity to forgive was infinite.

"I do love you, Janne, but it is very hard to love you sometimes."

But Aino's immediate worries were not over. Kasper had written that Emma was very sick. It was understandable that Aino should be worried about her brother and his wife, but as we were far away in Italy, there was little that we could do except send them our best wishes and pray for Emma's recovery. So I attempted to distract Aino from her worries.

"What you need is a, a change of air! Let us go to Florence!"

Aino looked surprised but she was interested in the idea, although I had not expected that she would be. And it was a blessing that we did go; for there were so many interesting places to visit, and we were able to enjoy being together. While we stayed in Florence, I also drafted a C-major theme that I thought I could use in my symphony.

From Florence, we continued to Vienna, where I received an invitation to conduct some pieces from the *Lemminkäinen Suite* at Richard Strauss's Heidelberg Festival. Then, finally, we went to Prague.

It was in Prague that I had the honour of meeting Antonín Dvořák, who was already an old man by then. I wanted to visit Prague to foster my contacts with the Bohemian Quartet whom I had met a few months earlier. The violinist of the ensemble was Josef Suk, and he suggested that we could pay Dvořák, his father-in-law, a visit.

I agreed to that immediately and I am very glad that I did; for he was one of the kindest people that I have ever met.

We spoke to each other in German, or rather he spoke and I listened; I was struck dumb in his presence, not knowing what I should say to this man whom I considered a genius.

"I am honoured to meet you. I – your Fifth symphony was – *is* – a ... masterpiece!"

"As is *Finlandia*! Come, let us sit down and have some refreshment. Now, tell me something about yourself."

"Well … er … there is not much to tell. I have, I have written a symphony –"

"No, no, tell me about *you*!"

What was there to say? I told him, briefly, about my childhood and youth and then about my studies in Berlin and Vienna, and he listened with great interest, his eyes twinkling and his lips forming a perpetual smile.

"In, in Vienna, I went to see Brahms, er, with a letter of introduction – from my piano tutor, Busoni – but … Brahms said that, um, he did not want to teach me!"

"Yes, he can be a cantankerous old fool when he wants to be, but I have to say that he has always been very kind to me. In fact, I owe him a lot. He was responsible for me getting an Austrian State stipend – he was on the panel of judges, you see – and he got his publisher to publish my works, too. He is not *so* impossible when you get to know him! But … now that I know a little about you, tell me about that symphony of yours!"

"Well, it was my first attempt. It is not, er … I suppose that I was influenced by … Tchaikovsky."

"Ah, the great Tchaikovsky! I met him two years ago, here in Prague. I gave him a copy of my Second Symphony, and then he gave me a signed photograph! 'To my dear and deeply esteemed friend Antonín Dvořák from a sincere admirer, P. Tchaikovsky' – that is what he wrote on it. It is something that I will always treasure. So … you evidently like Tchaikovsky's music?"

"Indeed. The *Pathétique*, it is so beautiful … so sad."

"And excellent orchestration! Quite remarkable and original. A *slow* fourth movement – *that* was original and most exceptional! Of course, one is always inclined to be influenced by others, so that it is not at all surprising that you should be influenced by Tchaikovsky, but one must find one's own voice eventually. No doubt, you will do that in your next symphony. Have you begun writing it yet?"

"Not yet. But I do have some ideas … to work on – when I return to Finland. I need to, I need to publish more music, er … to earn some money. I must not be a, a, a poor composer … for ever!"

"We are all poor at the beginning, I more than most! When I

went to the organ school at the age of sixteen, my father cut off my living expenses. You see, he did not approve of music as a profession, and so I had to pay my own way. Life was very hard … until I met Brahms, of course. By the way, have you been to England?"

"No. No, I have not."

"Then you must go! In England, they are most receptive to new music. *They* understand it. I have had quite considerable success there. *Stabat Mater* was very warmly received there some years ago, and, as a result, I was then invited to London. Yes, you must go to England if the opportunity arises."

"Hmm … yes."

"So, what is your music all about? Finland?"

"Yes … it is. But what I want is, well, um … I do not want to be a … Finnish Grieg."

"Oh, yes. Much of his music is based on old, Norwegian folk songs. But you want to write music that is representative of *you* more so than of your country? And why not!"

Dvořák understood me perfectly, and I felt as if the quandary about what my music should represent was greatly lessened. It was as if the great master had given me permission to focus on my personal experiences in my music.

Up to this point, Suk had sat listening to our conversation without saying anything, but then Dvořák patted him on the arm and referred to him as his 'very talented' son-in-law.

"He is a very gifted violinist, much more so than I."

"He always says that", said Suk, "but he is far too modest!"

"No, *you* are much better!" And turning to me, Dvořák said, "My little Otilka found herself a good man in Josef!"

They clearly got on very well together, which reminded me of my late father-in-law. This recollection caused me instant melancholy, and Dvořák must have noticed the change in my expression; for he said, "You have had a sad thought?"

"Yes … I was thinking of my father-in-law. He … passed away a few years ago."

"He was a good man?"

"Yes, he was a very good man."

"I sincerely hope that my son-in-law here will say the same of me when I am gone!"

"I am sure that he will say so!"

Suk was most fortunate to have such a kind-hearted father-in-law; Dvořák had the capacity to see into your very soul and to bring out all the good that he discovered there.

He was full of surprises, too. He asked me what my other interests were and he revealed that he was as passionate about locomotives and pigeons as he was about music!

"I breed pigeons as a pastime. They are remarkable little birds, and I have names for them all! Perhaps I should call one of the next brood 'Sibelius'!"

"Now that *would* be an accolade!" said Suk.

"Do you like birds, young Sibelius?"

"Indeed, I really do! I especially like swans – so graceful."

"Yes … and Tchaikovsky must have liked swans; for he wrote a ballet about them! They are, indeed, graceful birds."

"And they are one of the symbols of … Finland."

"Is that so? In that case, the pigeon should be a symbol of Bohemia!"

*Chapter 9*

# Music And Drinking

Meeting Dvořák was a source of great inspiration to me and, on my return to Finland, I was anxious to start working on the new symphony.

However, in the first instance, I had teaching duties to honour. These distracted me from my composing, but I could hardly give them up; our finances were not good. Admittedly, I had not been careful enough with money, particularly on our trip to the Mediterranean, and more bills of exchange had been added to my already considerable debts.

But the political situation at the time, and Carpelan's ingenuity, saved me. People were busy protesting about Finns now being conscripted into Russian-speaking regiments, and a petition was being passed from person to person. I am proud to say that I was one of the first people to sign it.

Carpelan was quick to recognize the significance of such a public protest by me. "I am certain that we can use that to your advantage," he said.

"What, what do you mean?"

He twitched his moustache. "Patriots will consider it their duty to support financially a man such as you who stands up for what they believe in. Leave it to me."

And it did not take long before Carpelan returned with good news; he had managed to secure me a regular quarterly allowance of five hundred marks! That meant that I could resign from my teaching duties and devote myself to composition.

So, with a new source of income, in the autumn of 1901, I began composing the symphony for which I already had some sketches, written in Italy. But when I looked at them now, I doubted whether I would utilize them. I had written in my notes: 'Jean Paul says somewhere in *Flegeljahre* that the midday moment has something ominous about it, a kind of muteness, as if nature were listening to the footsteps of something supernatural.' The question was, would I use this idea or not?

On another sheet of paper, I had described a fantasy that I had entertained, namely, that our Italian villa was the palace of Don Juan and that I myself was the amorous protagonist of that legend: 'Don Juan. I am sitting in the dark in my castle, when a stranger enters. I ask who he could be again and again – but there is no answer. I try to make him laugh, but he remains silent. At last, the stranger begins to sing. Then Don Juan knows who it is. It is Death.'

I suppose that this story was fresh in my mind after seeing a performance of Mozart's interpretation of this legendary character; I saw *Don Giovanni* in Berlin on the way to Italy. It was interesting, but would I use it?

And on a third piece of paper, I had the C-major theme that I had sketched in Florence above which I had written the word 'Christus'.

In the end, I decided that I would not write about Don Juan, but there was something in my notes that was perhaps worth working on: ominous, muteness, twilight, nature, Christus – these were words full of potential.

I lit a cigar and considered what I wanted to achieve with the symphony. First and foremost, I wanted it to be quite different to the First. Just as Beethoven had progressed musically with each successive symphony, so I wanted to do the same.

I thought that I would attempt something structurally innovative in the first movement. So, I decided to deviate from the usual exposition-development-recapitulation progression and I inverted it. Therefore, I introduced thematic fragments in the exposition, built them up in the development section and then broke up the material into its primary constituents in the recapitulation. Also, I decided not to have first and second themes, as such, but to have fragments of themes working together.

To put all this together in a seamless flow of musical expression required a lot of work and one revision after another. But, when the final version was ready, I was reasonably pleased with the first movement, considering it the most innovative piece of music that I had composed up this point. However, that was where the originality ended. The three other movements, though melodically rich and impassioned, were not as groundbreaking as I would have wished them to be. Consequently, I was not fully satisfied with the work as a whole.

Furthermore, after its première in Helsinki, in March 1902, the symphony was subjected to all sorts of interpretations and, due to its combative spirit, Kajanus, for example, decided that I had meant it as a declaration of Finland's heroism. In fact, nothing could have been further from the truth; it was actually much more about my own conflicts than about my country's, and about the devastation caused by Aino's sister, Elli, taking her own life – she was only 33 at the time.

However, to my surprise, not only did the public warm to my symphony, but it also received some very favourable reviews in the newspapers: Oscar Merikanto wrote in *Päivälehti* that the work was a masterpiece that exceeded 'even the boldest expectations'; Evert Katila wrote in *Uusi Suometar* that the symphony was 'like a broad river flowing majestically to the sea; and Karl Flodin said that it pointed in the same direction as Beethoven's symphonies.

This was high praise, indeed. I was suddenly elevated to hero status in Finland, and I was delighted by such positive reactions to my work, but, at the same time, it put me under enormous pressure. How could I ensure that what I wrote next would live up to the Second? And the fact that I had been compared to Beethoven made me feel extremely uneasy, and his portrait in Oskar von Haase's room at Breitkopf & Härtel came back to haunt me.

Hence, I could not help thinking that the higher I rose, the further I could fall. So, feeling confused and afraid, I decided, on a whim, to go off to Berlin to see Christian.

"Are you sure that you are not going there to drink?" said Aino.

"I am going at the bidding of my genius!" I told her. However, I did not believe that any more than she did.

"Meanwhile, I am left here on my own to look after the children!"

"Well, it is, it is too much upheaval for you, and for the children, to, to always travel with me. Besides, I shall be working, and their noise, it distracts me. Also, er … I need to meet conductors there. And arrange to get my music played."

"*And* you need to get drunk with Busoni!"

"No. I am going there for my music!"

"Oh yes! As you always do! And you know very well that I cannot prevent you!"

"No, Aino, I will be back before –"

"If the drink does not cause you to lose your mind and forget that you have a family here in Finland!"

"Now, now you are beginning to talk nonsense!"

"Then I shall not say anything further!"

"But Aino …!"

However, this conversation did not continue; Aino went into one of her sulks and did not speak to me again before I left for Berlin. So when I said goodbye to her and the girls, she did not honour me with a reply.

Christian, too, was unsympathetic. "I am not at all surprised", he said, "that Aino is not speaking to you. Of course, she is angry; she is worried. As a doctor, I have seen what alcohol can do to people. It is one thing to have a drink occasionally, and I mean 'occasionally', but it is quite another matter to be dependant on drink – I am sure that you know what I mean."

"I am *not* dependent on drink! That is nonsense! If, if I have had just, er, half a bottle of champagne, for example – and that is nothing! – before I conduct, *then* I conduct as if, as if I am God.

Otherwise, any nervousness – you see, there is no knowing how, how people will react to my music – so any nervousness, um, will impair my performance. Or, when, when I go to see the bank manager, I, um, might feel … a bit anxious – money is always tight. However, a glass or two of wine makes me feel relaxed. I feel more like myself."

"And how about at home? Aino has written to me saying that you drink at home, too."

"Well … I am always under pressure; a lot of expectations are put on me. A, a, a drink or two will relax me, and I can, um … get in touch with music much better. It helps me compose."

"But you cannot continue to run your life with the help of alcohol."

"Well …"

"Janne, if you could only see what I have seen when I have dissected the brains of alcoholics."

"Well … yes. But I am no alcoholic! Just a few drinks. To get me going."

"I think that you *are* an alcoholic. And from what you say, your marriage is already under strain, and things will continue to get worse if you do not attempt to stop drinking!"

He was very insistent, and I could see that he was not going to give up in his efforts to lecture me about the perils of drinking. And I started to get quite annoyed by all this, particularly coming from my younger brother, but I decided not to argue with him.

"I suppose that I could try …"

While in Berlin, I was obliged to stay with Christian who, I felt, kept on eye on me and where I went. Therefore, I could not very well spend much time with Busoni and the others.

I cannot say that I accepted any of what Christian had said about my drinking, and when I returned to Finland, I have to admit that it was as if the conversation between my brother and me had never existed. In fact, the more I thought about what he had said that I should do, the less I was inclined to do it.

Aino was heavily pregnant then with our fourth child, and even when she eventually gave birth to Nipsu[1], nothing in our domestic situation had changed.

---

[1] The pet name that Sibelius always used for his daughter Katarina. It roughly translates as a 'nipper'.

That was when Aino, together with Carpelan – for he communicated with Aino when I was busy – devised a plan to remove me from Helsinki and from all the temptations that it represented.

Aino's brother, Eero, was living with his family in Järvenpää[1]. So, Aino thought that, being far enough from Helsinki, it would also be a suitable place for us to live. Indeed, the idea of composing in rural surroundings was appealing to me, as was the idea of owning our own house. Furthermore, in Järvenpää, there would be Eero nearby to keep an eye on the family when I was conducting abroad.

Although, over the last few years, my debts had continued to increase, by 1903, my income had improved – I had my grant, my contract with Breitkopf & Härtel and regular conducting engagements at home and abroad. Therefore, I decided to risk borrowing a substantial sum of money – in the form of a mortgage, and bills of exchange guaranteed by my friends – to pay for a plot of land and for the design and construction of a fine house in Järvenpää. Lars Sonck[2] agreed to design it.

"Is it not an idyllic location?" said Aino when we went to see the plot. "An ideal retreat for a composer!"

"Well, yes. Just as long as … I can work in peace and quiet."

"But we are here away from anybody else. Why would you *not* have peace and quiet?"

"The children …"

"I am quite sure that you will be able to find a quiet corner to work in; it is going to be a two-storey house!"

"Yes …"

"And we can get fresh milk from the nearby farm. Janne, it is going to be such a wonderful place! For the children, too … so close to nature."

"Hmm … yes. That is the best thing here. All the trees … the bird song … the smells of the forest. And not far from the lake. What I would like is, is a green fireplace. In the dining room. Green – yes! – the colour of grass and leaves."

---

[1] At the time, a small village, 37 km north of Helsinki.

[2] Lars Eliel Sonck (1870-1956), an architect who played a major part in Finland's search for its architectural identity. Besides many public buildings, he designed, among others, Kultaranta, the President of Finland's official summer residence.

"Why not! And there is so much land to cultivate! I will be able to grow vegetables for the children."

"Ah, you must remind Sonck that, um ... there must be *wooden* gutters installed. If there was rain falling on metal –"

"Janne, I do not mind anything as long as you do not ..."

I thought that, Here we go, she is going to say 'as long as you do not drink', but, instead, it was:

"... spend *all* your time composing. You must sometimes spend time with the children."

"Of course. That is what I ... fully intend to do! We shall have very nice sauna evenings ... cooking sausages. And, and go for walks, and the children, they will learn about nature –"

"Right in the middle of the forest!"

"Right in the middle of the forest! Yes, I believe that, that we will be very happy here."


While the house was being built, I decided to give attention to the violin concerto that Carpelan had suggested that I write, albeit the Second Symphony, and all its deficits, was on my mind, also. In fact, the more that I thought about the symphony, the more I realized that I had failed in what I had wanted to achieve.

Firstly, there was far too much of Tchaikovsky in it, and the world did not need another Tchaikovsky. Indeed, there were echoes of him in each and every movement, the fourth movement, in particular, bearing too strong a resemblance to the final movement of his *Pathétique*. What is more, I even heard strains of his *1812 Overture* – not to mention something that sounded like a melody from Rimsky-Korsakov's *Scheherezade*.

Furthermore, the symphony was far too impassioned, and far too long and complicated; the fourth movement should have been cut by a half– it was far too repetitive and longwinded – and the first movement should have been less packed with ideas.

Bearing all this in mind, I came to the conclusion that if I were to be a really successful composer, and a happy one, I needed to find my own voice so that people would know instantly, from the first few notes, that Sibelius had written the piece of music that they were listening to.

I also concluded that this was going to be a very demanding

task, and I began to doubt myself and felt that I needed a drink; it was only when I had reached a level of inebriated assurance that I felt that I was I able to write my best music. Besides, I had even more money worries now that we had borrowed money for the house, so I needed a consolatory drink, as well as a confidence-boosting one.

Naturally, there were the usual arguments with Aino when she suspected that I had been drinking, but, fortunately, Nipsu took up a lot of her time, which took Aino's attention away from me.

Chapter 10

# Ainola

My violin concerto was conceived on a more symphonic scale than those of composers before me. Also, I wanted to explore the whole range of the violin and not just its upper register, the soloist's virtuosity being an important element in the music. I suppose that I was living out my fantasies of being a virtuoso player when I composed it. So, I wanted the concerto to have intricate passages, as well as moments of enigmatic unpredictability, which would make for a dazzling display by the person who performed it.

The first movement began as a depiction of Finland's lakes and forests in winter, the third theme in B flat minor and the sombre colours of the woodwind representing the long hours of darkness from mid-afternoon until late morning. As I immersed myself in its composition, my own gloomy thoughts and repressed feelings began to colour the music, also.

In addition, Aino, or more specifically the state of our marriage, was on my mind. Aino was quite clearly at the end of her tether, blaming my drinking, but I could not give it up; for I have always been weak-willed. Here I was, in the prime of my life, with great things before me, and yet I felt that it was only with the aid of alcohol that I could achieve them. The dissonances that appeared in the music seemed to me to represent my domestic strife and, as the music in the movement became more animated, that seemed to me to represent the arguments between Aino and me, which were becoming more and more frequent. Added to all this, I had money worries and my health was giving me cause for concern.

For some time, I had had a problem with my ears and I was beginning to fear that I would end up in the same situation as Beethoven or Smetana, who had both gone deaf. In addition, my throat was giving me trouble, too. I believe that, owing to all these factors, the first movement developed along very doleful lines.

The second movement was equally low-spirited. I decided that it would be opened by the clarinets playing in thirds, followed by the oboes, French horns and timpani. Then I put the violin to play a very sad melody, punctuated by ascending, scalic pizzicato lines in the violas and cellos, reminiscent of the Second Symphony. The bassoons and horns would be playing pianissimo at the bottom of their range.

As I wrote it, the music came from deep within me, almost as if it was composing itself; emotions that I could not and would never be able to talk about rose up from the depths of my very soul and found expression in those twenty-four minutes or so of notation.

In particular, my profound sorrow over the death of little Kirsti and the subsequent anger at the injustice of the situation burst out from heart onto the manuscript paper. When I wrote the final coda, bringing the movement to a close, that was my heartbreak. I knew that I would never be able to put into words to anyone what it was like to lose a young child, but in this concerto, I had come as close to describing it as was possible in any language.

I suppose that writing that second movement helped me to some extent but, after completing it and exerting myself to the limit, I could not bring myself to write the finale. Depressing thoughts over Kirsti's premature death, which the composition had resurrected, had weighed me down to such a degree that I could not bring myself to compose any more. What made matters worse was the deadline – the première of the concerto had been set for the autumn – but I knew that I could not keep to it, and it did not seem worth even trying.

Therefore, I could not resist going out to bars and downing quite a few whiskies. I remember Kajanus telling me, on more than one occasion, how he and Aino had gone looking for me and found me at a level of intoxication that required them to help me get home and to bed. Naturally, Aino had been livid. What I do remember is what followed, which is not pleasant to recall.

Instead of lecturing me, once more, on the error of my ways, she chose to ignore me; several days went by without a word from her – she did not even say 'Good morning' or 'Good night'.

This made the atmosphere in the house extremely oppressive. However, gradually, I came to realize that it was me only who was at fault and that my behaviour was hurting her, and the girls, beyond all measure. My poor family! How much suffering I had caused them! This life was not what they deserved, and something had to be done. So, in the end, I resolved to give up the drink.

Then, one evening, after several days of Aino not speaking to me, when the children were already in bed asleep, and Aino was sitting with her sewing, I went to the piano and played a tune.

"Is, is, is this what it feels like, Aino? Living with me ..."

"That is *exactly* how it feels!" she said. "Drat it! Now I have spoken to you!"

"I am so pleased that you have! It is, it is unbearable when you are not speaking to me. You *must* understand that it is not my, um, in-in-intention to hurt you. I know that, er, my, my drinking, it *has* gone too far – which is not easy to ... admit to. But I will try to stop."

"Janne, you must not destroy yourself! Do not throw away everything that you are capable of. It tears at my heart when I think of how much you could achieve, if only –"

"You *must* continue to believe in me, Aino. You faith in me, it, it is all that I have!"

"Please try –"

"I *will* try – for you, and for the children."

"When the need for drink arises, try distracting yourself. Go for a walk, for instance. I know how much being in nature relaxes you. Or play with the girls. Is that not better than being inebriated? And you must complete the concerto," she said.

"Yes, you are right, Aino. That is, that is what I must do."

Finally, I could detect Aino's sternness gradually dissipating. There was a sigh, and a faint smile appeared on her face. I knew that I was forgiven.

That smile resulted in the third and final movement of the concerto; I was so childishly happy that Aino and I were on speaking terms once more that I sat down the very next day and wrote what turned out to be a very energetic and rhythmic finale in $\frac{3}{4}$.

As the movement drew to a close, I threw in some final-sounding chords, but on the *second* beat of the bar, and, when the genuine final chords came, I put the penultimate one also on the second beat, subverting all expectations!

I think that I succeeded in making the music embody the feelings that spring evokes in Finland after the long hard winter – joy and thanksgiving – and I believe that I also succeeded in combining the violin and orchestral interludes effectively.

However, the most important thing about the whole concerto was that, in it, I had finally found my own voice!

"Is it not the loveliest house that you have ever seen, Janne?"

It was September 1904, and Aino and I were standing outside, admiring our new house in Järvenpää and, at the same time, breathing in deeply and savouring the smell of the pine forest around us. And, indeed, it was a fine house. It was a large, two-storey, bark-stripped timber villa. Initially, we only lived on the lower floor where there was enough room for us, and our servants; Aino, the housemaid and nanny, and Hellu, the cook. In the basement, there was a large cellar, and a spare room that was later to accommodate Heikki, our stableman and caretaker. We also had several outbuildings, including a stable for our horse, Vilkku, a shed for the cart, a pigsty and a chicken pen. Although the house was not quite finished, we were eager to move in.

"I still cannot believe that it is really ours!" said Aino, kissing Nipsu, whom she was holding in her arms. "And we have so much land!"

Järvenpää was still largely untouched countryside at that time, and we had a two and a half acre plot close to Lake Tuusula. Aino was planning to grow vegetables but she also intended to cultivate a flower garden, while the girls would have plenty of play areas and the forest to explore.

Back in the house, we found Eva and Ruth in the kitchen, helping themselves to some fresh *pulla* that had been baked by Hellu. Her real name was Helmi, but we all called her Hellu.

"Would you like some *pulla*?" Hellu asked. "It is fresh from the oven!"

"Indeed, I would!" I said. "I have, um, always been partial to cinnamon buns!"

"Eva has had two already!" said Ruth.

"And how many have *you* had?"

"Only one."

"Ahh, then you must have another!"

"How many are we allowed, daddy?"

"As many, as many as you can eat – unless your mother says otherwise!"

The girls giggled, and Ruth's little hand reached out for another *pulla*.

"Hmm," I said, "the house needs a name. It is your house, Aino – it was *your* idea. So, how about Ainola[1]!"

"Yes, mummy! Ainola!"

"Ainola it is, then!" I confirmed, turning to Aino who looked most delighted with the decision that the girls and I had made.

Leaving the others in the kitchen, I then went to look at the study. It was marvellous having a proper workroom. And the view from the window was most inspiring; no roads or houses but pure nature in its autumn colours.

"Do you like it here, Janne?" Aino had appeared at the door.

"Where is Nipsu?"

"In the kitchen with the others."

"Ah, then I have you to myself! Come and look out of the window! See the view! That is the view that, that I have when I work."

"Yes, it is lovely. So peaceful."

"It is good that the lake is, um … so close; we can have nice walks there. I can imagine the girls, er, skating on the, on the frozen lake. In the winter time. And think of us having a, a picnic there, in the summer, and the girls swimming."

"It is going to be lovely."

"Perhaps … we should also get some sort of boat."

[1] Aino's place.

"Hmm, that might be nice."

"Is there anywhere else in the world where, where I would get so much inspiration …?"

It did feel like an ideal place for a composer. And I am not only inspired by scenery, but also by the sounds of the countryside. They can produce a real symphony – the wind in the trees, waves flapping against the shoreline or the side of a boat, birds singing, insects buzzing. Even the complete stillness of the midwinter forest has a meaning; nature rests, but the occasional crack from a distant, frozen tree tells me that it is still alive, ready to be woken up, in the spring sunshine, by the babbling brooks made by the melting snow.

"Janne, we will soon be having Christmas in our new home!"

She looked so happy at that moment that my heart felt for her; I and my 'weak will', as she called it, had caused her so much anguish, and here she was, now radiant with joy at the prospect of Christmas.

"And Hellu will prepare a big dish of *lanttulaatikko* … and *perunalaatikko* … and *porkkanalaatikko!*[1]"

"Yes, it makes me hungry, um … just thinking about it. And I think, I think that I can smell the ham already!" I said.

"Soon the children will start talking about *Joulupukki*[2] coming. It is going to be a joyful time – if only we had more money …"

The thought of money was not a pleasant one; for we *would* have had more if I had not spent so much on alcohol.

But sensing my discomfort, Aino was quick to reassure me. "Even so, we will manage somehow."


We were living in a fine house and Aino and the girls were very happy there, but I was not as contented as I should have been; for I was still thinking about the disastrous première of the violin concerto earlier in the year.

I had convinced myself that it was the best thing that I had ever written, but the public did not share my enthusiasm for the

---

[1] Swede casserole, potato casserole and carrot casserole, respectively.

[2] The Finnish name for Santa Claus. The literal meaning of the word is 'Christmas Goat', reflecting its pagan origin.

piece. I wondered if the première would have gone better if the German violinist, Willy Burmester, had been the soloist, as I had originally intended, instead of Victor Novacek from the Helsinki Conservatoire, who had struggled to execute the piece effectively. But perhaps Willy would have found it difficult, too. Now I had to revise it.

But at least *Valse triste* and *Scene with Cranes* had proved to be a success. However, there was a problem with *Valse triste*; I would only receive royalties on my own versions. Fazer[1] and Breitkopf & Härtel were free to publish other arrangements for which I did not receive any money at all! It was a ridiculous situation – the publishers were getting rich, whereas I certainly was not.

My health was not very good, either. The doctors in Helsinki thought that I might have symptoms of diabetes, although this was not the diagnosis of Dr Klemperer, whom I had consulted in Berlin – he told me that I was a hypochondriac! I was *not* a hypochondriac and, if Dr Klemperer thought that I was, he should meet Carpelan!

Klemperer had also told me that I should stop drinking – that was easier said than done. I had made all those promises to Aino, as well, and I sincerely wanted to keep them, but how was I supposed to stop drinking just like that? The most worrying thing, however, was my hand tremor, which made writing more and more difficult.

Still, I now had a contract with Lienau[2] for four years, and he would pay me 8,000 German Goldmarks[3] for four major works per year. After building Ainola, my debts had gone up significantly[4]. So, now I would be able to reduce them, provided I could rise to the challenge. I had no idea yet what I would write, but I was thinking of writing a third symphony, which I had

[1] The Fazer Music Company was founded by Konrad Georg Fazer in 1897, brother of opera impresario Edvard Fazer and of Karl Fazer, founder of the Fazer confectionary company. Its publishing department began in 1898, and it has piano and guitar factories, a concert bureau, recording studios and teaching studios. It was acquired by Warner in 1993 and in 2002 by Fennica Gehrman, a subsidiary of Gehrmans Musikförlag Ab of Sweden.
[2] Emil Robert Lienau (1838-1920), a German music publisher. The Lienau publishing company was merged with the publisher Zimmerman in 1990.
[3] €41,000 in today's money.
[4] At the time, Sibelius's debts were nearly €300,000 in today's money.

decided would be considerably shorter than the previous symphonies. My aim would be to write in concise language so that every note counted; the music would be stripped back to its bare essentials.

"This is a good sauna!" I told Aino. "Big enough for our growing family ... and it smells good. Pine smells so good!"

It had taken a year to have the sauna built, which Aino had designed herself. Obviously, she was more technically minded than I was!

"Sauna!" said little Nipsu.

"Yes, it is the sauna! Nipsu knows all the important words!" Aino said, stroking Nipsu's hair.

"I wonder whether, um, Nipsu will get the taste for a *vasta*[1]. Perhaps we might go in the sauna. This evening. And, and cook some sausages on the stove. Er, what do you say?"

"Oh yes, the sauna will ensure that we will get a good night's sleep tonight!"

Later, we all went down to the sauna with some sausages.

"Can we go in yet, daddy?" Eva was impatient for the sauna to be ready.

"Go and check the temperature. If it is, um ... sixty degrees, you can go in."

Eva hurried in and out. "It is *eighty* degrees! I am going in!"

"Do not sit too high up!" said Aino. "Sit further down and then you will be able to take the heat longer!"

The rest of us followed behind Eva. Aino sat on the lower level with the girls, with Nipsu on her knee, and I went up to the top level with my *vasta*.

"Put your feet into a bucket of cold water if you feel too hot!" Aino reminded the girls.

"When can we have sausages, daddy?" said Ruth.

"Let daddy relax a little first! We will have the sausages all in good time."

I threw a little water on the stones, and we sat in warm

---

[1] Also called *vihta*, a bunch of leafy, fragrant silver birch twigs used to gently beat oneself in the sauna to relax the muscles, and cleanse and rejuvenate the skin.

contentment with all the worries of the world far away.

"Daddy, can we put the sausages on the stove now?"

## Chapter 11

# A Sibelian Symphony

"The English are, as we know, very well mannered and impeccably dressed at all times," said Carpelan, straightening his tie.

He was educating me prior to my first visit to England, to conduct the First Symphony.

"I should have gone there, um … months ago. But I had to postpone it; I was busy. Except that they wrote, in the English press, that, that the Russians would not let me out of the country!"

"I hope it does not ever come to that! But, as I was saying, you must dress smartly."

"Yes … but what will the, the weather in England be like, I wonder …"

"It will certainly not be like it is here. It will not be as cold and it will not be as bright, since they do not have any snow."

I walked over to the window and looked outside. Eva and Ruth were building a snowman, and the sun shone directly onto them, wrapping them in a blaze of light.

"I have heard that it rains a lot in England."

"Yes, it does, so you must bear that in mind when you get there. And remember to say 'please' and 'thank you' at regular intervals!"

"Yes … hmm … we Finns, we are not the most well-mannered people, are we?"

"Indeed, we are not, so there is something to be learned from the English. It is probably that we have been under Russian rule for so long; they tend to treat each other … almost like animals, and we have become similar to them!![1]"

"I suppose we have."

"In England, I have read, they have such a thing as 'small talk'."

"What is that?"

"It means that when you talk to someone, what you say does not have much content."

"No content?"

"No, just something trivial. When you meet an old friend and you just have a chat – yes, it is a chat, about the weather, for example, and not a proper discussion."

"I understand."

"And they do it with strangers."

"With strangers! Why?"

"I do not know. They just do it."

"How odd …"

"It is. But I wanted to warn you in case a stranger starts talking to you. You are expected to say something."

"Huh, I do not know about that. And I, I do not speak much English."

"Enough to get by, I am sure."

"Well … at least, they like the symphony – more than they do here. Bantock[2] said that, that it should receive a, um … warm reception. It did when, when *he* conducted it."

"Excellent, excellent, then you have no worries! But there is one more thing: you must make sure that you have medication with you in the event of sudden illness. It is difficult in a foreign country to explain about medical matters. If you are prepared for such situations in advance, then so much the better! You must

---

[1] In Finland, even today, there remains a 'shut up or put up' mentality. Hence, for example, abhorrent personal violations, such as child sexual abuse and gang rape, are not regarded as particularly serious and seldom result in the imprisonment of the perpetrators or even in the naming of them. The 'shut up or put up' mentality also means that, once a decision, however misguided, has been made by whoever is in charge, questioning or appealing against it is futile and frowned upon.

[2] Granville Bantock (1868-1946), a British composer of 'exotic' music who was influential in the founding of the City of Birmingham Symphony Orchestra. The Bantock Society was founded shortly after his death, and its first president was Sibelius, who dedicated his Third Symphony to Bantock.

make quite sure that you have everything with you that you might possibly need, such as headache pills and cough medicine, for example."

That was typical of Carpelan, with his health worries, but I hastened to reassure him: "Aino will take care of ... that sort of thing."

Carpelan was right in saying that the English were very polite. When I arrived in England in November 1905, a customs officer said to me, most courteously, "I am sorry about this, sir, but are you aware that the amount of cigars that you are carrying appears to be over the limit that you are allowed to bring into the United Kingdom? Regrettably, I have to ask you to pay duty of two pounds six shillings." He said this as if they, the customs officers, were being a nuisance to me, whereas in Finland we had got used to the officials being blunt, accusatory and treating people like criminals.

Politeness, as Carpelan had told me, was a strong characteristic of the English and, so therefore, whilst I was there, I never permitted my expression to betray my thoughts; in short, I behaved impeccably – and learned to dress appropriately.

I wore a brown suit in the morning, a long coat, a green waistcoat and grey-striped trousers to lunch and evening dress with a white silk scarf to dinner. I even ordered some dress shirts with only one button on the front; for they were the latest fashion. It was all quite an education for me, and I must say that I considered England thoroughly pleasing and aristocratic. Everyone whom I met treated me with the utmost respect and consideration.

Although I only stayed there for a short while, I had the opportunity of making several valuable contacts. Granville Bantock – who insisted on calling me 'Mr Väinämöinen' – introduced me to, among others, Henry Wood[1], Ernest Newman[2]

---

[1] Sir Henry Joseph Wood (1869-1944), an English conductor, best known for his association with the annual series of promenade concerts known as the 'Proms' at the Royal Albert Hall in London.

[2] Ernest Newman (1868-1959), an English music critic and musicologist, author of books on Richard Strauss, Edward Elgar and Richard Wagner.

and Rosa Newmarch[1], who would prove to be faithful friends and supporters for many years to come.

Rosa spoke to me in fluent Russian when we were first introduced to each other, thinking that I spoke it fluently also, which was certainly not the case. However, when we had put that particular matter straight, we had a most pleasant conversation; for she had published a study on Tchaikovsky and, what is more, she had spent time in Russia and knew Balakirev[2] and Stasov[3], which was fascinating to me.

All in all, the trip to England was most refreshing and, whilst I was there, I was already mentally working on the Third Symphony, the tone of which was much more high-spirited than that of the previous symphonies, which showed that I was feeling happier than of late.

On my return journey to Finland, I decided to seize the opportunity of widening my musical horizons by stopping off in Paris for a short while. As well as having the chance to better acquaint myself with French music, I was anxious to write down the ideas that had taken root in my mind whilst I was in England and which were now starting to mature. But, as it happened, I fell in with some other Finns and took to spending more time than I had anticipated in cafés and bars. And, somehow, time seemed to fly, and it was not until March in the New Year that I continued my journey home.

Back at home, all my gaiety dissipated; Aino was unhappy that I had not returned for Christmas – she did not believe my excuse that I had been busy in Paris, writing the Third Symphony – and, furthermore, our nation was facing political upheaval. The 1905 Revolution had spread throughout the Russian Empire, leading to a lot of restlessness in Finland, which had culminated in a general

---

[1] Rosa Harriet Newmarch (1857-1940), an English writer who championed Russian music in particular. She wrote concert programme notes and published books on Tchaikovsky and Sibelius.

[2] Mily Alexeyevich Balakirev (1837-1910), a Russian pianist, conductor and composer. He formed the group of composers called the 'Moguchaya Kuchka' ('Mighty Handful' or 'The Five') with Cui, Mussorgsky, Rimsky Korsakov and Borodin.

[3] Vladimir Vasilievich Stasov (1824-1906), a law graduate and the most respected Russian music and literature critic of his time. He was adviser to 'The Five' and to Tchaikovsky, advocating Russianness over European influence.

strike. To keep law and order, citizens' home guard militia groups had been formed.

I could feel tension in the air; not only were there protests against the common enemy – the Russian rule – but the home guard started to divide into the White Guards and the Socialist Red Guards, and it was only a matter of time before they would clash.

Although Axel Gallen had dealings with Russian activists, like Gorky[1], I preferred not to be involved with politics. I threw myself into composing, instead, and, whilst the ideas for the Third Symphony were taking shape, I composed *Pohjolan tytär*[2] and some incidental music to Hjalmar Procope's[3] play '*Belshazzar's Feast*'.

By the time that I actually began writing the Third Symphony, I found myself working to an impossible deadline; the London première was scheduled for the spring of 1907, but I knew that the symphony would not be ready by then.

I informed Lienau of this and, of course, he was extremely disappointed and frustrated. He asked me if I could possibly have it ready by June, but, unfortunately, I was not able to complete it by then, either.

How, I asked myself, was I supposed to write a really important work – and this symphony *was* important – under such pressure as this? It was a hopeless situation, and I felt that too much was expected of me in too short a time.

That is why I abandoned the whole damned project and went to Germany to drown my sorrows. And drown them I did, so much so that I did not even write to Aino while I was there – I was totally incapacitated.

Naturally, when I returned home, Aino was furious. "First you leave without telling me where you are going and then you do not even deign to write to me! Meanwhile, I am here on my own with three children to look after! Ruth and Eva have been asking

---

[1] Maxim Gorky (born Alexei Maximovich Peshkov) (1868-1936), a Russian writer, political activist and founder of socialist realism. He was an opponent of the Tsarist regime and a close associate of the Bolsheviks.

[2] *Pohjola's* *daughter* . * The North's.

[3] Hjalmar Johan Fredrik Procopé (1889-1954), a Finnish diplomat and politician from the Swedish Peoples' Party. He was the Finnish Ambassador in Washington D.C. during the war years (1939-1944).

'Where is daddy?' and what was I supposed to tell them? Well, Janne, what was I supposed to say?"

"I am sorry …"

"Sorry? You are *always* sorry! I know that I agreed, when we married, that you needed something more than just me and the children, but I did not think that I would have to compete with a bottle of whisky! Why is it that men are so weak-willed? Why are *you* so weak-willed? What would happen if *I* were to start drinking every time something went wrong? Where would the children be then?"

"Aino, you do not understand –"

"No, I do not! How can you do this to your own family?"

I wanted to tell her that she did not understand what it was like to want a drink and to know at the same time that it was wrong to want it. I could not help myself and, recently, I had been wondering which was the stronger impulse in me; was it to compose or to drink? Nevertheless, one thing was certain and that was that without the drink, I could not compose.

"I will not speak to you ever again after this!" Aino said.

She did speak to me, of course, but not until she had sulked for many days, making me feel, once again, ashamed and regretful for how I had treated her and the family.

This was how it always was between us: arguments, sulking and an atmosphere in the house that you could cut with a knife, then, finally, the forgiveness – until the next time.

On this particular occasion, Aino was not angry with me for *very* long; for the children had missed me, and she wanted things to return to normal for their sake. But it was only normal on the surface; it took a good two weeks before I could see Aino looking happy again.

I had abandoned the Third Symphony for quite some time but now I started to feel that perhaps I could start working on it again.

I had quite definite ideas about what I wanted in this one. First and foremost, I wanted it to be much more condensed in form than its predecessors had been. They had been too long and unnecessarily complicated – one hundred and sixty pages in the full score of the First Symphony and one hundred and forty-five pages in the Second. It was surely possible to say everything that one had to say in a way that was more economical. Therefore, I intended to fuse what would ordinarily be the third and fourth movements into one single movement.

Secondly, I wanted to have a lighter orchestration to give a luminosity to the music. This would mean that when it was performed, only about fifty or so players would be required – instruments which I dispensed with included the bass tuba that had featured prominently in the other symphonies. I also made the trumpets and trombones less conspicuous in the score and made the strings take precedence.

And thirdly, I wanted there to be a compelling forward movement, as in the symphonies of Beethoven, the rhythm being as important as the melodic material.

I had already long decided that the first movement would begin with a rhythmic melody in the cellos and double basses, after which the brass and remaining strings would enter, and I would emphasize the C-F sharp tritone in bar fifteen by a rinforzando marking. Then I would have a solo passage for the flute and a triumphant horn call over strings in the first of three major climaxes, the movement moving energetically forward like a river of semiquavers. The movement would be lively and upbeat, and would progress in a similar vein to Beethoven's Fifth.

Whilst I was writing it, I recalled some of the colourful characters whom I had met in Liverpool and, particularly, their cheery dispositions and their talkativeness. However, at the same time, I recalled the feeling of homesickness that always came over me whenever I was away from Finland. It was very windy whilst I was in England, and I think that that influenced the feel of the music, too.

The third movement, also, was full of fragments of memories: the rain in England, the freshness in the air after the rain, the seagulls squealing and the sight of ships entering majestically into the Liverpool docks in the evening mist. I thought of this movement as the crystallization of chaos, the chaos being a game of motifs and tempos, which recedes when a hymn theme enters.

I was pleased with the outer movements, but the central movement caused me a lot of trouble – until one day, when I was looking out of my study window.

I saw Aino outside, playing with the children, and she looked happy, but something struck me; a strong sensation crept over me of what it must be like for Aino to have such a weight on her shoulders caused by me and my drinking. So, it was this sensation that was to inform the writing of the central movement.

This was meant to be a happy symphony, but how easily had a sad theme found its way in! Nevertheless, I had achieved what I had set out to do: there were just seventy pages in the full score, the prevailing mood had remained surprisingly bright and cheerful, the texture was much lighter and the music as a whole had a greater clarity and simplicity.

Furthermore, I felt that, at last, I had written a symphony that was the work of Sibb – and not of Tchaikovsky – recognisable by a persistent rhythmical figure.

But even though I myself was pleased with it, the public evidently was not; when it was premièred in Helsinki in the September of 1907, it got a very cool reception indeed.

Perhaps they had been expecting the Third Symphony to be similar to the Second and so they were disappointed – I do not know. However, Flodin seemed to approve of it; for he said that it met all the requirements of a symphony as a form of art but, at the same time, it was new and revolutionary, and thoroughly Sibelian. I could not have hoped for better praise than this.

*Chapter 12*

# A Meeting Of Musical Minds

A short while after the Third Symphony's première, I had the opportunity of meeting Mahler when he came to Helsinki in November 1907 to conduct the Helsinki Philharmonic Orchestra.

I paid him a visit one morning at the Seurahuone Hotel and, when he opened the door of his room, I was somewhat surprised at his stature. He was much shorter than I had imagined; he could not have been much more than a hundred and sixty five centimetres, or less, in height. I myself am one hundred and seventy eight centimetres tall, so that it felt as though I was towering over him.

"Mr Sibelius, I recognize you!" he said in German, adding, "You speak German, yes?"

I told him that, indeed, I did speak German and I asked him whether, if he had the time, it would be agreeable to him to have a chat with me. Smiling and nodding, he invited me in and gestured me to be seated. Then, without any preamble, he began to talk about his activities prior to his arrival in Finland.

"I have just been to St. Petersburg. It is, by all accounts, a fascinating city, but I am afraid that I was unable to enjoy all that it had to offer; for I am quite unwell."

He seemed tense and spoke very quickly. "Yes, I have been diagnosed with a heart defect and I am forced to rest at regular intervals."

"Ahh ... er, if you wish me to go –"

"No, no, no! I am happy to talk to you! We could even go for a walk if you wish, but a short one. I should like to have visited the Hermitage in St. Petersburg and seen all the wonderful paintings, but I could not do so owing to the rehearsal schedule, which was from 9 a.m. until noon every day, and, after lunch, I needed to rest until 5 p.m. on the advice of my doctors. They said that I must not do too much – I am not the man that I was!"

"So ... you are conducting the Helsinki Philharmonic Orchestra?"

"I am, and it is an excellent orchestra, astonishingly good, in fact, and is a credit to Kajanus. He is a very likeable man, yes?"

"Yes ... he is – one of the rare men who have, er ... understood my art. But, um ... which works will you be conducting? This evening."

"I shall conduct Beethoven's mighty Fifth Symphony, the *Coriolan Overture*, the overture to *Die Meistersinger*, and the Prelude and 'Liebestod' from *Tristan und Isolde*. It is an interesting programme, is it not?"

"Most interesting! It, it will be, um ... a splendid evening!"

"What would you like me to conduct of yours?"

The question had come quite unexpectedly, and I did not know what I should answer. I did not want Mahler to think that I had come to see him merely to interest him in my compositions.

So, I just said, "Er – um – nothing."

But then I realized that he might have been offended by my reply; I knew that he enjoyed conducting other composers' works, and I had now turned him down. But his expression did not change.

"Ah, I see. Well, of all the composers, I value Beethoven as the sublime example and mentor of my own creative sense and intelligence in art. His music developed always, and every symphony that he wrote was a Ninth Symphony in terms of its excellence and innovation!"

"Yes, indeed! And one could say that he, he wrote programme music, whereas – I – um – his Seventh is a favourite of mine. In the second movement, there is – how would I describe it? – mystery."

"Yes, hmm ... I conducted the Seventh in St. Petersburg with the Marinsky Orchestra! It was truly wonderful! But you want to go for a walk, yes?"

We left the hotel, and I took him along Mikonkatu[1] to the Etelä Esplanaadi[2].

"If you have the time, there is an, an, an excellent book shop along here", I told him, "with books in many different languages. And, in, in this direction, we can get to the harbour. Or ... we can stop and, er ... have a drink, in Kappeli."

That was what we did; we went to Kappeli. By then, I could see that Mahler was already getting tired, at least physically. However, mentally, he was very alert, his nervous disposition making him talk incessantly, and in detail, about anything that entered his mind.

"I have just resigned from my directorship of the Imperial Court Opera of Vienna. And soon I shall take up the post of principal conductor of the Metropolitan Opera in New York, but it is a pity that, at the age of forty-seven, I am not in better health. My brother, Ernst, died after a long illness. I expressed my sorrow in my music then and I have been doing the same ever since."

"Yes ... we composers do that ... express our sorrow."

"My little daughter, Maria, died this summer. Such sorrows are sent to burden us. It was scarlet fever and diphtheria, both at the same time, and she was only five years old. It was a tragedy! It was

---

[1] Michael Street.

[2] South Esplanade.

an awful thing to happen – such sorrows! But, then, human existence is made up of so many things – good and bad. Regrettably, the tragedies that we have to bear are many."

He would have continued talking about sorrows if I had not stopped him. However, I had to stop him; for I did not wish to be reminded of Kirsti. So, I asked him what he had composed recently.

"Ah, I have completed my Eighth Symphony! It is a vast symphony, truly vast, and a very long symphony! It will require many musicians, many soloists and many choirs!"

"That sounds very impressive. And demanding! I have … just completed my Third Symphony. But, um … it is much shorter than, than my previous two."

"I see … so, what do you say are the formal qualities of a symphony, Mr Sibelius?"

"Er … its style and form, of course. And … yes, I believe, the, the profound logic that, um … creates an, an inner connection between … all the motifs. That is, I think, important."

But he said, in a most emphatic way, and I remember his exact words, "Nein, die Symphonie muss sein wie die Welt. Sie muss alles umfassen."[1]

He then paused as if to let these important words have the desired effect, before continuing:

"Also, Mr Sibelius, I have observed that, with each new symphony, I have lost listeners who had been captivated by the previous one! They expect that we will always write something similar to what we wrote before."

"Hmm … I, too, have observed that."

"And the critics do not always understand our motivations!"

"No. No, they do not! In fact, I always say that, um, no one ever put up a statue to a critic!"

"True, Mr Sibelius. That was magnificently said!"

Mahler paused for quite a while and he looked like he was savouring what had just been said, before continuing: "You are coming to the concert tonight?"

"Of course! Beethoven's Fifth – such a … masterpiece! Perfectly constructed."

"Yes, I would say that it is a veritable masterpiece from the pen

---

[1] 'No, the symphony must be like the world. It must encompass everything.'

of Mr Beethoven, he who inspires us all! I could talk about Beethoven endlessly, but I must refrain from doing so now; I must return to my hotel to rest before the evening. It has been a pleasure to talk to you, Mr Sibelius, but I must obey my doctor's orders!"

Mahler had praised the Philharmonic Orchestra, but I felt that it did not warm to him – this may have been due to his illness causing him to be quite withdrawn when conducting.

When he reached the podium, he was greeted by a fanfare and thunderous applause but, instead of being thrilled by this, he seemed to regard it with a certain amount of impatience. He went straight into Beethoven's Fifth as if he was saying to the audience: 'Never mind about the applause, let us get on with the music!'

Also, he seemed to keep his distance from the musicians, and his face showed signs of tension. Moreover, he was very economical of gesture. Perhaps he thought that the orchestra knew what it had to do and he simply left them to do it – I do not know.

Nevertheless, the concert went well, and I had the utmost respect for him both as a composer and as a man. It is true that we disagreed on the essence of a symphony, but I have always been open to the views of other musicians and accept that they may not accord with my own but are still valid. We are all artists in our own right.

Unfortunately, I did not see Mahler again before he left Finland. I learned later that he spent much of his time with Axel Gallen; Axel took him by motorboat to Eliel Saarinen's[1] villa, and it was there that Axel painted Mahler's portrait. No doubt, Mahler would have had plenty to say to Axel, although sitting for a portrait must have been very tiring for him.

Poor Mahler! It was a real shame that he had had the misfortune to be diagnosed with a weak heart at such a young age,

---

[1] Gottlieb Eliel Saarinen (1873-1950), a Finnish architect known for his art nouveau buildings in the early years of the 20th century. He designed, among other buildings, Helsinki railway station and the National Museum of Finland. He moved to America in 1923.

and I wondered how much longer he had to live. But, when Aino and I were in Moscow the following month, I began to wonder, also, whether *I* had long to live.

I had conducted the Third Symphony in St. Petersburg – to extremely unenthusiastic receptions and a hostile press that claimed that I had been infected with the decadence of Debussy and Elgar! But it was in Moscow, where I went to conduct it again, that I had a severe sore throat, quite unlike anything that I had experienced before. I sensed that something was not quite right.

I speculated as to whether my health had been compromised by the short trip to London that I had made a few weeks earlier – when the city was enveloped in smog. However, although I continued to have a sore throat, I tried to ignore it, until well into the next year, when Aino insisted that I should see a doctor.

"It is so unlike you to refuse to travel," she said, referring to my reluctance to travel to Berlin to conduct the Third Symphony. "I really do think that this has gone on long enough! We must go to Helsinki and have your condition investigated. The children will be all right here with Aino and Hellu. We *must* go before you get any worse!"

Hence, Aino and I travelled to Helsinki to see a specialist, Mr Elmgren, and we discovered that I had a tumour in my throat. After the biopsy, we learned that the tumour was benign, but I was recommended by Mr Elmgren to go and see a specialist in Berlin by the name of Dr Frankel.

"Well, it is expensive, the operation. We, we do not have the money," I told Aino. "And ... I am behind in my work. I should have delivered, um ... much more to Lienau than I have. And we have already borrowed ... so much."

"Your income is better than it has ever been before[1], so where is the money going? How much of it has found its way into the bars and restaurants in Helsinki? We moved here to Järvenpää to steer you away from temptation, but you still manage to find your way back to Helsinki without any trouble! And now you say that we cannot even afford to take care of your health! Nevertheless, we *must* do something ... and quickly!"

"Perhaps Carpelan can help ..."

"But at such short notice? No, there is nothing else we can do

---

[1] At the time, Sibelius's annual earnings were about €50,000 in today's money.

but visit the banks in Helsinki and beg *them* for money!" said Aino.

So, we went to many banks in Helsinki but we had no success and we were beginning to feel very desperate. I remember us sitting on a bench on Mannerheimintie[1], sighing and wondering what on earth to do next. Then, finally, we decided to approach the director of an insurance company to find out whether he was in a position to help us. And he, much to our surprise, very graciously donated the company's entire day's takings!

Dr Frankel had a very strong handshake. "Good day to you, Mr Sibelius ... Mrs Sibelius. Come, sit down. I count myself privileged to make your acquaintance! So, how can I be of help to you?"

We seated ourselves in the leather armchairs opposite the doctor, and I explained why I had come to see him: "Well – er – I – have had a, a very bad throat – for some time now. So we went to see a doctor – in Helsinki – and he told us that, that I had a ... tumour. He said that it *could* be, um, benign. But he referred us to you – here is a sample that he took."

"I see ... very well. Let us have a look at your throat, then."

I opened my mouth, and Dr Frankel looked down my throat. "Yes, there is a tumour. I shall examine the sample taken by ... Dr Elmgren, and you must come and see me again tomorrow."

On saying these few words, he rose from his seat, looked at his watch and walked with us to the door. "Until tomorrow, then," he said.

It had all happened in the blinking of an eye, and Aino and I were left dumbfounded.

"So ... we have to wait till tomorrow!" I said.

"Patience, Janne."

"And he is much older than, than I expected him to be. Do you think that, er ... he knows what he is doing?"

"I am sure that he does; Dr Elmgren would not have recommended him otherwise."

"I suppose not ..."

---

[1] Mannerheim Road. The most famous street in Helsinki, named after the Finnish military leader and statesman, Baron Carl Gustaf Emil Mannerheim.

However, after going to see Dr Frankel on five consecutive days, with no progress being made, I began to have serious doubts about him, especially when he said that 'it seems to be getting better. But it could also worsen, or not.'

"What on earth does he mean? *Perkele*! Who *is* this doctor!" I said to Aino.

"I agree that what he says does sound rather contradictory, but perhaps it is too early to say what will happen next. I do not know, Janne, but we must give him the benefit of the doubt. He did say, also, that an operation might be necessary."

"Well, I wish that he would just ... do it!"

Four days later, I found myself writing to Carpelan – I do not know why, except that I thought that he would be interested in news of my illness. And I told him that I had been to see Dr Frankel no less than nine times already, and so far he had done absolutely nothing!

Eventually, however, Dr Frankel did attempt to remove the tumour – on many separate occasions, in fact – until perhaps even he thought that it was beyond his capabilities. So finally, it was his young assistant who released me from the menace of the previous months. It was left to Dr Frankel to advise me that I should refrain from drinking alcohol for the rest of my days and, preferably, I should stop smoking, as well.

I knew that I ought to follow Dr Frankel's advice and, besides, the operation had shocked me into thinking that, perhaps, I myself had been responsible for putting myself through this ordeal. Besides, I had witnessed Gustav Mahler's bad state of health and I did not wish to compromise my own health when there was something that I could do to avoid being ill again.

I certainly did not have any inclination to drink or smoke at that time; for my throat was extremely painful and, for a long time, I could hardly speak!

## Chapter 13

# Two Russians And A Frenchman

Aino was, of course, delighted that I had given up the drinking and smoking, and the atmosphere at Ainola was much better as a consequence. Gone were the arguments and the sulking, and we became almost like a newly married couple. In fact, Aino was so much more cheerful in those days that we often used to dance together, quite impromptu, much to the amusement of the children!

We were one big happy family, and soon there was one more of us; on the 10th of September 1908, our fifth daughter, Jeanne Margareta, was born.

Little Margareta! I can still see her now, a tiny bundle, wrapped up in a brown and white blanket, looking like a little snow bunting. So, I always referred to her, and her younger sister, when she was born, as my snow buntings. When they were small, they even made the 'kilili' sound that the snow buntings made!

I loved the snow buntings; for they heralded the coming of spring, being the first migratory birds to arrive in southern Finland in late March. They moved in big flocks as they searched for food in the first snow-free spots and, when Margareta and her little sister played outside, poking at the ground with sticks, as children do, they were like these charming little birds.

But the arrival of Margareta meant that we had one more mouth to feed, and money was tight. So, with our ever-increasing debts weighing on my mind, I attempted to settle the backlog of works that I owed to Lienau.

Consequently, I spent the rest of the year working on *Night Ride and Sunrise* and, when this was complete, I started a string quartet, the heart of which was a long Adagio. However, it was becoming increasingly difficult to work at home when there were so many children around, and one cannot, after all, expect a baby not to cry. Therefore, I gradually began to feel that I needed to get away from Ainola for the sake of my music.

Of course, I did not wish to upset Aino by intimating that our girls were disturbing me when I was trying to work. That is why I explained my need to get away by saying that I had been stuck in Finland for too long, which compromised my development as a composer.

Hence, in the New Year, I went to Berlin, where I conducted *En saga* and *Finlandia* to great acclaim, and from there I travelled to England, where I conducted the same works, as well as attending a soirée at the Music Club in London.

It was the custom for the Music Club to invite well-known composers to their meetings, and I was asked to attend. At the start of the proceedings, I had to take a seat in the middle of the stage and be addressed by the chairman of the club, after which I took my place in the audience and listened to my music being played; Ellen Beck sang some of my songs. After that, we enjoyed a most delicious dinner. Apparently, the wine that was served as an accompaniment to the meal was excellent, too, according to my fellow diners, but I, of course, had to refrain from drinking it. And, unfortunately, I also had to turn down the brandy that was served with the coffee!

One thing that left me worried was that the songs that were performed were not among my best works, and I felt that now that they had been performed at the club, my reputation could be damaged.

But there was something that I had not expected on this trip; I had the opportunity of finally meeting Claude Debussy. We met at a concert at Queen's Hall at the end of February when he conducted *L'après-midi d'un faune* and his three nocturnes.

Unfortunately for Debussy, the concert did not go entirely smoothly; at one tempo change in *Fetes*, he lost his beat and indicated with his baton that the orchestra should start again from the beginning, but it just went on playing. However, the audience obviously sympathized with Debussy and, when the piece ended, there was such enthusiastic applause that they had to play it again!

After the concert, I went to the artists' room to pay my respects to Debussy. I had to converse in my somewhat limited French – for it was the only language that we had in common – but, nevertheless, we had a most pleasant conversation during which we expressed our mutual admiration.

"A magnificent concert!" I said. "The English, they like you!"

"Yes, in spite of my difficulties!"

"It does not matter. *Faune*, a masterpiece! It has a, er – how shall I say – an atmosphere. So dreamy!"

"Thank you for such kind words about my music. But your *Finlandia*! A real tour de force! So much power and majesty!"

"Well …"

"And I like very much the *Valse Triste*", he continued, "and *The Swan of Tuonela*. Chevillard conducted it in Paris before the première of *La Mer*."

Such unexpected praise from Debussy, France's greatest composer, was truly humbling. And I knew that we were birds of a feather when he began talking about his life as a composer:

"I reacted against any kind of formal training when I was young."

"I, also!"

"And I always delighted in playing 'forbidden' melodies, those, you know, outside the syllabus. I only wanted to compose for my own pleasure!"

"I, also!"

"I did not think that I would ever be able to cast my music in a rigid mould, so I attempted to liberate sound from the chains of conventional form. And I turned my back on the repetition of material – I aimed for perpetual variation. Why hear the same music again if you have already heard it before?"

"I understand you. Yes, we must question the, the old, um … principles."

"Yes, yes. Exactly, Mr Sibelius!"

Meeting Debussy was such a pleasure that, when it was his turn to be addressed at the Music Club, I decided to go with him as moral support. And, indeed, I noted his discomfort when he was addressed by the chairman – the latter proceeded to mumble something in incomprehensible French that I am sure Debussy did not understand!

When his ordeal on the stage was over, and his music had been played, we sympathized with each other about what we had endured for the sake of our art, and he was quite clear about his feelings regarding what he had just gone through.

"Heavens above, I would rather compose a symphony than repeat that experience!" he said. "However, I could see many beautiful ladies in the audience, which made my trial more endurable!"

"We must be thankful for, er … small mercies," I replied, and we both laughed.

Having met Debussy, I admired him even more than I had done before and, subsequently, I followed with interest his progress as a composer. And when I heard *La fille aux cheveux lin* and *L'Ill joyeux* at a Berlin piano recital a few years later, I knew, for sure, that something big and important was emerging from his music.

But meeting Debussy was not the only source of satisfaction for me during my time in London; a soirée was given in my honour by the beautiful Lady Bective[1], who told me that she had once been a friend of Emperor Napoleon III. Henry Wood and his wife had been invited, also, and the latter sang some of my songs. We did not leave Lady Bective's house until 3.00 a.m., and I had had a marvellous time, in spite of not having had any alcohol or cigars.

Having said that, I must confess that I did not find it easy to be without drinking and smoking. In fact, sometimes I found it extremely difficult – especially when I was constantly being offered alcohol and cigars. It was at that time that I began keeping a diary, which was my way of confiding my miseries onto paper. I wrote things such as, 'Do not give in to cigars and alcohol! In the long run, it is better so!', and I found that this helped me. Also, if my mood was low, I wrote about that in the diary, and I found that, in writing about it, my mood changed.

But, sometimes, depriving myself of a drink or a cigar made me feel as if I was living in hell. Nevertheless, I knew that I had to be strong and not give in to temptation and, every time that I had trouble in this respect, I wrote about it in the diary.

I thought of my diary as my 'jardin secret'[2], and it became some kind of substitute for alcohol and tobacco. It also served as a friend to whom I communicated my innermost thoughts. No doubt, my recent illness had something to do with my need for a diary, also; the fear of dying had made me aware of the fleetingness of life, and so I needed to record events to make them

---

[1] Lady Alice Maria Bective (1842-1928), the wife of Thomas Taylour, Earl of Bective, an Anglo-Irish politician and Member of Parliament from 1871 to 1892.

[2] Secret garden.

permanent.

What I had not expected, however, was to have even more fears about my health; the London smog did not agree with my throat – it started to feel uncomfortable. But I told myself that I could always travel to Berlin again to see Dr Frankel, before I went back to Finland.

In the meantime, I needed to take advantage of my time in London, whilst I had peace and quiet away from the children, and compose – namely, a string quartet. But this was not so easy; for when I moved out of the hotel into a private house on Gloucester Walk, it was impossible for me to concentrate owing to the piano playing of my next-door neighbour. She was attempting to play Beethoven's Piano Sonata in C sharp minor but she made rather a mess of it, and it was irritating to hear her playing the wrong notes over and over again. In the end, I moved to a flat in Kensington, where I did manage to work in peace.

Eventually, however, the need to see Dr Frankel became more urgent, and, regrettably, I had to leave London and I travelled, via Paris, to Berlin. But, much to my surprise, Dr Frankel informed me that everything was fine and that my health was not in danger!

So, buoyed up by this good news, I decided to stay on in Berlin for a while, and it was there that I conceived the idea for a new work. It was only an eight-bar sketch but it was interesting enough, I thought, to be the basis of a new piece that I would work on sometime in the future.

While in Berlin, I also tried to settle things with Lienau, but that proved impossible; he insisted that I had not fulfilled my contractual obligations and that our relationship was, therefore, unworkable. Hence, I was forced to change my publisher back to Breitkopf & Härtel.

While abroad, I may have been free from distractions by Aino and the children, but many problems remained. When I returned to Finland, Aino made it clear to me that she was at the end of her tether as far as our financial situation was concerned. I had written to her from London, telling her that if people came to the house, demanding money, she should send them away. She should tell them that I was not at home and that I did not concern myself with their bagatelles. However, this had not deterred them.

"Off you go on your trips abroad while I am here fighting off our creditors! I tell you, Janne, I am tired of it! No matter how much I try to economize, it makes no difference. Where has all our money gone?"

I thought that she was about to refer to the money that I may have spent on alcohol and cigars in the past but, if she was, she evidently thought the better of it.

"I am sorry, Janne, I do not mean to be angry with you, especially after your health concerns, but I cannot think of a solution to our problems, however hard I try – but at least you do not drink now, and that is a blessing."

"Aino, do not worry, er, unnecessarily. We, we will get the money, um … to pay off our creditors – somehow. But … let us not think about it, today. I wish to, to enjoy my wife's company, and play with the children."

Later in the year, in September, I travelled to North Karelia with Eero. We went to the village of Koli to climb Ukko-Koli, the highest peak of the mountain that soars two hundred and fifty-two metres above Lake Pielinen. In fact, it was on the opposite shore of the lake where Aino and I spent our honeymoon.

The scenery in the region is renowned, truly spectacular, and we wanted to climb high up to admire the lake and the forests, and marvel at the complete stillness. It was an opportunity for a composer and a painter to take their inspiration from the purest nature.

"It is a, a, a long time since I walked this far," I said to Eero, "but it feels good! And invigorating!"

"Yes, it is certainly good for the mind to be at one with nature, and we are lucky that, in Finland, we have the most beautiful nature in the world!"

"True – we have. Hmm, it, it is so quiet here … and yet the breeze plays a melody! I am really glad that we came here."

"Me, too!"

"And I shall be even happier when, when we get to the top!"

"But did Tolstoy not say that happiness lies not in achieving the goal but in striving towards it?"

"Um, yes … yes, he did."

Indeed, our 'striving' was most fulfilling. Mostly, we walked in silence, filling our senses with nature, occasionally stopping for a rest. Eero was good company; for he and I had so much in common. However, recently, I had not seen him as often as I would have liked, since we had both been busy with our work commitments.

Picking up a crooked stick, which he examined with interest, he said: "Do you remember how we used to talk about art and literature in the old days?"

"I do."

"You were particularly fond of Turgenev, were you not?"

"Yes, *and* Tolstoy."

"Did you ever read *What is art?*"

"I did … and I liked what Tolstoy had to say – that, um … art must create a, a spe-specific emotional link … between the artist and his audience. And that real art, it, um, has the capacity to unite people. All good art, he said, er … fosters feelings of, of universal brotherhood – which makes me think of Beethoven's Ninth."

"Hmm … and that applies as much to me as a painter as it does to you as a composer."

"Indeed. But … I do not agree with everything that Tolstoy said!"

"Ah, such as?"

"Well, namely, about Beethoven's Ninth! He said that, that Beethoven and Wagner were, um … overly cerebral artists, who lacked real emotion! Imagine, to say that about Beethoven! And about Beethoven's Ninth: 'It cannot claim to infect its audience as it *pretends* a feeling of unity.' Nonsense!"

"I agree, not everything that he said can be taken seriously; he even preached abstinence later in life. Someone who had fathered God knows how many children by that time!"

"Indeed!"

When we reached the top of Ukko-Koli, I must say, the view opening up was magnificent – Lake Pielinen, down below, glistening in the sunshine, and the forest, in all her different shades of autumn colours, reaching as far as the eye could see.

"Is it not spectacular here, Eero?"

"It is breath-taking!"

"But … standing here, strange as it may sound, I get a, a sense of loneliness."

"Loneliness …? But, why?"

"Well … perhaps it is the, the isolation – in this vastness of

104

nature. I can, er, truly feel the insignificance of man. It feels as if, as if nature offers only a passive indifference … to man's fate – whatever it may be …"

"Now you sound like Turgenev! If you remember, in *Nature*, he personified nature's indifference in the figure of a majestic woman, wearing a flowing green robe. And she says that all creatures are her children and that she cares for them equally. On the other hand, she also says that she destroys them equally and the life that she has given them 'she will take away from them and give it to others, to worms or to people'. So, in this sense, she does not care."

"Hmm … she does not … yes, while providing life and nourishment, she can, indeed, take life away … so easily. And at a very young age – as I have learned …"

"Yes …"

"I think that it was in, um … *On the Eve* where he went further in, in, in explaining how nature affects us."

"Yes, I remember. It was the Bensenyev character who described how nature excites a kind of restlessness … a kind of uneasiness, melancholy even. And he wonders whether nature makes us conscious of our incompleteness."

"Eero, I can relate to that!"

"Although I do not know about incompleteness, I, too, can relate to feeling uneasy and being melancholy. But can it be caused by nature? You see, there are people living in southern countries, close to nature, and they appear to be so happy. I would say that, rather, it must be the lack of light that we have in winter. That certainly does not lift my spirits."

"No, it does not lift mine, either! We Finns, we certainly suffer from melancholy – almost as a, a national trait – *and* we have long periods of darkness. I have to say that when, when spring comes, and the days get longer … and nature awakens … the birds start to sing, I feel full of joy. I feel … alive, through the long days of spring and summer."

"Me, too. Until the autumn comes."

"Until the autumn comes! But, of course, for a composer, and a painter, autumn and winter are not, er … without substance. In fact, they provide different and often glo-glorious tones … shades … and colours to work with. And, of course, um, to make sense of nature, we must incorporate *all* the seasons. In our art."

"We certainly must!"

"There was the character in the book – er … Shubin, I think it was – who said that nature 'may utter a musical sound or a moan, like a harp string, but we must not expect a song from her'!"

"Do you mean that nature only provides inspiration but she, in her indifference to an artist's needs, leaves the rest to him."

"Yes, in a way."

Eero laughed loudly. "We are getting too philosophical in our old age!"

"Getting? I have always been so!"

"Just look, though, Janne! Is there anything like the Finnish lakes and forests?"

"No, definitely not. And, er … these thoughts about nature, I have a feeling that, that they will come out in my next symphony!"

As I said this, Eero set up his easel and began to paint.

## Chapter 14

# A Financial Crisis

Soon after the trip to Koli, I began working on my Fourth Symphony but, before I could make much progress with it, Aino distracted me with desperate pleas for me to sort out our money situation.

"Er, I will ask Carpelan. He knows what to do. I am sure that he will think of … something."

"Carpelan? Why is it that you must always rely on Carpelan?"

"He, if anyone, will know what is required –"

"Have you any idea how much we owe, Janne! What on earth can *he* do about it? Really, Janne, it is not just a few marks. We owe a lot of money!"

"But I do not know what else to do."

Despite Aino's reservations about it, I got in touch with Carpelan, and he promised that he would come to Ainola to see us as soon as he could.

"He is so kind!" said Aino. "But I still do not understand how you expect him to get us out of this situation. But, nevertheless, we must at least make sure that he is fed whilst he is here. Hellu must make some *maksalaatikko*[1], and we can have it with *puolukkahillo*[2], with perhaps some *kiisseli*[3] for dessert."

When Carpelan came, he set to work immediately. There were papers strewn all over the table, and he went through them for what seemed like hours, doing endless calculations. Occasionally, he paused, stroking his tufty beard and looking very grave. I was anxious to know what his verdict on our situation was, but I did not dare disturb him while he was thinking.

Aino was busy with the children's lessons, so she had a distraction, but I could not bring myself to do anything while waiting to know the full extent of our debts. How could I even think of sitting down to compose any music in circumstances such as these?

I walked up and down, sometimes stopping to look out of the window, and I wondered whether Aino and I would ever be solvent. Here I was, supposedly an important Finnish figure, and I did not have a single mark to my name!

"Right, how would I put this?" Carpelan suddenly said, smiling nervously and clearing his throat. "I am afraid that your total debts appear to amount to close on 100,000 marks. In addition, your income has recently gone down substantially, to a third of what it was a few years ago. Hence, you can hardly cover your living expenses, and there is no money to pay off your debts. It is a very serious situation indeed; you are about to go bankrupt!"

"God help us! Is it that bad?"

"I am afraid so. Your present income is not enough to pay off these debts. We need to raise additional funds, quite a lot, from somewhere."

"But where? What is – what is – to be done? Even if I – were to write more music – the royalties, they are, um – so meagre."

"No, no, no, funds will have to be acquired some other way."

Carpelan looked at his calculations. "I think, and this is a

---

[1] Liver casserole, made of minced liver, chopped onions, rice, milk, eggs and raisins, flavoured with salt, pepper and syrup, and traditionally eaten with lingonberry jam.

[2] Lingonberry jam.

[3] A fruit dessert made of water, fruit, sugar and potato starch with a jelly-like consistency.

conservative estimate, that you need around 12,000 marks for your living expenses, 4,000 marks for mortgage repayments and … let me see … yes, 6,000 marks for interest payments. Unfortunately, your pension has remained static at 3,000 marks a month for the past thirteen years, and that is in spite of inflation."

"I can – I can count on 12,000 marks – from Breitkopf & Härtel. And, and, and around 1,000 marks – er, from other sources. But –"

"Then the shortfall must come from freelance earnings."

"And, and from further borrowing?"

"Absolutely not! You are already so heavily in debt! Any more loans, which would be impossible to obtain in any case, would make your situation even worse. That is not the answer."

"So, what are we – what must we do?"

"I cannot say for sure, at present, but I have one or two ideas."

"You do?"

"Yes, if only …"

"Yes?"

"I know a family in Turku, the Dahlström family. They are very wealthy and may be in a position to help you in the first instance."

"Do you think so?"

"Yes. I will write to Magnus Dahlström and tell him that your funds barely cover necessities and, what with Christmas coming and so on, you are in real need of help."

"And how long …?"

"Fear not, I will approach them without delay."

"Thank you! Thank you! Heaven knows how we can ever … repay you!"

"The lunch that Aino promised is payment enough!"

"You are so kind! So kind! Er, well, do you like *maksalaatikko*?"

"It is one of my favourites!"


On Christmas Eve, thanks to Carpelan, money arrived from Magnus Dahlström, which meant that we had a much brighter Christmas than expected. It also meant that I did not have to trouble myself to write ballet music and could, instead, concentrate on my symphonic writing.

I did not know how I could ever repay Dahlström for his kindness and generosity, but Carpelan said that I had no need to thank my patrons as such and that my thanks would be in new and beautiful works. He also added that he was looking forward to hearing the new symphony and that he would inform Dahlström just as soon as it was finished.

Hence, I continued working on the Fourth Symphony during the Christmas period and, by the New Year, it was fully underway.

Furthermore, in the New Year, Carpelan arranged a collection for me and managed to collect 29,000 marks. This helped to pay off a sizeable portion of my bills of exchange. Hence, to my great relief, the threat of bankruptcy was avoided.

However, there were all kinds of distractions that year; for example, I had to revise part of a tone-poem and a cantata for Breitkopf & Härtel, and Rosa Newmarch visited Finland, so I was duty bound to show her a few sights. However, when I took her to see the Imatra falls, it was useful; I heard the pedal points in the roar of the water, which I later transposed into the symphony's Finale.

It was not until the November of 1910 that I could finally work in peace. But when I got working, I became so engrossed in the symphony that I even missed the opportunity of meeting Fauré and Glazunov in Helsinki. And what I wrote proved to be unlike anything else that I had composed so far.

Originally, I conceived the first movement as *La Montaigne*, although it was not to bear that title in the final score. The movement opened with a motif that was as harsh as fate. I used it to develop the principal theme, which emerged on the solo cello and continued its development in canon, before the brass affirmed a shift of key to F sharp major. The mood of the movement was dark – with only a shaft of light just before the conclusion – and I wanted it to be played with all sentimentality excluded.

I told Eero at Koli that what we had discussed might come out in the symphony, and that is exactly what happened. Specifically, it was nature's indifference to man's fate – in my case, the loss of Kirsti and our hand-to-mouth existence.

But, the more harmonious atmosphere at home, which was as a result of my abstinence from alcohol, was also reflected in the symphony; in the second movement, there is a waltz-like motif in the flutes. As I wrote it, I had in mind the times when Aino and I danced together, and the cries of laughter from the girls as they watched us. However, the movement was not without darker undercurrents; for there was still friction over our money situation.

Even darker tones featured in the third movement. Here, the loneliness in nature that Eero and I had talked about at Koli served as a backdrop for my reflections on my own mortality. When I had been operated on for the throat tumour, I had found myself wondering what would happen to Aino and the children if I were to die. Thinking of Turgenev, I knew that the nature surrounding Ainola would be of no consolation to her. I expressed these oppressive thoughts using the woodwind, much in the same way as Tchaikovsky had done in his *Pathétique* symphony.

The final movement of the symphony was brighter, with pizzicato strings and even a glockenspiel – which gave an element of colour, its four notes of A, B, C sharp and B serving to counterbalance the Lydian figure and giving luminosity. Nevertheless, it was not enough to alter the sombre tone of the symphony.

To paint a musical picture that was stark and austere to the extreme, I dispensed with the rich orchestral textures that I had woven into the First and Second Symphonies. Also, compared to the Third Symphony, the Fourth was even more condensed in expression, and, for that reason, I was very pleased with it. Indeed, when it was finished, I could not find a single note in it that I could remove, nor could I think of anything to add. This gave me great satisfaction, and I was immensely glad to have written it.

In the final analysis, the Fourth Symphony was a work that described a mind that was at once desolate and oppressed. Perhaps that is the reason why I used the tritone – in the shape of C-F sharp – throughout the work and also why I scored a clash of tonalities at the main climax. These served as tools to reflect the state of my life at that time.

I was especially pleased with the ending, which was different to all the other endings in my previous symphonies; I rejected both the usual dramatic ending and also the slow ending, as sometimes used by Tchaikovsky and Mahler, choosing, instead, to end it abruptly.

This, I thought, was how life sometimes ended – when a person least expected it. Man's life, I thought, was but a brief moment in time, and the harshness of that reality was what struck me forcibly at that time.

But I am ashamed to say that the germination and writing of the Fourth was quite a strain on the family. It was difficult to get any peace to write when there were five children around, and it was hard for Aino to keep them quiet. She did complain that that was impossible to do, but how else could I have got any work done?

The Fourth was premièred on the 3rd of April 1911, and, exhausted, I awaited the response.

I recall Oskar Merikanto writing in the *Tampereen Sanomat* newspaper that new worlds were opening up for me as a composer of symphonies, worlds that I had not shown to others before and which, with my 'astonishingly highly developed sense of colour and melody', I could see and describe to others. However, the 'others' to whom he referred appeared not to understand or appreciate the symphony, which was extremely disappointing to me. In fact, in Gothenburg, the audience hissed at a performance conducted by Wilhelm Stenhammer! And when Paul Weingartner contemplated performing it with the Vienna Philharmonic the following year, astonishingly, the musicians refused to play it!

However, what annoyed me the most was the way in which the symphony was interpreted; either as a piece about Finland's struggle with Russia or as a piece about the friction between 'true' Finns and Swedish-speaking Finns. One critic even described it as if it were programme music, a Mountain Symphony! That was why I decided to write to *Hufvudstadsbladet*[1] to set the record straight; for such interpretations were totally incorrect.

The Fourth was a *psychological* symphony, inspired by the nature at Koli, and was a quest in the infinite recesses of the soul. I had climbed Ukko-Koli but, in my music, I experienced the mountain symbolically, looking back on the past and, not without a sense of foreboding, forward to the future. In the final analysis, climbing the mountain had resulted in the broadening of my symphonic horizons.

---

[1] *The Capital City News*, founded in 1864, it is the highest circulation Swedish-language newspaper in Finland. During the late 19th century, it was the highest-circulation newspaper in Finland.

However, people, with very few exceptions, did not understand any of that and, hence, they did not like the symphony and even seemed offended by it. I daresay that they found the structure of it elusive and mystifying; for, in place of clear themes, I had offered tiny thematic germs, only, and the rhythms were twisted and dislocated, resulting in a musical landscape that was perhaps too ascetic for them. I only hoped that, in time, they would see it for what it was – a work of deliberate restraint and austerity – and appreciate its uniqueness as a White Dwarf among symphonies.

But what right, I asked myself, did I have to expect a different destiny from other great talents before me. Composers had always been misunderstood: I was not the first and I would not be he last. Even Claude Debussy's music was called 'ugly' and impotent', so I was in good company, as far as bad reviews were concerned!

*Chapter 15*

# More Family Problems

All at once, things seemed to be conspiring against me; for, in addition, to the annoying misinterpretations of the Fourth, Aino, who was heavily pregnant at the time, was not very well and had to go into hospital to be treated for her rheumatoid arthritis.

And on the top of all this, I had expended all my creative resources in the Fourth and I now started to worry whether the Fourth could be surpassed, not to mention being in a quandary over whether I should write small saleable pieces to pay the bills or something more profound. The latter was the right course but, in the circumstances, it was impossible to put into effect.

Aino gave birth to our sixth daughter, Heidi, on the 20th of June 1911, and this resulted in neither of us being able to get a good night's sleep, let alone peace in the daytime. I was worried about Aino; she had been ailing for some time, and this latest confinement now seemed to have sapped her of any strength she had.

And, as if that was not enough to trouble me, Linda, my sister, came to visit us. Linda had been in a mental institution for five years but now she was allowed out for a holiday, and I had not had the heart to refuse her our hospitality; for she was, after all, my sister.

But, one morning, after another night tending to the baby, Aino said that she could not cope at Ainola any longer.

"I am so sorry, Janne, I know that Linda needs you now, but she makes me even more stressed than I am already, and I am sure that it cannot be good for the baby."

"But what – I mean – what do you want to do?"

"I was thinking yesterday that perhaps I could go and stay with Arvi's family for a little while, as they live nearby, and I would take the baby with me, of course."

Arvi Paloheimo, a lawyer, was Eva's fiancé, Eva being already grown up and on the verge of getting married and leaving home.

"If, if you think that that will help matters …"

"Worry not, Janne; Aino and Hellu will take good care of the children. It will only be for a short while."

"Well … do as you think best. But I think that what we need is, er, more space. The, the upper floor … we need to convert it."

"If many more children come along, yes – though, can we afford it? But I do not want to think about that now; I am so tired."

But Aino did not need to think about it; for while she was away, I made enquiries about the building work that would be required. And, by the time that she returned home, work was already in progress to add a new bedroom for Aino and me, a guest room and a new study to the upper floor, and to convert the downstairs study into a living room.

During the building work, I attempted to work on some saleable pieces to help pay for the conversion. And I did manage to get some work done, despite all the hammering and other noise – this kind of noise has always distracted me less than people talking or the sound of the wireless.

Firstly, I revised *Scenes Historiques I* and then I wrote a second set, *Scenes Historiques II*. The first piece, Metsästys[1], was highly rhythmic with horns heard through the mist, so to speak, whereas,

[1] *Hunting.*

in the second piece, *Love song*, I had muted violas leading to the main melody, which had a harp accompaniment. I used the harp in the third and final piece, *Nostosillalla*[1], also.

After all three pieces were completed, I wrote a new version of an old song of mine, *Rakastava*[2], for strings and percussion. Then later, I wrote Three Sonatinas for piano and Two Serenades for violin and orchestra.

But it was a depressing time, nevertheless. I began to think that I should never have married; for I could not provide for my wife in the style to which she was accustomed before we met. I attempted to relax and forget my worries by playing movements from Beethoven's trios on the piano, but it did not always help me.

"I am sorry, Aino," I said to her one afternoon when I was tired from working and had stopped to have a cup of coffee, "I cannot give you, um, what you want. Comforts … the same kind of comforts that, that you had got used to. Before you met me."

"I do not understand what you mean, Janne. I do not demand these things. It is not *me* who requires a grand lifestyle, rather it is *you*! You insist on spending money that we do not have. The upstairs conversion. Did we really need that?"

"I needed a new study. The children, there is always so much noise."

"And the shirts and so on that you order from London. Are they really *necessary*? They do *sell* shirts in Finland, and at a fraction of the cost. And why do you need white suits? They are so impractical! Janne, you are far too extravagant! And it is hardly a few months since Axel was here, telling us what a hopeless situation we are in. But you continue with your spending, regardless. First, it was the alcohol and cigars and, now, it is other things! I despair, Janne, I really do! Will you never learn to live sensibly and take more responsibility? Can you not do that for *me*? I cannot go on like his, Janne, I cannot!"

But what could I have said to her? Everything that she said was true, but I was loathe to admit it. And not only should I have been more *careful* with money, I should have written music that would have *earned* money. Yet, I was always reluctant to waste a good

---

[1] *On the Drawbridge.*

[2] *The Lover.*

114

motif on a trifle when it could have been put to better use in a symphony. The symphony was the supreme form of musical expression, and I disliked having to write mediocre potboilers that were saleable but were an inferior form of art. However, writing symphonies did not pay. My Second Symphony, for instance, had brought fame and credit to Finland, and yet I had only earned 1,500 marks from it. And my debts seemed to mount with every new symphony! But I thought then, and indeed wrote about it in my diary, that surely I had not been sent into this world just to pay off debts!

"Aino, things *will* improve."

She had calmed down a little. "I know it is difficult for you to work in a full household like ours, but I do try to keep the children quiet. They have learned to creep about the house when 'Papa is working' and they are silent at breakfast until you give them permission to speak. What more can I do? Poor Katarina cannot even practise the piano at home – she has to go to the Halonens! We have done everything possible to give you the peace that you need. And you hardly even have the time to play with the children these days."

She said this last sentence, I thought, to make me feel guilty. If that was the case, she had succeeded. But how would I have had the time to play with the children when I had so much to do?

Aino's dissatisfaction was growing and growing, and the atmosphere in the house was getting tenser by the day, so that it was with much relief when I was able to go away. I went to England in the autumn of 1912 to conduct at the first performance there of the Fourth Symphony, at the Birmingham Festival.

The rehearsals took place at the Queen's Hall in London, where I was assisted by both Granville Bantock and Henry Wood, who helped me to call out instructions to the members of the orchestra.

I was never one of those conductors who used grand gestures; I conducted lightly but did give the orchestra precise instructions. I would demand that the brass played with lustre and the strings with *Fühlung*[1]. When rehearsing a work, I might spend a long time polishing details in each section. But I did allow regular breaks so

---

[1] Passion.

as not to tire the musicians. Once all the details had been polished to my satisfaction, when it came to the actual performance, I trusted the orchestra and I focused only on keeping the overall sound as I had intended it to be.

After the final rehearsal, in Birmingham, I conducted the symphony on the 1st of October. That year, 1912, Elgar's *The Music Makers* was in the same programme.

Elgar's work touched me deeply; I could relate to the sadness and loneliness in it. That is why I would dearly have wished to meet him; for we seemed to have much in common. But, regrettably, he disappeared straight after the concert, so that I did not have the opportunity of talking to him. I considered him a great composer and I was disappointed not to have made his acquaintance.

Nevertheless, the trip to England had given me some respite from my domestic problems, and the symphony had been more warmly received in England than it had been in Finland. Also, Frederick Delius, who had been present at one of the rehearsals, said that it was 'no ordinary music', and I believe that he meant that as a compliment. Moreover, *The Times* reported that it was 'music that stood apart from the common expression of the time'. Only *The Standard* wrote in a less positive tone, saying that 'Mr Sibelius's music could be described as written in cipher, and, unfortunately, he has omitted to provide us with the key'.

Rosa Newmarch advised me to ignore that particular comment and she also advised me not to accede to Granville Bantock's request to write a sacred work for the 1913 Gloucester Festival. She said that she had 'a horror of festival commissions'; for that was how many of the best composers in England had been ruined. Elgar, she claimed, was 'going quickly downhill under the strain of commercial projects'. Neither did she want me to turn into a composer 'en vogue' as had happened to Dvořák years ago.

I owe a lot to Rosa; not only did she give me useful advice but she also tirelessly championed my music, and her letters were always most delightful and encouraging.

When I returned to Finland, I wrote a piece to which I gave the title *The Bard*. Whether it was as a result of the trip that I made with Rosa to Stratford, I do not know. I kept the orchestration similar to that of the Fourth Symphony, and it was a relatively short work, and I intended it to be so, but Breitkopf & Härtel rejected it on account of its brevity, saying that surely it was the first movement of something larger. However, I considered it a complete work in its own right and agreed only to revise it, not to rewrite it.

Having completed *The Bard*, I was ready to embark on a new symphony, but the Danish publisher, Wilhelm Hansen, had asked me to write music for a pantomime, *Scaramouche*, and, thinking that only a handful of songs were required, I agreed, if only to earn some money to appease Aino.

It was only much later that I realized the extent of the work involved; I had to write an hour's worth of music! So, once again, I resorted to writing in my diary about my frustration.

However, music was not the only thing on my mind then; there were other, more personal things. Eva was soon to marry Arvi, to whom she had got engaged the previous year, and it pained me to think that she would soon be leaving home. Of course, she was a grown-up young woman but she was still my little girl, and I did not like the idea of losing her.

Naturally, I did not wish to upset her by talking about it and, besides, what would I have said to her? How would I have put it into words? So, I composed an Etude for her as a souvenir from home and confided my feelings to my diary.

She had lived away from home before, when she moved to Helsinki in 1906 to start at the Suomalainen Yhteiskoulu[1], but she had always spent her weekends and holidays at Ainola, so that was not quite the same as leaving home for good.

"Just think, Janne," said Aino one evening when we were sitting outside to cool off from the sauna, "Eva and Arvi will marry on our twenty-first wedding anniversary!"

"Hmm, is that how long you have … put up with me?"

"Yes, twenty one years!"

"It is a long time. And, and I know that, er, it has been hard for you …"

"I daresay that it has been hard for you, too."

"Well … what, what has been hard has been … the money. The lack of it. But I have never regretted marrying you!"

"You have not?"

---

[1] A co-educational secondary school in Helsinki. Founded in 1886, it is the oldest Finnish-language school in Finland.

"No. Never! What I wrote to you once, from abroad, is true. Um, that you are a, a superb wife and mother. There are not many like you, who, who would have managed … so … well."

"Is that really true?"

"Yes, it is. And … as I once wrote to Carpelan, um … life can be wonderful – even if we are sent here to, er, suffer. And he is the richest spirit who can suffer most …! Still … the im-important thing is to keep one's spirits up, in, in spite of 'Alleingefühl'[1]."

Aino guessed what I was thinking. "Are you sad that Eva will soon be leaving us?"

"Sad … yes. It is difficult to believe that, that she is … already leaving the nest. It hardly seems five minutes, since she was born. Hmm … how the time passes so quickly …"

It pained me to think that I had had precious little time to spend with Eva while she was growing up.

"We must begin making plans for the wedding. We have to decide whom we are going to invite. Of course, it will have to be a modest occasion."

"Modest! For *my* daughter! It will be a grand celebration! With nothing but the best!"

"But Janne –"

"No, Aino, I will *not* scrimp on my daughter's wedding! Even, even if I have to write a, a thousand sheets of saleable nonsense, um, to pay for it! I just have to get that awful *Scaramouche* out of the way."

## Chapter 16

# Aallottaret

On the 10th of June 1913, I was the proudest man in Finland; Eva got married. I gave her a day to remember, sparing no expense to provide a lavish feast for eighty guests. It was the least a father

---

[1] Feeling alone.

could do for his daughter, and I was not about to let Eva go without on her wedding day. Hence, that day is a day that I can still look back on with satisfaction and contentment, knowing that I gave her the very best. Eva looked beautiful, and happy, and so did Aino and the other girls in their pretty dresses that were bought for the occasion. It was a magnificent day for us all and, for one day at least, we forgot all our troubles.

However, after the wedding, I soon had urgent matters to deal with, in particular the music for *Scaramouche*, which was a veritable millstone around my neck. In fact, I became so frustrated with it that I asked myself many times why I had agreed to write it in the first place, when I had much loftier aspirations to fulfil. Why did I allow myself to be weighed down by one stupidity after another? I was not enormously interested in this tale of abduction and murder – I was much more interested in writing another symphony. Nevertheless, I had accepted the commission and I had to honour it, so I struggled on and managed to complete it in the December of 1913 – and then the damned thing was not even staged until 1922!

Whilst working on *Scaramouche*, I wrote *Luonnotar*[1] for Aino Ackté[2], who went to perform it in England in the September of 1913. When I sent the score to Breitkopf & Härtel, they informed me that they were apprehensive at the idea of publishing such a long song – it lasted nine minutes – and, so therefore, it appeared in a voice-and-piano edition only, which made me think that it, too, had been a waste of my time.

My next work, however, was something far more interesting and satisfying to write and it came about following a request from Horatio Parker, who was a professor at The Yale School of Music. In the spring, he had asked me for some songs for use in American schools, and I had sent him three. Now he wanted me to write a fifteen-minute piece that would be premièred the following year at a music festival, financed by Carl Stoeckel and Ellen Battell-Stoeckel, in Norfolk, Connecticut.

They paid me 1,000 dollars for the piece, but I thought later that I should have asked for at least five times that amount; for

---

[1] *Daughter of Nature.*

[2] Aino Ackté, (1876-1944), a Finnish soprano and the first international star of Finnish opera to whom Sibelius dedicated his tone poem, *Luonnotar.*

they could have easily afforded it. However, they were wealthy and important patrons of music, and their sponsorship guaranteed my entry into American musical circles. So, the situation was not without its rewards.

I began to write the piece, to which I gave the title *Rondo der Wellen*, in Berlin in January 1914 – again I had had to escape from Ainola to get some peace and quiet – and, by early March, I had already finished it. So enthusiastic was I when writing it that the work grew to proportions that were much larger than what was required. Hence, I had to reduce it from its original three movements into one movement, which was eventually only eleven minutes long. I also elevated it by a semitone from its original form in D flat major to D major.

In Berlin, I was also listening attentively to music by other composers, noting that the latest trend amongst some of them was to imitate Mozart, which, in my view, was not very progressive. However, I was impressed by some of the music that I heard, such as that by Mahler and Schoenberg, but it was Debussy's work that influenced my writing the most at that time.

I would definitely say that *La Mer* was the inspiration behind *Rondo der Wellen*. I wanted to depict the sea in all its moods but I did not wish my work to sound like a mere imitation of Debussy's. Consequently, I explored the lower depths of the orchestra more than he did and scored to the bass instruments, with the double basses playing an entirely different role to the cellos. I also included the kettledrums, which were to play *piano*.

I reflected that perhaps Debussy wished to keep to the upper reaches of the orchestra to avoid his music becoming too heavy, but this was not a concern of mine, especially as I wished to depict not only a calm sea but also an angry and threatening one, when it could be beautiful and terrifying at the same time.

The piece started with a calm sea, which I described using muted strings over rumbling timpani, after which two themes – one for the flutes and the other for the oboes and cellos – came in fragments. Then, in the middle section, I scored the music to surge to a dramatic climax, before returning to the calm again at the end. In the main, I attempted, as I had also done with previous works, to eliminate the unessential, creating the effects that I had in mind using the limited devices of passages in thirds, the cross-hatching in the strings and long pedal points.

When I had completed the piece to my satisfaction, I sent the score to Horatio Parker, who wrote back to me, saying that Carl Stoeckel was delighted with it and asking me whether I would consider going to America to conduct the première of it, and perhaps conduct a few other short orchestral pieces besides. He told me that I would receive a fee of 1,200 dollars and I would also be given an honorary doctorate by Yale University, the ceremony being scheduled for June the 13th, two weeks after the première – coincidentally, the University of Helsinki had also decided to award me an honorary doctorate. This was an opportunity to establish myself further into American musical circles. So, I decided to travel there and I set sail on the 19th of May 1914 on the Kaiser Wilhelm II.

When I arrived in America, Parker put me in a suite in the Essex House, overlooking New York's Central Park, and he took me to press conferences and bought me dinners at Delmonico's, ensuring that I had a thoroughly enjoyable time. The rehearsals for the concert took place at Carnegie Hall, which was a most impressive building.

But after the first day of rehearsals, I thought – as I did so many times when I had written a piece of music – that I should alter the score; for I was not satisfied with it. The Atlantic crossing had given me a new insight into the nature of the sea, a new sense of its power, therefore, I wanted to incorporate it into the music before it was aired to the public.

I also decided to change the name of the work to *Aallottaret*[1], who were the water nymphs of Greek antiquity; for I had always been interested in Greco-Roman lore. In fact, I wrote on the manuscript that the title alluded to Homeric mythology – not to any creatures in *Kalevala*. I wanted to show the Americans that I was able to get inspiration for my tone poems from other sources besides the Finnish national epic. Perhaps, subconsciously, the title also appealed to me after I had seen a painting by Axel Gallen called *Aallottaria*, not to mention that *Aallottaret* would mean more to Finnish audiences than a foreign title.

When I entered the concert hall in Connecticut and saw the podium bedecked with the Finnish coat of arms, and decorated with the colours of America and Finland, I felt extremely proud

---

[1] *The Oceanides.*

and I sensed that the concert would be a success.

I was not wrong. The American people took *Aallottaret* to their hearts and they also enjoyed hearing *Pohjolan tytär*, *Valse Triste* and *Finlandia*. This was, in no small measure, due to the excellent musicians that I had at my disposal; Parker had gathered together players from the New York Philharmonic Orchestra, the Boston Symphony Orchestra and the Metropolitan Opera, ensuring that I had the best that America could offer. As a result, the concert was a great success.

And not only did the public like my music, but the critics were kind to me, also. Olin Downes[1] wrote in the *Boston Post* that *Aallottaret* was the finest evocation of the sea that had ever been produced in music! Moreover, *The American* said that I had been the most fascinating and popular conductor of all time in Norfolk. Then, two weeks later, I received a magnificent-looking doctorate certificate, in Latin, at Yale University!

But that was not all. I was dined and fêted in style, and I was the guest of honour at many different functions. I also had the opportunity to see the sights; I admired the skyscrapers in New York and stood in awe of the magnificent Niagara Falls – one of the most tremendous sights that I had ever seen in my life. Furthermore, I met many important, and interesting, people, including Walter Damrosch, George Chadwick and even the former American President, William Howard Taft.

Surely, I thought to myself, as I sailed back to Finland aboard the *President Grant*, I ought to return to America the following year for a concert tour.


The outbreak of World War One in 1914 was a complete surprise to me; I had never seriously imagined that the great nations would wage war on each other. Indeed, I had thought that the Franco-Prussian war was the last armed conflict that we would

---

[1] Edwin Olin Downes (1886-1955), an American music critic who was to become known as 'Sibelius's Apostle' because he championed the composer's music. In 1937, he was appointed Commander of the Order of the White Rose of Finland and was a guest speaker at Sibelius's 75th birthday celebrations in 1940. He published two books on Sibelius: *Sibelius* (1945) and *Sibelius the Symphonist* (1956).

see in our lifetime.

We had already been subjected to a second wave of Russification for a number of years. And now a war had started. Hence, we felt extremely apprehensive.

Furthermore, although the 1905 protests had resulted in the abolishment of conscription in Finland, many Finnish volunteers joined the Russian army. At the same time, the Jäger Movement[1], – the aim of which was to create a Finnish army to help Finland towards independence – was looking towards Germany as a possible ally, and a large number of young men went to train in the German army. This division amongst the Finns led to further tension and wide-spread unrest. Moreover, the economic state of the country was exceedingly bad.

My own circumstances changed for the worse, also; I lost the majority of my income. My music in Germany was no longer in demand – I was seen as an enemy national – and, in Russia, where Finns were seen as disloyal subjects of the Tsar, my having a *German* publisher meant that they were not going to tolerate my music, either! Even in America, I was no longer in favour due to by pre-war links with Germany, meaning that the concert tour, which I had so enthusiastically planned, was now out of the question.

In short, I felt that, as a composer, I no longer mattered, which was depressing, as was the fact that people were free to exploit my work in whatever way they wished; for Finland and Russia were not part of the Berne Convention.

All this meant that my debts began to accumulate again, and, under such pressure, Aino and I began to argue more and more frequently. A few concerts in Scandinavia were hardly enough to make a difference to our sad financial situation, and I could not secure a loan from anywhere.

The situation in which I found myself was certainly not conducive to creative work of any kind. And yet, what else could I do but compose?

---

[1] A Finnish para military organisation, founded in 1914.

## Chapter 17

# The Impossible Fifth

When Carpelan arrived at Ainola, I took him straight upstairs to my workroom where we could talk without being interrupted.

"Er, Aino – is – complaining again. And I – um, I – really need to, to earn some money. I have been asked to, um, write a tone poem. For chorus and orchestra. *King Fjalar*. And a, a ballet to something by … Juhani Aho. So, what do you think?"

"Do you want my honest opinion? If I were you, I would forget *King Fjalar, and* the ballet. Have you got anything that you have already written that you could sell? You could always change the opus number to give the publishers the impression that you have written it only recently."

"Well, I do have some pieces for piano."

"Good, they will do. Then you need to write a few more pieces, short ones that will not take up too much of your time."

"Ah, well, I *have* been thinking lately of … trees. Perhaps, I could write something inspired by trees."

"That sounds excellent! Yes, write a few songs and part-songs. That would be good."

"Hmm, except that, er … I would, I would rather work on a new symphony."

"That will take time, and you need to sell something *now.*"

"But my reputation, I might lose it by, um, writing in-in-inferior pieces."

"You will soon lose your wife if you do not write these 'inferior pieces', as you call them. Sometimes we must do what we do *not* want to do in order to be *able* to do what we want to do."

"Hmm … yes. Forgive me, I know that, that what you say is right. It is just that –"

"When you have written a few 'trifles' and sold them to publishers, *then* you can concentrate on a symphony!"

"Yes … very well. I will do as you think best."

I did sell some pieces in Finland, to Lindgren and Westerlund, and other pieces to Hansen, knowing that they were not of the highest quality, but it was a small price to pay to keep Aino quiet. That accomplished, I was able to start thinking about the new symphony. I had contemplated writing it as far back as 1912 and I had jotted down a few ideas, but that was as far as it went. Perhaps now I might be able to go further. I wrote in my diary that, although I was in a deep mire, I was beginning to see dimly the mountain that I would surely ascend. I had not been a regular churchgoer, but I hoped that maybe God could open His door for a moment and let His orchestra play my next symphony, the Fifth.

Then I got the impetus that I needed to settle down and write it properly; I was commissioned by the Finnish government to write a new symphony to commemorate my fiftieth birthday on the 8th of December 1915. They also declared my birthday a public holiday! This really raised my spirits, and I threw myself into composing.

Writing the symphony, however, proved to be much more of a struggle than I could ever have envisaged. I lost count of the number of times that I had to rewrite and edit it, and I would never have believed then how long it would take me to resolve the question of what form it should take!

I even had doubts as to whether the symphony was the appropriate vessel for my ideas or whether I should write an orchestral fantasia, instead. Besides, was the word 'symphony' the right one to describe my music? It had perhaps done more harm than good to my previous 'symphonies'. But surely, symphonies should decide their own form and not be tied to tradition. So, I decided that I would write what is called a symphony, but it would be my own form of symphony. And it was going to be my most innovative thus far.

The inspiration for the Fifth came when I was standing outside our house one day in the spring of 1915. The air was crisp, the day was bright and the sun shone on the last patches of snow that were gradually melting, revealing the previous year's fallen leaves, now dark and fragile, through which new greenery was emerging. It was the kind of weather that, in Finland, can be deceptive – Aino used to always tell the children that they should still wrap up warm in the spring, even if it was sunny outside; for spring was the time of year when they could easily catch cold.

Then, and I remember it to this day, it was at ten to eleven when I saw sixteen swans in flight – I know that there were sixteen; for I counted them. It was the most beautiful and majestic display that I had ever seen in my life. Their call was the same woodwind type as the cranes', but without tremolo, or perhaps it was closer to the trumpet. In any case, in their swan song, I had discovered the motif for the finale. This was the inspiration that I needed.

From that moment onwards, I seemed to have an abundance of ideas. I wrote in my diary that it was as if God the Father had thrown down the tiles of a mosaic from Heaven's floor and asked me to determine what kind of picture it was.

However, fitting the pieces together proved to be a difficult task, and struggling with writing the sketches was more than I seemed to be able to cope with, which is why I resorted to having a cigar from time to time to help me concentrate. I was more cautious about drinking, but Eva's husband and I had indulged now and again, when we were away from spying eyes, and I had not suffered any ill effects. So, I decided that it would not do me any harm if I had a drink to steady my nerves when I was battling with the symphony. In fact, I doubt very much whether I would have ever completed the symphony at all had I not had the drink as my support.

To begin with, I scored the Fifth in four movements, but I was not satisfied with this form. To that effect, I wrote in my diary that I was wrestling with God and that I wanted to give my symphony another, more human, form. But I was distracted from getting to grips with this; I had conducting engagements in Sweden and Norway that I had agreed to earlier, which I was reluctant to cancel. In addition to this, I was beginning to wonder whether it was worth trying to perfect the symphony when I knew that I would no longer have the delight of working with a really first-class orchestra, as had been the case in America. The situation was very depressing, indeed.

Nevertheless, I did get the symphony into reasonable shape and I conducted the première of it in Helsinki, with the Helsinki Symphony Orchestra, on my fiftieth birthday. However, although it was very well received, I was still not completely happy with the score. I felt that it needed more work done on it.

It was then that I began to feel the impact of not being able to travel to Berlin, where I had so often gained inspiration for my work. After all, it was the centre of European music where so many ideas were exchanged. Subsequently, I grew more and more restless and needed more and more alcohol to get through the day.

Of course, Aino was not at all pleased by my drinking, and arguments erupted constantly.

"I should have known that I could not trust you to stay sober!" she said, with a look of disgust on her face. "I had seven years of happiness, but now that is at an end, and there is only utter misery ahead! And how can you write proper music when you are always the worst for drink? Really Janne, do you not think that I have suffered enough? Must you put me through all this *again*?"

"But, er, the symphony, it is difficult –"

"Difficult? And how difficult is our life going to get now? And there are the children to think of! It is not good for them to see their father drinking, and making himself ill in the process! And it is not good for them to see that their father is so weak-willed, either!"

With these words, she left the room, banging the door behind her and saying that she was going to stay with Eva and Arvi, which did not come as a surprise to me; for she had left me before in similar circumstances.

In the following weeks – having returned from Eva's and Arvi's apartment – she told me time and time again that she was throwing her life away, and she cried constantly. But did she not realize that I, too, had my problems? How could I work when I had a hysterical wife berating me all the time instead of supporting me?

I would not have said so to others but, sometimes, I seriously contemplated the idea of us separating – so unbearable did the state of our marriage become. It was only the knowledge that, deep down, Aino believed in me that prevented me from doing something drastic.

On the top of that, for the second time, I was heading for bankruptcy. The bailiffs had already visited Ainola, making a list of everything that I owned, including my new Steinway that I had received for my fiftieth birthday from a group of music lovers.

To save me from financial ruin, a collection was arranged, yielding the sum of 43,000 marks. That enabled me to reduce my debts to half of what they had been at their maximum in 1910. So, at least financially, I was now able to breathe freely for a while.

Nevertheless, my heart was full of sadness due to the state of my marriage. But I struggled on with the symphony, and, by November 1916, the second version of it was ready and it was performed at the beginning of December in Turku with me conducting the orchestra of the Turun Soitannollinen Seura[1].

By this time, I had changed the form of the symphony significantly. The first two movements I had fused into one – I had removed the opening span's inconclusive close as well as the first sixty bars of the scherzo, and had then inserted a connecting bridge between the two parts. The third movement, a slow-paced set of variations, had also been substantially rewritten, and I even changed much of the finale, expanding it so that it was in balance with the first two movements.

However, I was still not entirely happy with it and I wondered how much longer I would have to struggle to get it right. I felt as if I had been led up a blind alley and I asked myself how I had got there.

But the difficulties that I had with the symphony were not the only thing worrying me. I, like the rest of my countrymen, was extremely disturbed by the continuing political unrest in Russia. When the Bolshevik revolution took place in 1917, Finland ceased the opportunity and declared independence. Although the Russians eventually accepted that, and we were now, finally, a free nation, this was not to be without major repercussions.

Indeed, it was not long before civil war broke out, in 1918, between the Reds and the Whites.[2] Privately, I hoped that the Finns would unite with Germany to oust the Russians – even though some of Russian troops had gone home, many of their garrisons were still in Finland, lending support to the Reds. However, I was wary about a march that I had written being hijacked by the pro-German White faction at a concert in Helsinki; I feared that this would put my family at risk. So, I was horrified when Red Guards appeared at Ainola one day and insisted on searching it. Unknown to me at the time, they had already shot someone in our neighbourhood. I knew that they were looking for hidden food and arms and, in fact, I had a

---

[1] Turku Music Society.

[2] The Reds were now actively supported by the Russian Bolsheviks, and the Whites by Germany.

revolver, hidden in a room on the ground floor, but they did not find it.

Not surprisingly, Aino and the children were terrified; for the guards behaved in a very aggressive and threatening manner, and we all feared for our lives. However, what was strange was that they did not appear to know who I was – which was just as well.

Nevertheless, one thing was clear: we were not safe in Järvenpää, and it was imperative that we should get away. We therefore fled to Helsinki where, fortunately, we were able to take refuge in the psychiatric hospital where my brother Christian was senior physician – somehow or other, he managed to keep the Red Guards from occupying the hospital – but food was scarce, and we often went hungry.

Eventually, there was a German bombardment of Helsinki. It can only be described as a crescendo that lasted thirty hours and ended in a fortissimo – it was horrible, but grand!

And so, by mid May 1918, the Red forces collapsed, the war was over and we were able to return to Ainola. But the war had taken its toll; the scarcity of food put up prices, and more of my already meagre earnings went on buying essentials – although the high inflation did, at the same time, reduce my debts substantially.

Furthermore, Aino was depressed, and our marriage was under immense strain. It was no wonder that I needed a drink to calm my nerves and help me compose, which was something that I had to do, however bad our circumstances were.

I went back to working on the Fifth and, the more I looked at it, the more I felt that I still had not achieved what I had set out to achieve. Hence, I began to revise it yet again, and it is fair to say that I virtually recomposed the whole thing! The first movement was totally new and the finale I made leaner, but even when I had finished the revisions, I still had reservations about it. I therefore abandoned it for a while and, when I returned to it later, I decided to overhaul the second movement completely; for Carpelan had told me that he thought that it was too complicated and needed to be simplified. And I was surprised by the outcome; I felt that the symphony was now complete.

This final version of the Fifth, I thought, was the best that I could achieve, and in it I had fulfilled my desire to condense my musical ideas as far as was possible. I now had a symphony that was my second shortest to date – the Third had been less than thirty minutes long, the Fifth exceeding it by only a minute or two. The symphony was now well balanced and cohesive. I remember sitting back in my chair, lighting a cigar, looking at the score, and feeling quite pleased.

At the beginning of the first movement, the horns were in expansive mood, followed by the woodwinds in thirds before the entry of the strings. The dramatic tension of the tremolo strings then led nicely to the second subject, and the solo trumpet theme was a suggestion of what was to follow in the finale. Here, the prominent use that I had made of the brass had lent a more heroic aspect to it than to its prototypes.

The second movement, in the form of a G major theme and variations, I was now happy with, also – it had the folk-like theme for *pizzicato* strings and flutes, the brass coming in towards the end and subtle hints of themes yet to come in the finale.

But it was the finale that was the crowning glory of the work. The dance for high strings at the beginning led to the most beautiful part of the symphony, where the horns played the swan theme, accompanied by a complimentary theme from the woodwind. Then, later in the movement, there was the swan theme again, this time on trumpets, initiating a long, slow crescendo. For the final flourish, I ended the symphony with a series of sledgehammer chords punctuated by long silences, so that the music seemed to hold its breath, before a brusque two-note cadence brought the symphony to a close.

Although all my symphonies were a struggle, this one had surpassed them all in terms of the time that I had had to spend on it. But, after all the rewrites and revisions, I now had a work that I was pleased with.

## Chapter 18

# Ups And Downs

The children were eagerly eating their breakfast porridge, but I had no appetite.

"I … cannot believe it. Carpelan is dead …"

Aino sighed. "I cannot believe it, either. Poor, dear Axel."

"Lately, I have been so, um … preoccupied. I, I did not fully realize … how serious it was. His illness."

Aino gave me a look that meant: 'Since when were you *not* preoccupied?'

I hoped that she was not going to start blaming me for ignoring Carpelan, and she must have read my thoughts; for, on beginning to say something, she changed her mind and became silent. I suppose that she could tell that I was upset and that it would be inappropriate for her to start criticizing me at such a moment.

"I feel guilty that, um … we always used to say that he was a … hypochondriac. But his illness was real."

"Yes, it was. And he suffered from malnutrition and ill-health as a child, so he was not very strong otherwise."

"No, he was not. But he was a very good friend to me – a *very* good friend. And, and he gave me good advice. Such advice I would not have got, um, from, from many other people. Yes, he was quite an exceptional man!"

"He was. And where would we have been without him helping with our money matters …?"

We were quiet for a moment, and then Aino said, "He devoted so much of his life to you. Think of all the help that he has given to us over the years."

"Yes … I was very dependent on him – for his musical advice, also. He believed in the Fifth Symphony. From the very moment that … I told him about the swans."

"Yes, he did. Poor, poor Axel."

"It was the one work that, that he truly believed in. And it is so sad that … he will not hear the final version of the Fifth. He certainly understood music. So … for whom shall I compose now …?"

Carpelan's death hit me hard. I felt that I was left on my own, deprived of the support and unbending loyalty that he had given to me so generously. He had appeared, all those years ago, apparently from nowhere, and now he had vanished almost as suddenly, leaving me sad, and uncertain about the future.

I also carried guilt around with me as I had not always replied to his letters immediately, and I knew that there had been at least one or two occasions during the course of our friendship when he had been offended by my inconsideration towards him.

Furthermore, although I had appreciated his devotion to music, I had not been so happy about his lectures on the evils of alcohol; after all, *he* was not the one writing the music, therefore, he did not understand the frustrations that that entailed. So, sometimes it felt as if he was a nagging wife, and I had one of those already! Even so, I missed him.

Aino had kept up the correspondence when I had been busy, but now I felt that I had taken his kindness for granted, and thoughts of his possible disappointment in me caused me immense guilt and anxiety.

In hindsight, was it the death of Carpelan that also led me to have fresh doubts about the Fifth Symphony? Would he have approved of it? And was it, after all, everything that I wanted it to be? Somehow or other, I had the feeling that it was not, although I could not decide what was wrong with it; I simply had vague, niggling doubts about it. I started working on sketches for a sixth symphony and, indeed, for a seventh, but I was still pondering over the Fifth.

After a while, I decided that perhaps I should dispense with the second and third movements of the Fifth altogether and keep only the first movement as 'a Symphonic Fantasia', but then I changed my mind.

Also, I was not completely satisfied with the finale, so I thought that I might still have to work on it. But I soon grew tired of grappling with the problems that the symphony was causing me. Hence, I either worked on trifles to earn some income or I took myself off to Helsinki to have a break from it all – which did not please Aino; for she knew that there were temptations that I would eventually give in to.

Of course, I had a few whiskies in Helsinki but what else could I have done to cope. Carpelan was dead, my money matters were constantly on my mind, other composers were now more in demand than I was and, more often than not, Aino was complaining about something or other. And worst of all, it seemed that the Fifth Symphony was destined to for ever remain unfinished.

One day, I went for a walk along the lake shore in an attempt to clear my mind. And, as I looked over the expanse of the water and listened to the silence, I decided that I owed it to Carpelan to finish the symphony and to do it in a way that he would have approved of.

I did not go back to work on it straightaway; I decided to let my mind rest for a while, taking in the smell of the pine forest and allowing the lake's serenity to work its magic on me. In the evening, I would light the sauna and relax in the heat. There is nothing like Finnish nature for soothing a troubled soul, and nothing like the sauna for taking one's cares away!

So, I went through all these calming rituals and slept well, waking up refreshed the next morning. Then, immediately after breakfast, I retired to my study and began to work, so that by the time Aino announced that lunch was ready, I had done all the revisions that I had wanted to do. I had completed the symphony! And, this time, it definitely was the final version.

At last, on the 22nd of April 1919, the symphony was ready! And I knew that this was so; for, almost as soon as I had put down my pen on the table beside the finished score, I saw through the window a flock of swans flying past. I took this as a good omen.

I was now eager to hear what the symphony would actually sound like in a concert hall but, at the same time, I was worried as to whether the public would like it or not. But I need not have worried; for when it was performed on the 24th of November – with me conducting the Helsinki Symphony Orchestra – it was, to my immense relief, enthusiastically received by the audience. But what a shame, I thought, that Carpelan was not there to enjoy its success.

However, to my dismay, the critics did not pay much attention to it. In *Hufvudstadsbladet*, they were too busy praising the likes of

Selim Palmgren and Moses Pergament. I had done my utmost to push the boundaries of musical expression and, in my opinion, I had succeeded. To be left unnoticed was a very hard pill to swallow.

It was then that I reached for the bottle more than I had ever done before. Since June, there had been prohibition in Finland, but, luckily, there was plenty of moonshine, as well as illegally imported alcohol, available. In addition, I knew several doctors who were able to prescribe me medicinal alcohol in emergencies. So, I spent my days inebriated, wallowing in anything unpleasant that had ever happened to me. All kinds of things irked me now, especially people and how petty they were. For example, how cashiers mistreated or even refused to serve customers if they did not hand over the right change. This even happened at the Akateeminen Kirjakauppa[1] that I had patronised for years! In Helsinki, I also heard a dreadful arrangement of my Berceuse No 5 for violin by a 'musician' in a café! There should have been a law against that sort of thing to prevent artists' works being molested in such a way!

Then there was a host of old, unpleasant memories for me to rake over. For example, some years ago, the Finnish-speaking students had refused to take part in the annual honouring of Runeberg. I telephoned that fanatical, Fennomanic conductor, Heikki Klemetti, and told him that the students would not be performing in my next concert. Then *he* threatened *me*, saying that, if the students were to be banned, he would have no part in forming a choir for my forthcoming concert – it was to include the Impromptu for women's voices. Furthermore, he hinted that if my view became public, many of the members of the Suomen Laulu Kuoro[2], that also often took part in my concerts, would not wish to sing with me as the conductor, as they had done in the past.

Finally, he had the gall to write a letter to me, asking how, in the present circumstances, could Runeberg stand as a national poet when he was worshipped by 'those elements' who had turned

---

[1] The Academic Bookstore, founded in 1893. The Helsinki branch is the largest bookshop in Finland.

[2] Finnish Song Choir.

their back on national unity. It was at Kivi's[1] grave and at Lönnrot's[2] statue, he said, that students should assemble, 'undisturbed by Swedish nationalities'.

I was enraged at his comment, deciding that the less I had to do with him and his orchestra, the better.


"Er ... I must go to Helsinki."

Aino frowned. "What, again! Huh, you seem to spend more time there than you do here. What is the attraction? As if I did not know!"

I ignored her reference to my drinking. "There are things to do in Helsinki. Kajanus, he has scheduled concerts. All five symphonies. I, I *have* to go!"

"Well, if you *must* go. But I am not happy about it and I know that you will be drinking and making a fool of yourself. As you did in Copenhagen!"

"But they asked me to *pay*! For the champagne. The, the festival organizers, *they* should have paid!"

"Be that as it may, but it was not necessary for you to get into a rage and throw your money on the floor! That is not how a gentleman should behave in public! If I had not been there to control you, Heaven knows what you would have done next!"

After that outburst, Aino picked up the newspaper and we sat in silence. But what she read only served to fuel her anger: "I see that Ståhlberg[3] is in the news again. It is a pity that even he does not set a good example to his citizens! It is rumoured that alcohol is served at his state banquets, in spite of the prohibition! How can

---

[1] Alexis Kivi (born Alexis Stenvall) (1834-1872), a Finnish author of the first significant novel in the Finnish language, *Seitsemän veljestä* (*'The seven brothers'*), which took him ten years to write.

[2] Elias Lönnrot (1802-1884), a Finnish physician, philologist and collector of Finnish oral poetry. He is best known for compiling *Kalevala* from national folk tales he gathered during expeditions in Finland, Russia, Karelia, the Kola Peninsula and the Baltic countries. He was a founder member of the Finnish Literature Society in 1831 and compiled the first Finnish-Swedish dictionary (1866-1880).

[3] Kaarlo Juho Ståhlberg (1865-1952), a lawyer, academic and the first ever President of Finland (1919-1925).

we combat the drunkenness in this country if the President himself encourages people to indulge?"

"It is difficult, a difficult thing to enforce –"

"And not something which *you* would want enforced!"

In spite of Aino's protests, I went to Helsinki on that occasion, and on quite a few other occasions, as well. At that time, the social life in the capital was picking up after the war, and I was in demand again. Eliel Saarinen invited me to a function, and even President Ståhlberg himself wanted me to conduct at a gala concert, after which we enjoyed a few glasses of quality champagne.

But although these invitations helped to alleviate the restlessness that I felt on the completion of the Fifth, they were not enough to make me forget my financial predicament. I had continued to write a few minor works, such as the *Maan virsi[1]*, but they did not make much difference and, what is more, with the German currency collapsing, the royalties that I received from Breitkopf & Härtel were virtually worthless. I tried to explain all this to Aino, but she, of course, claimed that all our money had gone on alcohol, which was not true.

So, I decided to change my publishers. Breitkopf & Härtel, quite understandably, were not pleased, but what else could I do? The Danish crown was a stronger currency, and Hansen offered a better price for the Fifth. I only did what any other composer would have done in the circumstances.

Then, out of the blue, I received a letter from America, offering me a professorship at the Eastman School of Music, in Rochester, New York State. One month later, on a rainy day in the September of 1920, the school's director turned up at Ainola to negotiate the terms of my employment.

"Good day to you, Mr Sibelius. I am Alfred Klingenberg, from the Eastman School of Music. And … this charming lady must be Mrs Sibelius."

Aino smiled. "Come in, Mr Klingenberg, out of the rain!"

I looked at his rain-soaked coat, thinking what a pity it was that he had come all the way from America at the time of the year when the weather was at its worst in Finland. I hung his coat up in the hall and led him into the dining room for some coffee and

---

[1] *Hymn to the Earth*, with words by Eino Leino.

*pulla*.

"It is such an honour to meet you, Mr Sibelius."

"Thank you. We are pleased to meet you."

"I have seen no sign of Father Christmas since I have been in Finland."

Aino laughed – it was the first time that I had heard her laugh for months. "It is too early in the year for him to come, but if you can wait until Christmas Eve, *then* you might see him!"

"Sadly, I am here for a very short time only. But I must say, Mrs Sibelius, this coffee has an interesting taste."

"I am afraid that it is not as good as real coffee, but what with the war just over, who would have guessed that we would be drinking coffee made of acorns and dandelion roots!"

"Yes, quite so. And what is this called? It is very much like the *boller* that my mother made in Norway. That is where I was born and grew up."

"How interesting! This is called *pulla*. It was made by Hellu, our cook – she is a very good cook. I will ask her to prepare Karelian stew for us. It has both beef and pork in it, and onions and carrots, and is cooked slowly in the oven. I hope that you will like it."

"It sounds wonderful."

"So, when did you move to America?"

"I emigrated to America in 1902! I, and a friend of mine, Hermann Dossenbach, formed what was called The Institute of Musical Art in 1912. Unfortunately, it was never on a sound financial footing. Therefore, George Eastman bought it from us, and it became the Eastman School of Music, but I stayed on."

"But do you not miss living in Norway?"

"I do not miss the winters! Living in Finland, you, undoubtedly, know what I mean!"

Klingenberg looked at me. "So, how would you feel about being a music professor for a year?"

"Er ... what would it entail?"

"Well, you would be required to do some teaching, and also we would expect you to conduct at five concerts."

"I see. The teaching, er ... I am not sure about that."

I did not tell him that I had not particularly enjoyed teaching in the past. And now I was being asked to teach abroad, which was more than a little unsettling.

"But surely that should not be a problem, and we will pay you well — $20,000, to be exact."

"Ahh ... well, I suppose I could consider it."

"I was hoping that you would say that. It would be a great honour for us if you would agree to take up the post."

"Hmm, I must think ..."

"Of course, take all the time that you want, at least today!"

I rose from my chair and paced the room while Klingenberg talked to Aino. I noticed that she was enjoying his attention; she was certainly a lot livelier than I had seen her of late.

"I am, um ... interested in the offer," I said, "but — it, it is difficult — for me to say — I wonder if it would be, er ... possible to have ... an advance. On the salary."

"But Janne —"

"No, it is quite all right, Mrs Sibelius, it is a perfectly reasonable request. How much would you require?"

"Well, I was thinking perhaps, um ... something like $10,000?"

"I will see what the school authorities say when I return to America. Would you, then, be prepared to accept the post on that condition?"

"I believe ... yes, I would."

"In that case, I will let them know of your request. Thank you, Mr Sibelius, I am sure that you have made the right decision! I am so pleased! And ... now I look forward to tasting the Karelian stew!"

## Chapter 19
# Indecision

Not long after Klingenberg returned to America, he contacted me to say that my request for an advance on my future salary had been agreed to, although the money would only be paid into an American bank when I was ready to travel — this was not exactly what I had had in mind.

However, at least the prospect of going to America inspired me to start composing again, as did a letter from Rosa Newmarch, in which she put forward her proposal that I should conduct a series of concerts in England in 1921.

I had been thinking about a new major work, for which I already had a substantial amount of sketches, and had contemplated giving it a descriptive title – *Runes historiques*. But to be able to concentrate on that, I decided to quickly write some lighter pieces first, to ease out money situation for a while. So, I started by reworking the song for two sopranos and orchestra, *Autrefois*, which I had written the previous year. However, Aino had her own views on what I should have been composing and she was not slow to air them.

"I cannot understand why you waste your time on minor pieces which do your reputation as a serious composer no good," she said.

I tried to explain to her that I had to write these 'inferior' works, as she called them, to keep the money coming in to put bread on the table. I thought that she understood this; it was her who was always complaining about the lack of money. It was not that I *wanted* to write them, but if I did not, we would soon be destitute.

"Huh, what would you have me do, then!" I said.

"I want you to write music which would do justice to your talent! The money from major works would be more than enough, if only you did not squander it."

It was the same old story; she accused me of 'squandering money'. Her female, illogical mind failed to understand that it was not a question of my necessary expenditure, but of how much money was coming in. I was trying to do my best, but it was not enough for her, and I started to feel that, in her eyes, I could no longer do anything right. It was no wonder, I thought, that men said that they did not understand women.

Of course, all our arguments did not fail to have an effect on me and my music; they took away my desire to compose and made me more prone to reaching for the bottle, which I kept in my study where Aino could not find it. Many a time I had to resort to having a drink after one of our quarrels.

Worry made me drink, also. Amongst other things, I was anxious about the first foreign performance of the Fifth

Symphony – my brother-in-law Armas was to conduct it in Stockholm.

But such worries were nothing compared to what happened next; Nipsu, who was still only sixteen, contracted pneumonia. We were fearful that we would lose her.

Aino and I each dealt with this latest blow in our own way – she bustling about, calling for the doctor every day, sometimes more than once, and me either going for walks or, more often than not, sitting alone in my study with a drink. And I prayed to God, asking Him to keep our daughter alive.

I could not speak to Aino about what was on my mind, but I am sure that she must have guessed; surely, Nipsu was not going to be taken away from us in the same way as Kirsti had been? It was an unbearable thought and one that I could not get out of my mind. If Nipsu died, I did not think that I would ever have the strength to compose again. One should not have favourites amongst one's children, but if I had a favourite, it was Nipsu – we were very close. I could not bear the idea that I might lose her.

She did not seem to be getting any better, but then one morning, when I was outside feeding the birds, Aino called me in.

"Janne, her fever has subsided! She is going to be all right!"

"Ohh, thank God. Thank God. I thought –"

She clasped my hand. "I know how worried you have been."

"What would I have done … if –"

"Do not think about that now. She will recover."

I put my arms round her, and we embraced out of relief. And what a relief it was. I had had such sleepless nights, thinking the worst.

I rushed to Nipsu's bedside to see for myself that she was getting better. She smiled at me, and I sat on the bed and held her hand. My beautiful Nipsu was out of danger, and I was so happy.

But, despite sharing this happiness, I knew that it was only a matter of time before our problems would force Aino and me apart once more. Then, I would do what I always did; sit and stare in front of me and think depressing thoughts. And when the situation became intolerable, only a drink would console me. Aino would then avoid even looking at me, but I would be able to feel her silent reproach.

Even when Nipsu was well again, I could not concentrate on composing. I was also perturbed by the mixed reviews of the Fifth in the Swedish newspapers. This, in turn, made me procrastinate on sending a description of the Fifth to Rosa Newmarch for her programme notes, which resulted in her sending me numerous letters in which she expressed her frustration at the delays.

But I was in a terrible state of anxiety and indecision. I did not even know what to do about the professorship in Rochester. Even when I telegraphed my formal acceptance, I was still not sure whether I was doing the right thing.

However, I went to England at the beginning of the February, and that at least offered me some respite from my problems back home; for I was extremely busy and I did not have much time to brood on the state of my marriage or worry about the professorship.

Not only did I have concerts in London and Birmingham, but I also had some in Bournemouth, Bradford and Manchester, and my music, much to my delight, was very well received. The English audiences particularly liked *Finlandia*, *Valse triste* and *The Swan of Tuonela* and, to my immense relief, they reacted positively to the Fifth Symphony – unlike the audience in Stockholm.

But the best thing about being in England was seeing my old friend, Busoni, again. *That* really lifted my spirits.

"I am really happy to see you!" I said.

"Of course, you are, my friend!" he replied with his usual gaiety. "Come, let us go and have a drink, and you can tell me what you have been doing since I last saw you!"

"Struggling. Struggling to compose."

"Such is the fate of an artist! We all have to struggle."

We found a public house, and Busoni ordered a bottle of champagne.

"There is no point in doing things by halves," he said, "let us celebrate to the full!"

"Celebrate what?"

"Is our being reunited not reason enough?"

"Well, yes! It certainly is."

"Now, how are you, Sibban?"

"Er, all right – I suppose. Although, my finances, they are troublesome. As always."

"Is that so? I myself have hit hard times, too!"

"You have?"

"Yes, I have. I have had to teach in order to earn a living but I would have much preferred to compose."

"Of course! But … even then, it is, er, depressing when you have really struggled – sometimes for a very long time – to create something new. And innovative. And you, you never know whether the public … will like it. Or turn against you!"

"Ah, the public! They do not always understand modern music. I heard Stravinsky's *Histoire du soldat* in Lausanne, and it was a masterpiece! But while I stood up and applauded, everyone else was hissing!"

"Indeed? Well, that happened to my Fourth Symphony, in Sweden!"

"Your Fourth? But –"

"Yes. It was terrible. But, but luckily, the Fifth seems to have found more favour. The Fourth, it was, er … too far away from, from what they are used to."

"Yes, but the function of the creative artist is to make new laws, and not to follow laws already made. He who follows old laws ceases to be a creator!"

"I agree! It is just that, er … every time that I fail to impress the public, I feel that, um, it is time to … give up."

"*That* you must never do! Never. Do not let the public dictate what you should compose. And, besides, they are notoriously fickle."

"Hmm … yes, you are probably right."

"And when I think about it, in new works, we avoid the old mistakes but we make new ones! Therefore, with the beginning of each new work, one is timid and awkward again."

"Yes, that is exactly so! But, um … it, it is difficult to forget the public. Although, here in London, I … feel freer. The audiences, they are already receptive to new ideas."

"Of course, they are; London is not a backwater, like Helsinki. And it is not like Italy, either. I could never abide the provincial mentality of Italy!"

"No. Incidentally, I shall be going to America soon."

"America?"

"Yes, you see, I have been invited to be a, a professor at the Eastman School of Music, in Rochester."

"And you have accepted?"

"Well, yes. I am afraid that … I need the money!"

"And they will pay you well, no doubt."

"$20,000!"

"Hmm, that is a good sum of money! I would have accepted it myself, except that the post was not offered to me! Well, in that case, let us drink to your appointment!"

"By all means; this *is* exceedingly good champagne!"

"And when this bottle is finished, we shall order another! Now, let us drink a toast! To your post in Rochester! Cheers!"

"Cheers!"

"*And* to composing! As I once wrote to Gerda, composing is like a road; now beautiful, now difficult, but one on which we cover long distances. We can reach and surpass an ever-growing number of places, but its ultimate destination remains unknown and unreachable."

"To composing!"

We drank a lot of champagne that evening – and a few whiskies besides – and I was grateful for the fact that, although he had sometimes mentioned her in passing, Busoni did not talk about his wife on this occasion. If he had done so, then he would have inevitably asked me about Aino, and what would I have said to him in the circumstances? But we had other, better, things to talk about.

I must admit that it was the best evening that I had had for a very long time. And, when Busoni and I left the public house, we were both drunk and in very high spirits, behaving like two schoolboys as we walked along the streets of London.

I left England at the beginning of March and returned to Finland via Norway. En route, I was thinking about what Rosa Newmarch had said to me just before my departure. She was of the opinion that I should *not* go to America. Consequently, I began to have doubts about it, too, especially after my success in England. I thought that I might spend more time there, instead.

I decided to weigh up the matter with Aino – if we were back on speaking terms. Fortunately, we were, so, after I had been at home for a few days and had recovered from my journey, I mentioned it to her. In fact, she was already aware of Rosa's reservations; for she had received a letter from Rosa in the meantime.

"She does not think it wise for you to accept the post."

"No. She said that, that I should not waste my time, er, teaching young Americans. And, in any case, they could find out about ... h-harmony, and orchestration, by, by studying my works."

"That is exactly what she wrote to me."

"Yes. And, and she told me that I was a composer. Not a pedagogue. Which is true. And that I should, er, concentrate on writing a sixth symphony!"

"So, what do you intend to do?"

"Hmm, I do not know. I am not fond of teaching. Composing and conducting, *that* is what I should be doing. I think that ... er ... I think that I will, um, withdraw from the post. I will tell them that, that I cannot teach. Full stop."

Hence, I wrote a letter to Klingenberg, but he telegraphed me just over a week later to say that, instead of teaching as such, I could evaluate the students' compositions.

"What do you think, Aino ...? Should I accept? If, if there is no actual teaching involved."

"I do not know. A year is a long time for you to be away from home. What about the children? And *me*? And the temptations you are going to succumb to, over there – where *I* cannot keep an eye on you?"

"But $20,000! And we need the money."

"Nevertheless ... but it is for *you* to decide."

I did decide – in favour of going to America – but, a week later, I changed my mind.

## Chapter 20

# Pure, Cool Water


"I am not at all surprised that they rejected them. They are not exactly masterpieces!"

Aino was talking about the pieces that I had recently offered to

Chappel in London, and I could barely hide my anger and disappointment.

"They, they, they were as good as *Autrefois*! Perhaps even better!"

"Evidently, Chappel did not think so, and the other publishers did not think so, either. Have you not read their comments? I have said before that you write such nonsense nowadays!"

"The *Valse chevaleresque*, it will do well!"

"Nonsense! Your mind was soaking wet from the drink when you wrote it!"

"No, that is not true! I shall offer it to Hansen!"

"It *is* true, and it will be rejected again!"

"It is a good, saleable piece. Hansen will take it!"

"Are the replies from the publishers not evidence enough that what you write is not good enough?"

"Hansen will take the *Valse chevaleresque!*"

I was right: Hansen did take it, and a few other pieces besides. But that did not put an end to the arguments in our household, and I began to lose my self-confidence when Aino was constantly berating my music. I also missed Katarina, who was studying in Stuttgart at that time; for she was the one who cheered me up when Aino was against me.

Then, just as I was at my lowest ebb, Christian became seriously ill, and he was told that he was suffering from pernicious anaemia, for which there was no known cure.

It was more than I could bear and, without Katarina at my side, I found it difficult to get through the day, let alone compose. My mind went back to the times when Christian, Linda and I were young and played our music together – Good Lord, Christian was a doctor, saving people's lives, and yet he could not save himself.

It seemed unjust that such a fate should befall my brother. It should have happened to me, I thought; for I was wretched in every sense of the word – I could not give up the drink, I could not compose and I had let Aino down. Everything was futile, and my life was a mess. Surely, Christian deserved to live more than I did.

When he died, on the 2nd of July 1922, I could not bring myself to talk to Aino about how I was feeling. She offered a few sympathetic words, but her tone was far from friendly, so I poured out all my grief and sorrow into my diary. And I took many long walks in the forest where I could be alone with my thoughts and attempt to find some consolation in nature.

Winter had already set in, and the snow, which had first fallen in mid-October, had made everything clear and bright outside after the dull and rainy autumn. It was extremely cold, but I wrapped up warmly and headed into the sanctuary of the pine trees.

It was good to be outside, away from the oppressive atmosphere in the house, but, outside, I became more mindful of my deep melancholy. This was melancholy that reached down to the very depths of my soul. It was no wonder, therefore, that the first movement of the Sixth Symphony was to contain within it the saddest melody that I had ever penned.

When I had originally planned to write the Sixth, I had intended it to be wild and passionate in character – at least, that is what I told Carpelan in 1918. Now, things turned out differently. When I put down the notes on paper, for the first movement at least, something entirely different materialized. The sad string passage reflected not only my sorrow over losing my brother but also the state of my marriage and, in addition, it described my eternal longing for Kirsti, which I kept to myself.

The first movement had other elements in it, though; for when I was busy writing the sketches, Margareta and Heidi were often outside, playing in the snow, their faces a picture of carefree delight. Their energy and exuberance inspired the livelier passages in the movement and also much of the third movement in which the forward motion related to their sleigh rides down a track that I had made for them.

How I wished then that Aino and I could have been as happy as they were. But the slightest thing could provoke an argument between us, and it would flare up until Aino had had her final say, after which the inevitable silence ensued. It was all extremely oppressive. The silence was the worst part of it, and the more often it occurred, the greater was my need to escape into the forest, however cold and unforgiving it was outside.

Towards Christmas, on some days, even in the daytime, the temperature could fall as low as minus twenty degrees, but the purity of the snow-covered landscape was always something that made a deep impression on me, and I wanted to capture it in my music. The peace and stillness of the forest, snowflakes fluttering down in the few rays of winter sun – this mystical atmosphere I put into the second movement.

The distinct mood of nature as dusk was falling was also something that I wished to have in the symphony, and this I decided to incorporate into the final movement. But, for reasons unknown to me, the wild and passionate nature that I had originally envisaged for the symphony also materialized in this movement. Rising patterns competing with falling chords that grew more and more vigorous and emphatic seemed to find their way onto the manuscript paper almost without my authorization – sometimes I found myself wondering if my problems were driving me insane.

Occasionally, after an evening walk, I returned to the house to find Aino and the older children still up, but, more often than not, they had already gone to bed, and I went up to my study, where I poured myself a drink and worked on the score.

Quite frequently, I worked through the night, taking advantage of the silence. And on more than one occasion, Aino found me asleep at my desk the following morning, surrounded by discarded sketches and an empty alcohol bottle, which I had forgotten to hide.

It is fair to say that the Sixth symphony was written during one of the less harmonious periods of my life, so that is perhaps why it did not have the heroic quality of the Fifth. But, surprisingly, on the whole, the Sixth turned out to be reasonably tranquil in character and outline, so that my walks in the winter forest must have had a positive effect on my state of mind.

I always said of the Sixth that, whereas so many other composers were concocting strange cocktails of outlandish colours, I was influenced by the simplicity of Palestrina's music, and offered my listeners pure, cool water. To my mind, a symphony was not just a piece of music in this or that many bars but it was rather an expression of a phase in the composer's inner life. During the Sixth's gestation, my inner life was characterized by my increased self-awareness. And the process of expressing my emotions in music resulted in the feeling that my soul had been cleansed and refreshed.

By the New Year 1923, I had completed the first three movements and, by February, the whole symphony was ready, just in time for the première in Helsinki on the 19th.

But unfortunately, although Aino liked the symphony, she disapproved quite strongly of the programme for the concert.

"Huh, why on earth did they have to include all those minor works, as well! The *Valse chevaleresque* is hardly one of your better works. They should have left that out!"

"Well, that is how it has been arranged."

"They should be playing another symphony!"

However, in spite of Aino's reservations, the concert was a success, and the Sixth Symphony was well received. Even the *Helsingin Sanomat* music critic, Evert Katila, wrote about the symphony in positive terms. He described it as 'milder, more compact, less harsh than the Fifth' and he said, also, that it was 'a poem within the framework of a symphony', which I took as a compliment.

After the première of the Sixth, I was due to give a number of concerts in Europe, starting in Sweden. Worried about the state of our marriage, I suggested that Aino should go with me.

"Er ... perhaps, if you were to, to accompany me, you, um ... might not feel ... so neglected," I told her.

"And what about the children? Who is going to look after the children?"

"Margareta is already fourteen now. And Heidi is twelve –"

"Heidi is eleven! You see, you are so preoccupied that you do not even remember how old your own children are!"

I ignored her outburst. "Surely they are old enough to survive, um ... for a short while. Hellu and Aino are here."

"It is not just that."

"Am I – are we – are we – not, not important any more?"

"Why are you suddenly talking about whether *we* are important or not? It has not mattered to you before!"

"No, it has! You have – you have *always* been – important to me. I – know that – I, um, have been a, a disappointment to you. And, and I am sorry. Truly. But please come with me! You, you have not been out of the country ... for years. It would do you good!"

Before Aino had a chance to reply, I walked over to the piano and played a few bars of music. "That is how I, um ... will feel if,

148

if you do not agree to come," I said.

"Hmm –"

"Please, Aino …! We may, we may even have time to take a … short break. Somewhere … nice. In between the concerts. You *must* come with me! It has been, um, so hard lately, for both of us."

She relented. "Hmm. It has been hard, and … perhaps I have been too hard on you."

"No, I deserved it. So …? You will come with me?"

"I will come, on condition that you behave yourself! I shall have to have a word with Hellu and Aino about the girls, though. And I will have to be sure that the garden is tended in my absence, otherwise, Heaven knows what sort of state it will be in by the time we return."

And so Aino and I set out for Sweden in February 1923, this being the first time that she had been abroad for twenty-two years.

We arrived in Stockholm on the 25th of February and, at the beginning of March, I conducted four evening concerts and a matinée. My music was very well received, and the Swedes seemed to like my new symphony. Aino and I also enjoyed ourselves at the various dinners and receptions to which we had been invited. It had been a long time since Aino had attended any social functions, and I was pleased to see her looking so happy.

Our tour then continued south for a few more concerts; first, we went to Berlin and then on to Rome. Generally, I was pleased with the response to my music and I did receive some positive reviews.

We were then due to return home via Gothenburg and Tallinn. But as there was plenty of time before the concerts in Gothenburg, I decided to take Aino for a short holiday on the Isle of Capri.

In Capri, it was quite like in the old times before we had the children. We walked around as if we did not have a worry in the world. There was nobody making demands on us, and we could do what we liked and when we liked, without having to keep to a timetable. We spent our time exploring, resting and tasting the local cuisine. We talked and we laughed – on neutral ground, our cares were forgotten. But I could not manage without drinking, which I did in secret. Whether I succeeded in keeping it hidden or whether she  knew about it, but did not say anything, that I do not know.

## Chapter 21

# Aino's Letter

"That was strange. Why! Why did Busoni not want to see me!"

"It was rather strange, I agree."

"He had ... never snubbed me before."

Aino and I were referring to the odd way in which Busoni had come to the door of his apartment in Berlin, saying that he could not invite us in. After our holiday in Capri, Aino and I had retraced our steps and travelled via Rome to Berlin. We had intended to pay Busoni a visit before heading to Gothenburg, where I was to conduct more concerts.

"I am his friend. Or, at least, I thought that I was. So ... why did he slight me? In, in, in such a way."

"I do not know, Janne. But he *was* very evasive."

"Well, I shall, I shall not go out of my way to see him again!"

"But there must be a good reason for him to act so. Surely, there is a rational explanation, although I cannot think what it might be."

Whatever the reason for Busoni's odd behaviour had been, I did not have the time to ponder the matter; I had the concerts to conduct in Gothenburg and I needed to focus on those. The Second, Fifth and Sixth symphonies were to be on the programme, as well as *Aallottaret*, *Pohjolan Tytär* and *Rakastava*.

The first concert in Gothenburg went exceedingly well. In fact, Aino wrote to the children, telling them that things were going well and that their father was marvellous.

However, before the second concert, something happened that annoyed Aino and embarrassed me, thus spoiling what had so far been a most pleasant trip. After the morning rehearsal, I went to town to relax. Unfortunately, while I was there, I lost track of the time, and Aino had to came searching for me. She was worried that I would be late for the concert.

"Of course, I should have known better! The concert is about to start, and here you are, eating oysters and drinking champagne, as usual, and spending money that we do not have! You always have to spoil things!"

"Huh, I hhhave had ... just a *drop* of ... chhhampagne. With my ... with my meal," I am supposed to have said.

"You are not the President of Finland! And judging by the state you are in, I would say that you have had more than a drop! Really, Janne, will you never learn? How are you going to conduct properly in that state? Who ever heard of a drunken conductor?"

"I am NOT! Drunk! I ... asshure you that ... that I am quite capable. Of conducting!"

Admittedly, I might have been a little merry, but that has never prevented me from working or conducting. Quite the opposite. It was just that I temporarily forgot that it was a concert and not a rehearsal and, hence, at one stage, I stopped the music. So, therefore, people said that I was drunk.

When we were leaving the concert hall afterwards, I saw Aino looking at me with angry, accusing eyes, which made *me* angry. So, I took the small bottle of whisky from my pocket, which I carried with me for emergencies, and I smashed it on the steps in front of everybody.

"Janne, this is the last straw!" said Aino.

It had been a spur-of-the-moment reaction on my part to smash the bottle, but it was something that I would live to regret. Even when we returned to Finland, Aino was still so angry with me that she refused to speak to me – although she made it clear that I was a complete disgrace and that I should be thoroughly ashamed of myself.

I then found myself in a vicious circle. The more oppressive the atmosphere became in the house, the more I felt inclined to drink, and this enraged Aino even further. Thus, we avoided each other's company, and I confined myself to my study.

I attempted to write some music, but I did not make much progress, which meant that I needed a drink to console myself and a drink to help me concentrate. Also, I had to have a drink to steady my hands so that I could get onto paper what I did manage to compose. I thought then how tragic my life as an aging composer was.

But what else could I do? Composing was all that I knew. So I was forced to persevere and, eventually, I managed to get into composing proper; I continued working on the Seventh, to which I gave the title *Fantasia sinfonica*. It later became known simply as the Seventh Symphony, a symphony in one single movement, the pinnacle of condensed musical expression that I had worked towards in my previous symphonies.

I had first mentioned the Seventh in my diary in 1917, even before the Fifth Symphony was in its final form, and, indeed, I had sketches for it from as far back as 1914. One sketch had 'Aino' written on it; for that was what the music represented. It was a theme for the trombone that I wished to be prominent in the symphony.

I envisaged the Seventh in various different forms during the time it took me to write it, but, eventually, it became one single movement with much of the material deriving from the planned second movement. The ending, I recall, was particularly difficult to get right, and I rewrote it many times before I had a version with which I was satisfied.

Rewriting something many times over was, of course, nothing new to me. I always found that writing down my ideas on paper, rather than working on them in my head, helped me to better see how different elements fitted together and whether, as a whole, the piece represented what I wanted it to say. This meant that I had several versions of the piece to consider. And, when I heard the orchestra play my music the first few times, I still found parts that needed fine-tuning. But it is not to say that any piece would ever be ready as such; I would often hear my old compositions and think that there was something in them that I could have expressed better. However, when I wrote my music in a condensed form, consisting of its essentials only, I found that there was very little that I would have wanted to change, not even years later.

And the Seventh was such a piece of music. After the introductory flute theme at the beginning, I centred the music on the strings, and it was as if that passage placed the listener before the face of God – I truly believed that.

Then, the music became more intense, leading towards the first appearance of the C major trombone theme. It was, at this point, that the pulse of the music changed to *vivacissimo* and led into the second appearance of the trombone theme – this time in C major. After this, the tone lightened and became dance-like and gradually *accelerando*, eventually reaching *presto*, before broadening into the C major trombone theme.

Finally, I recalled the motifs from the beginning in the coda and ended the piece with a C major chord – and there it was, a symphony in one concise movement!

When I had finished it, I wondered what Gustaf Mahler would have thought of it; for he had written symphonies that were, in some instances, over two hours in length! But I had said everything that I had wanted to say and I was most delighted with the result. In fact, I would go so far as to say that it was one of my most supreme achievements: it was the symphony that I had always wanted to write!

The première of the symphony was scheduled for the end of March 1924 in Stockholm, and, naturally, I was eager to hear what the public and the critics though of it. I also wanted Aino to go with me but I did not think for a moment that there was any possibility of that, considering what had happened on our last trip.

Aino gave me a letter, a long letter, and then, with an expression on her face that was guaranteed to disturb me, she quickly disappeared from the room. I thought that it was probably a letter from one of our creditors and was about to throw it aside, but something – I do not know what – made me open it.

When I did so, I was totally dismayed by what it said, and I had to sit down.

She started with: 'Are you dear to me? Yes, when I remember those beautiful moments in our life when we could and wanted to look each other in the eye, heart to heart.'

But then she moved on to talk about 'a layer of sorrow between us' and about how difficult her life was; for I was at a dead end, my work being the product of 'artificial inspiration'!

Here I stopped reading; I recalled that she had said those very words – 'artificial inspiration' – to me once before.

She continued, giving me a long sermon about my way of living and working, and how her supporting me had been worthless and how I could be described as a weakling: '… this is how a weakling would behave; it lacks strength and it is a great waste of valuable, or rather sacred, time.'

She went on to say how much she had suffered on my behalf and how, if I did not change, I would go under. She begged me to 'break free from that which is dragging you down': 'Do not destroy yourself. Do not throw away all that you are still capable of achieving. If only you knew what you are like when you are not thinking straight. Your own judgement is then paralysed. Trust me and be aware that in such a state you cannot create anything permanent.' And, according to Aino, not only was my composing rubbish, so was my conducting: 'Even when you are conducting and everything seems to be going splendidly – it is not really like that.'

Regarding the forthcoming trip to Sweden, she said that she could not suffer again and that '… you no longer have the slightest appreciation of the advice of your only real friend. I, and your works from earlier times, shall remain here.'

Aino finished her letter by referring to my habit of saying that I was a miserable person, and asking how did I think it made her feel. Her final words were: 'It tears my heart, but I cannot stop believing that you will be able to tear yourself away once more from that which is bad. You have been granted the strength of a great man. Cannot your sense of responsibility start the change? …. I pray to you on my knees and I believe that you can succeed if you really want to.' The letter was signed: 'Your life companion, Aino.'

I put down the letter, feeling totally ashamed and helpless. Aino had not spoken to me lately but she had clearly been thinking a great deal. She must have spent a considerable amount of time preparing in her mind what she would eventually put down on paper, and now she had written, in detail, about my offensive actions and my bad judgement.

I picked up the letter and read it a second time. It was a very candid and heartfelt rendition of her attitude to our situation, and she had left no doubts as to her feelings.

What really disturbed me, however, was this repeated reference to my 'artificial inspiration' – as she called it. But how would I ever have survived all life's torments without drinking? Did she know that? Besides, far from inhibiting my work as a composer, it was the only thing sustaining it! She was telling me to 'break free of that which was dragging me down', but how much further would I have sunk without it? She said that I was in such a state that I could not create anything permanent, and, yet, my recent symphonies had been applauded and praised!

I was a weakling, which was true. But, as to her claim that even if I did complete a few compositions in the future, they would be nothing compared to what I would have accomplished without the aid of a drink from time to time, that, I thought, was questionable.

I did realize, of course, that my behaviour had been, at times, not what it should have been, but I was not a saint and I had never claimed to be one. I was only too aware that it had been very hard for Aino to see me reaching for the bottle every time that I felt depressed or unsure of myself, and she was right when she said that there was a layer of sorrow between us.

She was also right about my conducting not having been very good recently, and I wondered whether she had noticed that my hands shook when I had not had a drink. No doubt, she had; for nothing escaped her attention these days.

Nevertheless, I had attempted, as far as possible, to only drink when I was away from home, so as not to upset Aino and the children, or I had refrained from drinking at home, at least when the children were awake. What more could I have done?

Hour after hour, I thought about Aino's letter, and my opinion of it changed all the time; sometimes, I thought that it was a very cruel letter but, at other times, I thought that she had been justified in writing it and that it contained nothing but the truth.

But one thing was certain: if I had not fully realized before just how much Aino had been hurt by my reluctance to give up the drink, I certainly realized it now. No one would write a letter such as the one that she had written to me, unless they were utterly desperate. And she was right: I was weak, miserable and irresponsible.

Nevertheless, although our life had descended into the depths of hell, I felt that there was little that I could do about it. Of course, I knew that, for the sake of our marriage, I had to find it in me to somehow live without the drink and I told myself, out loud, that I would do it. But the mere thought that I would have to manage without alcohol immediately made me feel distressed and anxious, and, in the next breath, I was saying, 'No, I cannot do it!

It is totally impossible! I will not survive!'

I thought about the situation a lot but I could not help feeling how hopeless it was. And I supposed that Aino was waiting for some sort of response from me. She was perfectly entitled to one after pouring out her heart, but I could not bring myself to give it to her – and, besides, what would I have said? Nothing that I could have said would have made any difference.

Once or twice, when she looked at me questioningly, I was on the verge of saying something about the letter but I just did not have the heart to begin a conversation that would almost certainly have resulted in an unpleasant scene. So, weakling that I was, I let the chances pass me by and I kept my thoughts to myself. I do not know what Aino expected of me, but whatever it was, she must have been extremely disappointed. No doubt, she told herself, many times over, that writing the letter to me had been a waste of time. Poor Aino, she deserved so much more than she got from me!

And so I brushed the whole matter of the letter under the carpet and I did not speak to Aino until I eventually attempted to persuade her to change her mind about going to Stockholm. And then, as usual, I was not very eloquent in the way I phrased things, unlike Aino, whose mind and mouth were in complete harmony.

"Er, Aino. About Sweden. Are you – I mean, will you go to – um, Sweden – with me?"

"No, Janne, you know very well how I feel," she said, and her tone of voice said: 'Have you not read the letter? I made it plain enough!'

"But –"

And she could not resist mentioning the Gothenburg incident again: "You made such a spectacle of yourself in Gothenburg *and*, no doubt, you will give a repeat performance!"

"Ahh … so, you will not reconsider …?"

"No, I most certainly will not!"

"Er … I will have to go alone …?"

"Yes, you will!"

"But –"

"There is no point in you protesting! My mind is quite made up. And I would advise you to read my letter again! You do not appear to have understood any of it!"

## Chapter 22

# No One But A Norseman

Going to Sweden on my own in 1924 proved to be much worse than I had expected; for I did not have Aino to commiserate with me on the difficulties that I had to face. Owing to the ice on the Baltic Sea, my arrival in Sweden was delayed, which meant that the Violin Concerto – with Professor Julius Rutström from Kungliga Musikhögskolan[1] as the soloist – had to be performed at the first concert without any rehearsal beforehand and, as a result, it did not go well at all. And I did have nightmares about it later. However, the new symphony – described in the programme as *Fantasia sinfonica* – was very well received. Indeed, I wrote to Aino that it had been a great success.

But I was not prepared for what happened next. While I was arranging concerts to be held in Bergen and Copenhagen, I received news that shook me to the core: Busoni was dead. He had died on the 27th of July.

I was in shock. I could not believe it. It seemed like only yesterday that we had been together in London, and now he had died of a kidney disease. How could it be? I had not even known that he was ailing. But when I thought about it, he had looked a little thinner when I had last spent time with him. Perhaps he was already ill then, and, by the time Aino and I called on him in Berlin on our way to Gothenburg, his health had probably taken a turn for the worse. Now I realized that that must have been the reason why he had not wanted to invite us in. He may have been too tired and even embarrassed that we should see him looking so ill.

How guilty and sad I felt when I thought of poor Busoni, and he did not even wish to trouble me with his health problems. But why had his wife not told us? Had Busoni requested her not to do so?

My thoughts went back to our days at the institute and to the

---

[1] The Royal College of Music in Stockholm.

way in which he had dazzled us all with his flamboyance and wit. I also thought about our social gatherings. How he had captured us with his exuberance and zest, and had amused us with his opinions on other composers! And how pleased and humbled I had felt when he had praised *my* compositions!

Busoni was one of the best friends that I had ever had. He understood me as a man and as a composer, and we also had enormous fun together. And he was much more open, and much livelier, than Finns, and I liked that.

What made his death so very difficult to come to terms with was that I had no one to talk to about it. I could hardly confide in Aino, and my darling Katarina was abroad. In the past, I might have unburdened my heart to Carpelan, or to Christian, but they had passed away, too. The only friend that I had to console me and calm my nerves was my bottle of alcohol – and that remained faithfully at my side.

I wondered how Busoni's wife, Gerda, was coping. Busoni did not talk much about her, but he once told me that he had fallen in love with her at first sight and that she was the one and only love of his life – like Aino has been for me. Interestingly, some variations for cello and piano that he had once dedicated to her were based on a Finnish folksong called *Kultaselle*[1], and they showed, he said, how passionate his love for her was.

Busoni had passed away at the end of July, and I had not even had the opportunity of attending his funeral; for the news of his death had reached me too late. However, I vowed to myself that I would one day pay my respects at his graveside – I knew that he had been buried at the Stadtischen Friedhof III in Berlin.

At the end of August, I was back in Finland and waiting for Katarina to return from Stuttgart. In normal circumstances, this would have been a reason for me to be joyful – and I certainly needed something to lift my spirits – but her return was tinged with sadness for me; she was to marry Eero Ilves. It was not that I did not like Eero or that I did not wish them happiness, but I was forced to accept that my darling daughter was starting a new life and that, in a sense, I had lost her, too.

I had been a little concerned, initially, about the age difference between Katarina and Eero; he was thirty-seven and she was only

---

[1] *To my sweetheart.*

158

twenty-one. But she was mature for her years, and Eero was at least solid and dependable. He was a bank manager and very prudent with his own finances, so I knew that Katarina would be well provided for and would want for nothing. She would certainly not have all the worries over money that Aino had had – perhaps that was why she had chosen to marry someone like Eero.

Katarina's wedding made me think, again, about how difficult it had been for Aino during our marriage and, as I led Katarina down the aisle, I wondered what Aino was thinking. Perhaps she wished that *she* had married a banker, rather than a composer, and I would not have blamed her if that was what she had wished. I am sure that she had hoped and wished for something more than I had given her. And what *had* I given her? I had given her endless years of worry and insecurity.

Of course, we had a tacit understanding between us that, on our daughter's wedding day, we would act like a happily-married couple, but that was purely for Katarina's sake; we did not want to spoil her big day with any outward signs of our unhappiness. However, once the festivities were over and the newly-weds had left Ainola, the silence between Aino and me resumed; for to be left in each other's company was not something either of us wanted. But that was all the company we had; even our youngest daughter, Heidi, was no longer living at home – she was at school in Helsinki.

Fortunately, I had conducting commitments in Copenhagen in September so that I was able to escape the oppressive atmosphere at home. But, when I arrived in Copenhagen, in spite of everything, I missed Aino and I wrote letters to her, asking her to come and join me. I told her that I loved her even though our recent difficulties had prevented me from saying so, and I was thinking that perhaps we might attempt to effect some kind of reconciliation 'on neutral ground'. I reminded her that there were no children at home any more and, therefore, nothing to keep her in Finland and, surely, she would appreciate a change of scenery. Also, I had been feeling as if I was suffering from nervous exhaustion and I had consulted a doctor, so I hoped that she would sympathize with my plight and would feel obliged to come.

At one point, it seemed as though I had succeeded persuading her to join me, and she said that she might, indeed, come to Denmark but then she changed her mind. So, I was left to drown my sorrows, alone, and I have to say that I have never, in all my life, felt so lonely as I did then.

It was not at all what I had expected; Aino came to the door to greet me on my return from Denmark, and I was overjoyed that she was speaking to me again. Words cannot express how happy I always was when my wife began talking to me after days, sometimes weeks, of silence between us.

"How was the trip?"

"It ... went well. Yes, it went well. But I, um ... missed you!"

"I suppose that I missed you, too. After all, we only have each other now."

"I have, I have a gift for you. Somewhere ..."

"But you must first have something to eat and drink."

"No, the gift. The gift first!"

I lifted my suitcase onto the table and found the little box inside a sock where I had put it to prevent it being damaged in transit.

"This is for you ..."

Aino opened the box and took out the brooch that I had purchased a few days previously. "It is beautiful, Janne! You always did have very good taste!"

"Well ... I do not know about that. But ... now I will have what, um, Hellu has prepared!"

"She has cooked roast veal and peas, your favourite!"

"But that is what we have on, um, Sundays. It is not Sunday, today."

She smiled. "So you would rather eat something else?"

"No, no. Roast veal is good!"

Though we were chatting amiably, our conversation that day was on trivial matters only, and neither of us spoke of the things that had driven us apart. The 'layer of sorrow' that Aino had mentioned in her long letter to me was still there, but we buried it, for the time being, under the relief and joy of being reunited.

Aino laid a tray on the table and handed me a doughnut and a glass of *sima*[1] – we always had doughnuts and *sima* on May Day, according to the Finnish custom.

"Who is the letter from?" she asked.

"Wilhelm Hansen. He, he is asking me if I have ever written music for, er … *The Tempest*. By William Shakespeare."

"Oh?"

"Yes, er, it seems that the Royal Theatre, in Copenhagen, is … putting on a production of it. At the end of the year. And, and they want me to write the music for it."

"That sounds interesting. Do you think that you will do it?"

"Well … I do not have anything else to do, at present. And, and conducting the new symphony in England, it has, er, fallen through. Rosa said that, that they are having difficulties in funding the concerts. So, any concerts there are … highly improbable – if, if not impossible."

"So, what do you think?"

"Well … I rather like the idea. In fact, Carpelan, poor soul, said, years ago, that, er, I should write music for *The Tempest*! And, and, and now it looks as though that is, um, pre-precisely, what I will do – although they do not give me much time to, to do it. I shall have to read the play first, of course."

Adam Poulsen, who was the producer, asked for thirty-four pieces of music of various lengths. The first scene of the play was to depict the tempest, and appropriate 'stormy' music for that was required. The rest of the music needed to express the different personalities of the various characters.

Reading his letter, I began to think that this project might prove interesting, and challenging. I liked the idea of fusing music with drama of this calibre, so I replied to him, saying that I would be pleased to accept the commission. Aino's support, I had to admit to myself, was an added bonus, and I thought that anything that she approved of was conducive to a better relationship between us.

Hence, I started working on *The Tempest* in the autumn of 1925. I found that there were many instances when I had motifs that I would have wished to develop more, but I could not do so within

---

[1] A lightly brewed, Finnish drink made of water, lemons, brown sugar, raisins and yeast. It is drunk in the summertime, starting on May 1, on which occasion it is traditionally accompanied by a doughnut or a special May Day funnel cake.

the confines of the play. However, I accepted the limitation and, in any case, I was used to concise musical expression and, therefore, I was not troubled by it.

By my sixtieth birthday, in December, I had written the majority of the pieces. So, I planned to travel to Italy in order to avoid any fuss on my birthday, but that did not materialize and, instead, I found myself sitting at home, opening letters, the contents of which were startling, to say the least. One informed me that a nationwide collection to raise funds for me had yielded over 150,000 marks, and another revealed that my annual pension was to be raised from 30,000 marks to 100,000 marks! For the first time in my adult life, I was to be free from debt! Not only that, the Finnish government had awarded me the Grand Cross of the Order of the White Rose – a high accolade, indeed!

In the New Year, I continued working on *The Tempest*, and it was premièred in Copenhagen in March. Unfortunately, after all the hard work, I was not able to attend the première; by that time, I was working on a commission from Walter Damrosch and the New York Philharmonic.

I had received a telegram requesting me to write a short symphonic poem for their 1926-27 concert season and I had begun working on it straightaway, giving it the English working title of 'The Wood'. That was until Aino, whose knowledge of foreign languages surpassed mine, pointed out that the correct translation for what I wanted was 'The Forest'!

I promised the score to Breitkopf & Härtel; for, now that the German economy was stabilising, they promised me, if I agreed to have them as my publishers, better royalties than Hansen would have given me, and they said that they would publish it as soon as possible.

However, once I had sent the score to them, I immediately felt dissatisfied with it and told them that I needed to make cuts in it. They were not at all happy about that but, reluctantly, they agreed. Perhaps, at that stage, I already had the feeling that I would not compose many more works in my lifetime and I needed to be absolutely sure that my last creative efforts would not be found wanting. Usually, I did not put the final corrections to a score until after the première; for it was only then, after conducting it, that I could see what needed rectifying. However, in this instance, this was not possible since Walter Damrosch would be conducting it, and not me.

This work – which I eventually named *Tapiola*[1] – captured the spirit of the Finnish pine forests, where I had sought comfort and refuge so many times in the past, and so I supplied the publisher with a description to clarify what the music represented. Someone at Breitkopf & Härtel then expressed it in the form of a poem. As well as in German, in the final score, it was also in French and English.

'Widespread they stand, the Northland's dusky forests,
Ancient, mysterious, brooding savage dreams;
Within them dwells the forest's mighty God,
And wood-sprites in the gloom weave magic secrets.'

I wanted people, when they listened to *Tapiola*, to experience the mythological aspect of the northern forests. I wanted them to sense the mystery of the forest – with its nymphs and woodsprites – the frightening aspect of its stillness and the idea that something might be pursuing them. Whenever I went for a walk in the forest at night-time in the winter, I was struck by the eerie atmosphere there that came from the snow reflecting and intensifying the nightglow. It was as if the trees were like people, staring at you and making you feel uneasy. In the parts of the forest where the tall trees gave way to denser bushes, it seemed to me that there could quite easily be something hiding, waiting to come out and pounce on anyone walking there.

I wanted all these impressions to be in *Tapiola* and I think that I succeeded. As a result, when Walter Damrosch wrote to me after the première, he said that, in his opinion, this latest work was one of the most original and fascinating works to come from my pen. He clearly appreciated the poetic imagery and 'the variety of expression'. He even went as far as to say, 'No one but a Norseman could have written this work.'

But what pleased me most of all in his letter was where he said that he could feel the icy breeze sweeping through the forest and that it made him shiver. I could not have wished for a better reaction than that. And then, some critics had the audacity to write that I was running out of imagination!

---

[1] The kingdom of Tapio, the forest God of Finnish mythology.

## Chapter 23

# Isolation

In 1927, Aino and I had just enjoyed a brief holiday in Paris and, on the way back to Finland, we had stopped over in Berlin. It was there that I developed a nasty cough. By the time we reached Ainola, I was feeling extremely tired, my limbs were aching and I had a fever.

"You must go to bed immediately!" Aino said. "I am worried that you have influenza. I will call the doctor."

When the doctor came, he confirmed Aino's suspicions and said that, immediately, everything possible should be done to bring down my temperature – after all, there had been many deaths from influenza in recent years. He recommended, therefore, that I should try to sweat it out in bed under several blankets, take aspirin and drink copious amounts of blackcurrant juice.

"Poor Janne!" said Aino, once the doctor had departed. "But we shall soon have you fit and well again."

She noticed my anxious expression and added, "Do not worry! You will not succumb to this! You are as strong as a bear!"

It was true; I had a strong constitution and had seldom been ill in my life, save for the growth in my throat. Besides, I had a conscientious and determined nurse in the shape of Aino, so that my chances of recovery were better than for most people.

"It is a blessing that the children have all left home. Otherwise, they would catch it. You have to drink this, and we must make sure that you eat well to preserve your strength."

But I did not have any appetite whatsoever. Nevertheless, I would have done anything then to please Aino; for it was wonderful that she was fussing over me – it proved to me that she still cared about me, in spite of all our disagreements and arguments in the past, and I was anxious to maintain our new-found harmony.

True to her word, Aino did get me fit and well again, but then things began to go wrong.

It started with Kajanus's odd behaviour, which I found hard to understand, given that he had always been the one to laud my music when others had criticized it. He conducted the Seventh symphony, the prelude from *The Tempest* and *Tapiola*, in Finland, but then when he went to the Nordic Music Festival in Stockholm, for some strange reason known only to him, he conducted only the *Song of the Earth* cantata and no major works! What *was* he thinking? Why did he not conduct the symphony? Did he doubt its merit? Or was there some other reason why he should ignore it?

Of course, this was disastrous for me; people began to suspect that I was running out of ideas and that I could no longer write anything of any significance.

I have to say that, from that point onwards, I lost my trust in Kajanus – I felt that he had done me wrong – but I also started to have fresh doubts about myself. Consequently, I did not seem to be able to find any inspiration for a new major work.

In addition, I felt that I was losing my last remaining friends. But Aino said that, as far as losing friends was concerned, I only had myself to blame. Quite what she meant by that cryptic comment, I do not know, but she muttered something about Carpelan.

I thought, why was she now harping on about Carpelan. It was true that I had not always replied to his letters, but he had known that I had been too busy, composing. Besides, Aino took care of our correspondence in the meantime. Nevertheless, she attributed his occasional silences to my insensitivity – even though I had pointed out to her that Carpelan had been *oversensitive*.

I had also lost some friends when my reputation abroad began to soar – for Finns are very envious of each other's success – and others seemed to fade away now when I was no longer young and the hero of the day, and they could not bask in my reflected glory, anymore.

And, on the top of everything else, the tremor in my hands was getting worse. I needed a drink to steady them, but Aino, of course, stopped talking to me when she discovered what I was doing.

I did try to have alcohol-free days and I noted in my diary when I managed without a drink. But, I would quickly lapse back into my daily habit, especially, when I thought about how lonely and isolated I felt and how I was a falling star whilst others were in the ascendant.

Who, in such circumstances, would be able to take on the huge task of writing a new symphony? Even ideas for one eluded me, and so, eventually, I embarked on writing two concert suites from The *Tempest*, simply to have something to do to pass away the time. And even doing that proved an ordeal, akin to having to do one's school homework all over again! What a lamentable state of affairs it was!

Even a letter from Olin Downes did not succeed in raising my spirits in the way that it would have done before. He wrote to me, saying that my music was held in high regard in his country; for I was the epitome of all that was best in modern music. He was inviting me to go and conduct in America, but how could I possibly have done that when my hands shook and I had totally lost confidence in myself?

I did think about his proposal and, on better days, I thought that I might accept his invitation. However, on other days, I thought otherwise. Finally, about two and a half months after I had received his letter, I cabled him to say that, regrettably, I could not do a tour at the present moment.

He, however, was undeterred by my refusal and he duly wrote to me again, saying that if I could not go to America, he would undertake to persuade other conductors to present my works, instead. The result was that Leopold Stokowsky[1] conducted the Fifth Symphony, and Sergei Koussevitsky[2], no less, conducted several of my other works.

The opportunity to thank Koussevitsky arose when he came to Finland during a European tour. I went to Helsinki to see him, and we spent a very pleasant evening at a hotel. We had a few drinks, but my ability to tolerate large amounts of alcohol was no

---

[1] Leopold Anthony Stokowski (1882-1977), a British conductor best known for his association with the Philadelphia Orchestra, and especially noted for his free-hand conducting style without the need for a baton.

[2] Sergei Alexandrovich Koussevitsky (1874-1951), a Russian-born conductor and composer who had a 25-year long tenure with the Boston Symphonic Orchestra. He became a United States citizen in 1941.

longer what it used to be, and so I was no match for him!

I had first met Wäinö Sola[1] at the Freemasons' Suomi Lodge. A very gentle-looking man with a smart appearance, he was a well-known opera singer, and a teacher at the Institute in Helsinki. At one of the brotherhood dinners, he suggested that I should write a special ritual piece for the Masons, the Lodge being prepared to support the project financially. I agreed to do that, but, unfortunately, when it was performed for the first time at the Lodge, the Mannborn harmonium did not produce enough *forte*. I would have wanted the piece to sound more rousing.

Sola also proposed that I should write a new work, perhaps a symphony, for the inauguration of the hydroelectric power station in Imatra. This was, after all, an important engineering project to provide power for the young nation's industry.

"I know that you have always admired the Imatra Falls; surely, this would be an ideal project for you to consider."

"Ah, the Imatra Falls! Yes, such elemental, almost primeval power! It might be something to consider."

"It could be called *The Water Symphony* or *The Imatra Symphony* or something of that sort."

"Hmm ... I will have to give it some thought. It is a, a possibility ... yes."

"I could get in touch with Malmi, the chief engineer at Imatra, and see if we could arrange a commission."

"Yes ... by all means."

"So, shall I talk to Malmi, then?"

"Yes, talk to him."

Sola's idea did appeal to me, but a few days later, I wondered whether it was such a good idea, after all. I had already written *Aallottaret*, so I was not entirely sure whether I really wanted to write another work about water. Besides, by that time, I already had a few motifs dancing in my head, which I thought that I might use in a possible eighth symphony, and I wanted to develop those. Also, although the Imatra power plant was a major industrial

---

[1] Jalo Wäinö Sola (born Sundberg) (1883-1961), a Finnish tenor who played over 100 roles, directed 65 operas and translated 25 librettos into Finnish.

feature for the nation to be proud of, at the same time, I felt distressed by the inevitable destruction of the Falls, which were a magnificent natural landmark. Hence, I declined to write the music.

However, I found it difficult to concentrate on writing *any* music at that time. The discord over the language question in Finland was still ongoing. In addition, and worse still, the emergence of the radical *Lapuanliike[1]* at Lapua at the end of 1929 escalated violent confrontations between the nationalists and the Communists. We had already been through one civil war, and not that long ago; hence, I, along with many others, was concerned about whether we would have to face another one.

As far as the language question was concerned, I still disapproved of the conflict; I did not see why the Swedish and Finnish cultures could not exist amicably side-by-side. And regarding the political situation, I thought it right and proper that the leader of the *Lapuanliike*, Iisakki Kosola, should rally his supporters to persuade the government to introduce anti-communist legislation. However, some of their activities went, in my opinion, beyond the line of decency. What did abducting President Ståhlberg and his wife, and handing them over to the Soviet border guards achieve?

Furthermore, it did not help me to concentrate on music, either, that, earlier in the year, Aino's mother had died, which had plunged Aino into a deep depression. Regarding the funeral, I did not attend; Aino told me that she did not want me to go but she did not give a reason, and I did not press her to explain herself. I suspected that she was afraid of me turning up in a state of intoxication.

However, later, when Axel Gallen died, I was one of the pallbearers at his funeral. For the occasion, I wrote a short commemorative piece, in memory of our Symposium days, which I called *Surusoitto[2]*. I based it on a melody that I had sketched out for the slow movement of the Eighth Symphony.

At the funeral, I recalled how Axel, Adolf Paul, Kajanus, Armas and I had spent the days of our youth, and I was overcome

---

[1] The Lapua Movement, a Finnish radical nationalist and anti-communist movement founded in and named after the town of Lapua in the west of Finland in 1929.

[2] *Funeral Music.*

by a desperate sadness and a longing for those times. The world had much to offer then, when we were young, whereas now there seemed to be nothing but disappointment, frustration, disillusionment and, above all, loss on the horizon.

<br>

<br>

<br>

## Chapter 24
# A Struggle

<br>

The Eighth Symphony was slow in materializing; for I had so many distractions whilst trying to compose it. Or, at least, that is what I told myself. In hindsight, I suppose that the main reason for its slow progress had more to do with how I felt about my own capabilities as a composer.

The tremor in my hands was getting worse, and I now had cataracts in my eyes, as well, so that it was not easy for me to write down the score – I had to acquire manuscript paper with extra large staves on it.

But what was worse than the physical limitations was the fact that, most of the time, I was unsure of whether I had it in me to write another symphony, and I told myself that there was no point in writing it if it did not prove to be better than the one that came before it.

There had been a time when the compulsion to compose had been so strong that I had had to submit to it totally. Even in the middle of a social gathering, I had sometimes been forced to leave my guests in Aino's capable hands while I went to my study to write something down. As a young man, I had felt the urge to write music completely overpowering; it was like a strong pulse, energizing my entire body. But now the pulse had grown weak and seemed to be in danger of stopping altogether.

But, when I thought more about it, I realized that I had a problem that few famous composers had had to face. Beethoven and Mozart, for instance, had both died relatively young and had not had to deal with the lack of compulsion to write that came with old age.

What made me feel guilty was that the state was paying me a generous pension, but I could not produce what was expected of me. And it felt as if the piano, the record player and the manuscript paper were looking at me with silent reproach – perhaps they, too, were disappointed in me.

Of course, I could have endeavoured to convince myself that I was satisfied with all that I had achieved so far. But I could not do that and I doubt whether any musician's past achievements can compensate for the loss of joy in creating new major works. Besides, Richard Strauss, for example, was still producing them. This only made my sadness all the greater.

I had had a dream where I was conducting the Eighth Symphony, but is that all it would ever be – a dream? How many times had I discarded the sketches for this symphony? Three times? Four times? I could hardly remember, any more. But perhaps it was an indication that the Seventh symphony would be my last. In any case, I had only published half of what I had composed – so would one more unpublished work make any difference?

It did not help, either, that there were letters arriving at Ainola constantly, from conductors and publishers alike, pestering me as to when the symphony would be completed, and would it be ready for this-and-this season of concerts.

"*Perkele*! I wish that they would just leave me alone! To get on with it!" I said to Aino one morning – on one of the days when she was talking to me.

"I think that you are putting too much sugar on your porridge," she said.

"Ah, yes. Well, I was just thinking about when, er, Olin Downes was here. And, and he, um … brought up the symphony!"

"You spoke to him quite irritably, as I recall. The poor man had travelled all the way from America to see you, and you were not very nice to him!"

"These things, they, they, they cannot be rushed! I *told* him that, um, I had written the first two movements. And, er … the rest of the symphony, it was in my head. He, he cannot expect me to, to complete it … just like that!"

"He was simply making enquiries about your progress."

"Yes, well, he will be notified … when it is ready!"

"Actually, he said that he was astonished at how reluctant you were to discuss your music. 'Art, philosophy, literature, science and so on. He is willing to talk about anything except his music,' he said to me. I think that he was quite disappointed."

"I do not like discussing my music! You know that!"

"Even so, you could have said *something*! You have written the first two movements, did you say?"

"Er, in a fashion … but I shall have to rewrite them. At one stage, no doubt. They, they are, they are *not* how I would wish them to be. I may even rewrite them *now*. Sometimes, it is, um … not worth trying to salvage what is … essentially rubbish!"

"Rubbish? Surely not!"

"It is! For each symphony, I want to develop, um … something … special. Something unique. I do not want anything that, that I have written before. So … I may have to travel to Berlin."

"If you think that it will help, although I doubt that it will, once you get to the bars."

I did travel to Berlin for a short visit and, to my relief, I found inspiration there. Consequently, I wrote to Aino to tell her that my work on the symphony had been fruitful and that it promised to be wonderful.

But when I returned to Finland, I started to have grave doubts about the score. I even tore up some of the sketches. So, when Wilhelm Hansen decided to ask me about the symphony's progress, I told him that it was still in my head. This was not a lie; by this time, I did have a wealth of ideas, but whenever I put any of them onto paper, they did not satisfy me.

Why, I do not know, but in the summer of 1930, I promised Sergei Koussevitsky that the symphony would be ready to be performed in Boston in the 1930-31 season of concerts. Perhaps I thought that giving myself a deadline would be a good way of making me complete the symphony once and for all. However, I quickly realized that I had made a very rash promise and I knew that the symphony would not be ready even then.

The following year, I returned yet again to Berlin, and inspiration came to me, again! I even envisaged writing a choral symphony – albeit one that would be quite different to Beethoven's – and once more, I wrote home to Aino, telling her how engrossed in my music I was and that the symphony was making great strides.

So, when Koussevitsky wrote to me, asking if the symphony would be ready for the *next* season, I assured him that it would be ready by the spring of 1932 – which, of course, it was not.

By this time, Olin Downes was requesting the printed score and, in London, the symphony was already on the programme for the spring of 1933. Furthermore, Koussevitsky was constantly making 'further enquiries', and I was making more promises that, I knew, I could not keep. Basil Cameron[1] also asked me about the symphony, and I told him that it would soon be ready, but, by then, I knew that, in all probability, it would *never* be ready.

Musically, these were very frustrating times for me. Olin Downes's visit to Ainola had been a pleasant distraction for me at the time, apart from his questions about my music. However, his devotion to me had a detrimental effect in the long term; it put me under enormous pressure and increased my anxiety as to whether I could produce another symphony or not.

And that was not all. Downes's praise for me in American music circles served only to arouse resentment amongst the followers of Stravinsky, and it also prompted venomous attacks from the Schoenberg camp. Subsequently, the émigré theorist, Theodore W. Adorno, said harsh words about me, claiming that, not only was my work overrated but, also, it fundamentally lacked any good qualities by which musical standards were measured! He said that if my music was good, then all the categories by which musical standards were measured should be completely abolished!

This vitriolic attack on me caused me so much anguish that, for a long time, I abandoned all attempts to compose. What was the point in me working on a new symphony when all the signs pointed to a demise of my music? And even among my own followers, I believed that there were those who would criticize me if the quality of the Eighth did not match that of the Seventh, and what was the use of publishing a symphony that would let down its predecessors?

But, in spite of everything, gradually, I started to be drawn

---

[1] Basil George Cameron (Hindenberg) (1884-1975), an English conductor who was born in Berkshire, son of a German immigrant family. He dropped his German surname at the start of World War I.

back into the struggle with the symphony. However, during my break from composing, I had become accustomed to other things occupying my time, which also kept Aino happy – she even remarked that I was a member of the family again! And I enjoyed that time, so that, when I started working again, I did not feel so obsessive about it; I worked in moderation, leaving time for other things, as well.

The girls were often visiting us then, and we spent much of our time outdoors, weather permitting. I also went on long walks with Eero and, from time to time, we all went to an art exhibition, well supplied with sandwiches and my favourite toffee cakes for a picnic on the way back.

By this time, the girls' nursery had been converted into a library by Heidi's husband, Aulis Blomstedt, and, in the evenings, and sometimes in the daytime, as well, I liked to sit in a chair in the corner of the room and listen to the wireless. I often tuned in to foreign wireless stations and heard my own works being performed.

"The swan theme is one of the most beautiful things that you have ever written," said Aino, on hearing the familiar strains of the Fifth Symphony when she joined me in the library one evening after dinner. She had brought me my usual coffee and cognac.

It might sound surprising that she should bring an alcoholic drink for me, considering how she had always viewed my drinking, but she knew that I needed a small drink to steady my hands and that I could not take a large amount of drink any more, like I used to. So, an after-dinner cognac was more or less acceptable.

"Yes, it was a, a wondrous moment! When I saw those swans. So powerful … and poetic. But … this orchestra, it does not quite capture it."

"Yes, perhaps this is not the best rendition of it."

"And the *tempo* is wrong. Why! Why do they never get the tempo right! It is, it is either twice as slow as it should be, or … much too fast. But hardly ever right!"

"Do you think so?"

"Yes. The conductors of today, they, they, they do not seem to know how a *real* Adagio should sound! I shall have to write to this one. And, um … put him straight! Sometimes, I even wonder whether they do it on, on purpose. Perhaps, they begrudge me my success!"

"I am sure that that is not the case! But I have certainly heard better versions than this one. Still, it is very pleasant to sit here like this. You have had a lot of difficulty with your latest work, but it has been nice spending more time together."

"Yes, it has … indeed. And, and perhaps I am getting too old to … compose. A composer, he should know when he has, er … wr-wr-written his best works. And leave it at that. I do not think that, um, I am up to composing … anything. Any more. Sib is finished!"

"I am not sure that I believe that! You say that one day, but then you will be sitting at your desk the next day!"

"I do not know why! All my sketches, they end up in the waste paper basket! Nothing seems to work. I do not think that, that this symphony will *ever* be written. Every sketch is … total rubbish!"

"Now you are too harsh with yourself. Every symphony that you have ever written has caused you trouble. What is so different about this one?"

"The expectations! The, the 'when-will-it-be-ready' questions! It is hopeless … perhaps I have run out of ideas."

"I hardly can believe that!"

"It is true! Perhaps I have said everything that, that I have to say."

This was honestly how I felt that day. However, as Aino had predicted, a few days later, when my despondency had lifted, I was sitting at my desk, making another desperate attempt to write the symphony. I had not run out of ideas, but what appeared on the staves in front of me was still not right.

Also, I scarcely recognized my own handwriting now. Whereas before, my scores were always neatly written, nowadays the tremor in my hands made them resemble childlike scribbling. Soon nobody would be able to read my music. In fact, the situation was getting so bad that when people wrote to me, requesting my signature, I asked Aino to forge it. Not only was I no longer able to conduct properly, but I could not even sign my own name!

I suppose that there were some bright spots, however. Round about that time, the New York Philharmonic Orchestra carried out a survey about the musical preferences of its listeners of Sunday concerts and, when the results of the survey were published in *The New York Times*, apparently, they said that their favourite composer was me! Also, in Germany, I was awarded the

Goethe Medal and, in Finland, there was a banquet in my honour to celebrate my seventieth birthday – Aino sat next to Mannerheim[1]!

However, these events were only a temporary distraction; not long afterwards, Olin Downes was knocking at my door again, pressing me to tell him when the symphony would be ready. I tried to be polite to him but, in the end, I am afraid to say that my frustration got the better of me and, eventually, I blurted out in German, 'Ich kann nicht!'[2] The poor man left Ainola most disheartened and, no doubt, thinking that he was fighting a lost cause.

I have to say that none of the people with whom I had dealings in public, Downes included, knew of the problems that I was having in private. And no amount of honours made up for the inadequacy that I felt at not being able to compose or to take care of my affairs. I could not even keep up with my correspondence any more.

"A secretary. I think that, er ... we should have a secretary again," I said to Aino one morning, after I had spent a sleepless night considering the matter. "All this, all this correspondence. I cannot deal with it. And, and, and I cannot expect you to deal with it all. We are, um, not getting any younger ..."

"Yes, I think that is a good idea. You are right. There are too many letters for us to answer, what with the ones from the publishers and music people, and then there are so many letters from ordinary people."

"Arvid, he said that he knew someone ... suitable. Someone who, who works at the bank. *And* who comes from a, a musical family. Arvid said that he was a very, um, a-a-amiable man. A photographer, he said."

"Well, if Arvid thinks that he is the right person, then he must be."

And that was when my life changed for the better.

---

[1] Baron Carl Gustaf Emil Mannerheim (1867-1951), a Finnish military leader and statesman, regarded by the Finns as the father of the modern independent state of Finland. He served as the military leader of the Whites in the Finnish Civil War and as Commander-in-chief of Finland's defence forces during World War II. He was the 6th President of Finland (1944-1946).

[2] 'I cannot!'

## Chapter 25

# Santeri

It was a hot day in July 1938 when Santeri Levas first walked over the threshold.

"You must be thirsty. I will ask someone to, um, bring us a, a cold drink. From the cellar," I said, leading him up to my study to discuss what his duties would entail.

"I would, particularly, like to make it plain that, er … I *never* talk about my music."

"I understand and I am not capable of talking about such matters, in any case. I spent some years in the orchestral class of the Conservatoire, where I mostly played the violin, but I do not play much nowadays and I cannot remember much of what I learned in the way of theory. What I *can* offer are my organisational skills and a reasonable knowledge of foreign languages. But I shall be pleased to help you with whatever I can."

"No, no, I – er – did not mean – that. I do not – um, consider you – unworthy. No, no. It is just that, um … I do not speak to … *anyone* about my music. My, my music, it is a closed book … so to speak."

"That is quite all right; I am here as your secretary."

"Yes, and, and very welcome you are. It will be a, a great relief to have someone, who, um, can put my papers … in order. In fact, there was one secretary who left … after a week!"

"I see. I rather hope that I will remain longer than that!"

"Well, yes. I am still composing, you see. Even, even if some people think, um … that I am not. And, and I shall complete one more … major work. Before I die."

Santeri looked worried, and I could see that he was scrutinising my bald head and my wrinkled brow, and wondering what illnesses I could be suffering from.

I therefore hastened to reassure him: "Not, not that I intend dying, soon! No, there is life in me … still. Nevertheless, it, it will cause some, er – what is the word? – con-con-consternation when a sinner like me ... enters Heaven! Everyone will be asking what I am doing there!"

Santeri smiled. "I have no doubt that you are a good man."

We had been just standing there, so I asked him to be seated and I proceeded to tell him about the vast amount of correspondence that I had to deal with.

"Ah, the correspondence. There are, there are letters from conductors ... journalists ... photographers ... various organisations. And people asking for testimonials, er ... people wanting manuscripts and autographs, that sort of thing."

"That is a lot of correspondence."

"Yes, and other composers, they write to me, also. Even, even lunatics write to me ... enclosing their, um, 'compositions', for me to correct! Then there are all the, all the people who send me gifts. Yes ... and Americans. Well, they write to me with, with all kinds of strange requests."

"It all sounds very interesting! But, what strange requests?"

"Well, yes. Er ... one lady, for example, she, she wrote and said that, um ... she had read, in the newspaper, about me – that I was a composer. And could I send her a, a new piece for her to play on her piano!"

"Now it sounds even *more* interesting!"

"Hmm, some of the letters that, that I receive are quite ... extraordinary."

"Indeed!"

"It is a strange thing; many people, they write to me, er ... asking me to, to advise them on, um, their personal matters ... marital problems, and so on."

"They obviously trust your judgement!"

"Well ... or they are insane! And, and what do *I* know? My own marriage, it has not always been ... that easy."

"But ... you have been together a long time."

"Yes, no one else would have me! And I do not know what, what I would have done, um ... on my own. You see, I am careless with things, and very untidy. But, er ... my wife, she keeps me in order! However, the correspondence, it, it, it has become too much for her. And ... of course, she, *she* is not getting any younger, either."

"Of course."

"So, what you see here is, er ... co-complete disorder. And,

and I dread to think that, um, when I die, how are they able to … sort out my papers. Keeping things tidy, I never learned that! And, and that, of course, includes my, my correspondence. That is why, um … I need someone. To put it in order."

"Of course, and I will be glad to do that."

"You see, sometimes, when, when the girls visit, they help. But, um … it is my wife, *she* is the one who has been, er … struggling to keep up with it – though it is not really her … responsibility. I would never have been able to do my work … without her. She appreciates the needs of an artist. And, and she knows every bar of my symphonies, from memory!"

"That is most remarkable!"

"Indeed."

"So … is that all that my work would entail?"

"No, er, there is something; you must never tidy my worktable. And, and there are some letters, I will deal with them – they are in my green box."

"The green box?"

"Yes, green. Little boxes. I, er … like them. I have one that, that I keep my handkerchiefs in – it smells of juniper. And, and I have a box, just a small matchbox, of moss. I carry it in my pocket, um … wherever I go; for the smell is … some-something wonderful."

"So, *you* will reply to some letters, and *I* will deal with the rest?"

"Yes … and your salary, er, I will pay you myself. My wife, she pays the bills … generally. But, but *I* will take care of your salary. And the expenses. You must let me know about … po-postage stamps … telegrams … and so on. Um, as well as any other things that, that you need to purchase."

His secretarial duties having been made clear, we went on a tour of the house, so that he could familiarize himself with the layout.

"You can work in here," I said to Santeri when we reached the library, which was to be his place of work.

"Ahh! There is so much space here and so much light, as, indeed, there is in the whole house!"

"Yes, it is a nice room. Many windows. Er … you can spread the papers out on, on this table here. And … when, when you get tired, you can have a rest in the armchair."

"Oh, yes."

"And … if, if there is ever anything that you need, er … let me know. Or Hellu – if you are hungry or thirsty, let Hellu know!"

"Hellu?"

"Hellu, our cook. Well, Helvi, her name is, but, er … we have always called her Hellu. In fact, she has been with us a, a long time – ever since we moved here. And, and she will be with us … for ever, I suspect."

I could see that Santeri was eyeing the bookshelves. "By all means, take a look at the books. You can borrow … whatever you like."

"Thank you. You have a remarkable collection of books, if I may say so, and in so many languages! You are quite the polyglot!"

"Well … I would not say that. And … most of them are in Finnish. Some of the books are the children's, um … given to them when, when they were small … and not so small. And some of them are my wife's. That one, for example – Olavi Paavolainen's[1] *The Cross and The Swastika* – our daughter Ruth gave that to her. And, er … the Somerset Maugham, I gave that to her."

"This one looks interesting."

"Ah, that is the Japanese edition of, of *Kalevala*! Yes, there is a dedication in it by the translator, um … Ku-ku-kukita Mo-morimoto."

Santeri ran his fingers over the books. "Goethe … Homer's *Odyssey* in Latin … Horace … Shakespeare …"

"Yes, that is Shakespeare – the complete works. Ruth played the part of … Ariel when, when the, um … Finnish National Theatre, when it staged *The Tempest*, you see. If you can find *The Tempest*, there is her, her handwriting in it. She made all kinds of notes in the … margins."

Santeri flicked through the pages and found *The Tempest*. "Yes, she seems to have made a lot of comments!"

He replaced the book and turned his attention to the Finnish literature. "Juhani Aho …"

"Huh, my love rival!"

I did not know what prompted me to say such a thing,

---

[1] Olavi Paavolainen (1903-1964), a Finnish essayist, journalist, travel book writer and poet. He was the central figure of the literary group *Tulenkantajat* ('The Flame Bearers'), which represented liberal and Europe-oriented views on culture.

particularly, to a man whom I had only met for the first time just a short while ago. But I felt unusually comfortable in Santeri's company.

He looked at me in surprise and as if he was curious to know more but was too shy to ask.

"Oh yes! He … was in love with her, at one stage. He, he even wrote about it. In a book. When, when we were engaged."

"Ahh."

"Yes! Huh, for everybody to read about it! But … fortunately – or perhaps, for her, it was not that fortunate – she chose me!"

But what could Santeri have said to that! So, he just gave a few nods and smiled, and then continued looking along the line of books. "Hmm, Aleksis Kivi … Eino Leino[1] …"

"Yes … but she did choose me …"

"F. E. Sillanpää[2] …"

"Yes, books, um … there are some … interesting volumes there."

"Indeed."

"Er … it is a pity that, um, I have not had the time to, to read them much. There is … one of August Strindberg's[3] books, somewhere. Between the pages, there is a, a manuscript – which Strindberg sent to me – the, the, the revised ending of the story."

"How very interesting!"

"Read it, if you wish."

"I think that perhaps I will. I see, also, that you have a copy of Erik Furuhjelm's[4] book."

"Ah, you are familiar with him … yes. There was a, a second copy, but I gave it to my sister, Linda, at some stage … Karl

---

[1] Eino Leino (1878-1926), one of the pioneers of Finnish poetry. His poems combine modern and Finnish folk elements and are frequently on nature, love and despair.

[2] Frans Eemil Sillanpää (1888-1964), one of the most famous Finnish writers. He was awarded the Nobel Prize for Literature in 1939 for his 'deep understanding of his country's peasantry and the exquisite art with which he has portrayed their way of life and their relationship with nature'.

[3] Johan August Strindberg (1849-1912), a Swedish playwright, novelist, poet, essayist and painter. He is considered the father of modern Swedish literature, and his book *The Red Room* has frequently been described as the first modern Swedish novel.

[4] Erik Gustaf Furuhjelm (1883-1964), a Finnish composer and music critic who was a teacher and, later, deputy head at the Music Institute (the Sibelius Academy).

Ekman's[1] books are there, as well."

Santeri continued going through the books but then he stopped and looked at me questioningly: "*Mein Kampf*?"

"Ah ... yes. Well, um ... it was curiosity that, that made me acquire it. I ... browsed through it, but ... I must have torn, at least, a hundred pages out of it. The, the, the racial doctrines ... of the Nazis, I, er, condemned them ... without question."

"Of course – no humanity ..."

We lapsed into silence and, no doubt, we were both thinking of the savagery of Hitler's ideas, as I led the way into the drawing room.

"This is where I used to write. In this very room. The Third Symphony ... *Pohjolan tytär* ... *Voces intimae* ... they, they were all written in here. In this modest room. As you see, the, the only luxury things are the paintings. And, um, the Steinway. Of course, the Americans, they think that men like me live like, er ... lords! But we do not ... live in castles."

"But this is a very nice house and certainly in a good location."

"Yes. We were lucky that, er, there was a plot of land here ... for us. There is plenty of wildlife here; hares and foxes ... even the occasional elk! And we have ... mountain hens ... moorhens ... and, um, all kinds of other birds. I, I particularly like birds!"

"Hmm, yes ... they are delightful."

"Indeed. Sometimes, I feel that, um ... in my, in my previous life, I must have been related to ... swans and wild geese!"

"Ahh."

"Yes. Hence, um, I often walk to the lakeside. I just love to watch them ... flying over the lake – I use my bi-binoculars, you see. Somehow, er ... I feel so, so drawn towards them. Once – Christmas Eve it was – I saw a flock of, of about fifty swans! They flew over the house, very low."

"Fifty!"

"Yes! I could hardly have thought of a, a better Christmas present!"

"No, I suppose not."

---

[1] Karl Ludvig Ekman (1869-1947), a Finnish pianist, conductor, teacher and critic. He and Sibelius once played in a chamber music concert together to improve their finances. There was a sizeable audience and a big celebration afterwards, which Ekman described as 'neither cheap nor boring(!)'.

"So, you see, I do like it here. Very much. And ... although, although it is quite remote, we get many visitors. But, thankfully, not every day; for, um ... I need peace and quiet ... to compose."

"Of course, you do. So ... you say that you have had secretaries before?"

"Yes. But ... as I said, not for long. None, none of them, um, stayed with us very long – like Hellu and our other staff have. I think that, er ... it was too much for them ... to, to deal with all the correspondence. Particularly, all the letters, um, arriving from abroad."

"Ahh."

"But I can tell you ... something amusing. There was one young lady and, and, on her first day, she played Liszt, on the typewriter keys, and, er ... she destroyed the typewriter in the process!"

"Hah! Perhaps she should have played some Debussy, instead?"

"Yes, perhaps so! But ... we never saw her again!"

I decided that I liked Santeri from this point onwards. He gave me the impression that he would be efficient, but he also had a sense of humour, which I considered indispensable. I thought that we would get on very well.

He, perhaps, had decided likewise and he seemed to be relaxed in my company; for he asked me about my daughters. And when I had told him a little about each of them, he was quite forthright with his next question: "Would you have liked a son?" But I told him no; for my daughters were so dear to me and, besides, my wife had said that she needed no other son than her husband!

"My daughters, they, they help me, you see. Sometimes, they even ... represent me, abroad."

It was quite late in the afternoon, and I wondered whether Santeri was getting hungry, but he said that he had already eaten. I myself was hungry; for I had postponed my lunchtime in order to wait for him, so that we might lunch together. I did not tell him this, however; for it might have caused him embarrassment. So, instead of lunch, we drank a cup of coffee with some pie, made of the first blueberries of the season. Afterwards, I offered him a Havanna, but he said that he did not smoke.

When Santeri left, I stood on the veranda and waved goodbye to him, thinking that he was a godsend. I had found his company very reassuring and amiable. I soon began to look forward to his visits and I discovered that I could talk to him at ease on a variety of subjects – I even found myself saying things to him that I would not have said to anyone else. In short, I came to regard him as a good friend.

*Chapter 26*

# War

Aino had begun to pine for our daughters and she wanted to move to Helsinki to be nearer to them. This was understandable; she had devoted her life to them – not only caring for them, but educating them, as well – and now her life seemed empty.

Being fully aware of how I had neglected her in the past, I resolved that now I would not push her needs into the background; I would see to it that she would get what she wanted and that she would be part of our daughters' lives, once more.

Hence, I rented an apartment in the Töölö district of Helsinki, on Kammiokatu[1], and we moved there at the end of September 1939. It was well worth the trouble just to see the look on Aino's face when she looked around the apartment – she was clearly delighted.

"It will be quite like old times!" she said. "We could have all the girls round to celebrate us having a new apartment, and I will cook something nice."

She did cook something nice – *silakkalaatikko*[2] – and we enjoyed a family gathering of all of us: but who would have known how short-lived our stay in that apartment would be? Since the

---

[1] Kammio Street, now Sibeliuksenkatu, Sibelius Street.

[2] Herring casserole.

Molotov-Ribbentrop Pact[1] in August, the Baltic states had been worried, and, once Poland was divided between the Soviet Union and Nazi Germany, the Finns had been very anxious about a Soviet attack on Finland.

Indeed, Aino and I had been living on Kammiokatu for only two weeks, when the people in Helsinki were asked to send their children away from the capital. Consequently, we, together with our children and grandchildren, all returned to Ainola.

It was then in November that the Soviets made their first move and demanded that the Finns push back the border 25 km from Leningrad and grant them a 30-year lease on the Hanko Peninsula – for the construction of a naval base. In exchange, we were to have a tract of the Karelian wilderness. This was like exchanging gold for dirt, and, when the Finnish government declined, the Soviets amassed approximately one million men along the Finnish border.

I knew how deceitful the Soviets were, and what they did next was typical of them; they shelled their own town, Mainila, and accused the Finns of doing it. They then used this as their excuse to cross the border with 450,000 men to attack the Finns. The Winter War had started.

Once more, the country was looking for a national symbol, and they turned their attention to me. What this meant was that all sorts of people were clambering for the Eighth Symphony all over again, including the Royal Philharmonic Society, which wanted to raise money for the Finnish Red Cross.

But how did they expect me to produce another major work in the midst of all this turmoil? I was more concerned about whether Finland, and indeed our family, would survive rather than thinking about composing. I was offered asylum in the United States and in the Nordic countries, but that was not something that I considered; I was not going to abandon my country at the moment of danger, however frightening the situation was.

And, of course, it was a hard fight for the Finns. We have to remember that our army numbered only 180,000 men and it had

---

[1] This non-aggression treaty between Nazi Germany and Soviet Union included a secret agreement to divide Romania, Poland, Lithuania, Latvia, Estonia and Finland into German and Soviet spheres of influence and anticipating potential 'territorial and political rearrangements' of these countries.

far inferior weapons and much fewer aircraft than the Soviets had. But, by utilizing local knowledge, white camouflage and skis, they did manage to inflict a surprising number of casualties on the Soviets. They also managed to immobilise the Soviet tanks – they stole to the side of the tanks and put logs inside the caterpillar treads – and then offered rounds of Molotov's cocktails! In that way, they destroyed over 2,000 tanks!

But, by early 1940, the Soviets' massive artillery bombardments breached the Mannerheim Line – our southern defensive barrier that stretched across the Karelian Isthmus – and we knew then that we had failed in our effort to defend our country.

When peace came, it was a relief, but the war had cost us dearly; it had left behind devastation and loss of lives, not to mention the large areas of land that the Soviets took from us. We lost half of Finnish Karelia, including Viipuri, an area in Lapland and some islands on the Gulf of Finland.

On the top of this, as soon as the war had ended, a personal tragedy hit our family; Eva's husband, Arvi, died. Eva was distraught with grief, and I felt for her deeply – as I did for all my children when they were distressed – but I did not know how to comfort her. Words were inadequate, and even music did not come to my aid. Consequently, I grieved alongside her, and it was left to Aino to comfort us both.

During the war, we had stayed at Ainola, but now we moved back to Helsinki. But it was much noisier in the capital than at Ainola and, also, memories of the war intruded on my thoughts. So, I found it difficult to work there. What I did manage to compose, I kept in a safe.

But the peace time, we felt, would not last; the Soviet threat remained. Finland sought defensive arrangements with Sweden and Britain, but to no avail. So, we were forced to ask Nazi Germany for military support. Germany agreed to this, promising that Finland was to remain an independent state.

What happened then was that, when the German offensive against the Soviets started in 1941, for which they also used Finnish airfields, the Soviets bombed Finland, albeit military targets only. To stop the conflict escalating, Finland promptly declared neutrality. However, the Soviets responded by launching a massive air raid that included the bombing of Finnish cities. It was then that we declared war against the Soviet Union and allowed the Germans to attack the Soviets from Lapland. It had been a short period of peace: the 1941-44 Continuation War had started.

What was going to happen to a small country like Finland? We were at the mercy of the other, bigger powers.

Even Britain, which had declared war on Germany in 1939, bombed Petsamo[1] in 1941; there were German – but also Finnish – merchant vessels in dock. This was to show Britain's support for their ally, the Soviet Union. Luckily, there were not many vessels in port, but fifteen British aircraft were shot down. Four months later, Britain declared war on Finland! Naturally, I was taken aback by this until I later discovered that it had been under duress from the Soviets. Indeed, Churchill had sent a personal, apologetic letter[2] to General Mannerheim, warning him of the impending declaration of war. Fortunately, nothing came of Britain's war against us.


The war years were terrible. I was supposed to protect Aino and the rest of the family but how was I to do that? I was now an old man in my late seventies. But how was *anyone* able to protect his family in such circumstances? Finland was now part of the chess game between the Soviet Union and Germany, and it was impossible to predict what would happen from one moment to the next.

I was concerned about the growing presence of the Germans in Finland but, at the same time, I knew that it was necessary to keep the threat of communism at bay. Certain members of the *Eduskunta[3]* should have kept that in mind, too; for when they voiced their hostility to the idea of becoming dependant on Germany, they were imprisoned for treason!

---

[1] The battle of Petsamo, in the northeast of Finland, was fought between the Finnish and Soviet troops from 1939 to 1940. In 1944, Petsamo became a part of the U. S. S. R. It is now one of six administrative districts in Murmansk Oblast, Russia.

[2] Winston Churchill sent a personal, apologetic letter to General Mannerheim, informing him of Britain's pending declaration of war against Finland. The letter is kept in Britain's Imperial War Museum.

[3] Parliament.

Although we were supported by the German troops stationed in Finland, it became apparent that, again, we were fighting a losing battle against the Soviets. After many years of fighting, albeit sometimes very successfully, Finland had no choice but to surrender.

But that was not the end of the war. Under the armistice agreement between Finland and the Soviet Union, we were obliged to expel German troops from Finland by the 15th of September 1944. In fact, Finland and Germany made an informal agreement and schedule for German troops to be withdrawn from Lapland to Norway. However, the Soviets did not accept this 'friendliness' and forced Finland to take a more active role and speed up the expulsion of the Germans from Finland.

I would have thought that the Germans – our former war comrades – would have left in peace, but no. Why did they have to torch down all the towns and villages in Finnish Lapland and turn our co-belligerence into the 1944-45 Lapland War? Their destruction of Lapland was as horrific as the Soviets' bombing of our towns had been. It seemed as if the Germans were punishing us for losing our fight to the Soviet Union!

The peace agreement with the Soviets was costly to our country. In addition to the border being pushed back to where it had been before the Continuation war, we lost Petsamo and, hence, access to the Barents Sea.

But what saddened me the most was the lost of young lives. During the war years, winter and summer, graves were dug in villages and towns all over the country for young men[1] brought back from the front line. It was a sombre era in Finnish history.

Then there were all the evacuees[2] who were forced to leave their homes for ever. I have travelled in many places and have stayed in Berlin, in particular, for prolonged periods, but I have never considered moving away permanently. For Karelians, having to leave their homes in a hurry, and with the only possessions that they could carry, must have been very hard.

Many people did not want them to move to other parts of

---

[1] Between 1939 and 1944, 90,000 Finnish solders died or were lost. 2,000 civilians also died in Soviet bombings.

[2] 420,000 people, almost all Karelians, representing 11% of the Finnish population at the time.

Finland at all. Ryti[1] and Tanner[2] were among those who wanted to leave the Karelians behind and for them to become Soviet citizens (!), so as not to cause a housing problem in Finland.

And what awaited them was the dubious hospitality in other parts of Finland. The Finns did not exactly welcome Karelians with open arms; although the Karelians were part of the Finnish tribe and they spoke a Finnish dialect, the Finns found it difficult to accept the lively Karelian temperament and culture. It is particularly regrettable, from my point of view, that the people in Swedish-speaking parts of Finland altogether refused to allow any Karelians into their towns and villages! And they say that wars and disasters bring people together!

As for Aino, me and our daughters' families, we lived at Ainola through the war years as best as we could. We had to endure food rationing along with everyone else. Meat was scarce, as was flour and fruit, although we were lucky in that we had the vegetables that Aino grew. Everyone, at that time, was encouraged to grow tomatoes in order to get vitamin C – such was the scarcity of fruit.

But it was not just that times were hard; my reputation as a composer suffered, as well. In 1942, Joseph Goebbels[3] had founded the Sibelius Society in Germany 'to strengthen our countries' cultural ties'. I had also been awarded a German pension – worth half the average German annual income – and I had accepted an invitation from Goebbels to become vice-chairman of the Europäischer Schriftstellerverbund[4] in the Third Reich. Indeed, I was the most popular foreign composer in Germany. However, such links with Germany attracted

---

[1] Risto Heikki Ryti (1889-1956), a lawyer, politician and, 1940-44, the fifth president of Finland. In 1945, under the peace agreement with the Soviets, he was among politicians charged for 'crimes against peace'. He was sentenced to 10 years in prison but, in 1949, he was pardoned.

[2] Väinö Tanner (born Thomasson) (1881-1966), a leader of the Social Democratic Party, minister in several cabinets and Prime Minister in 1926-27. Like Ryti, he was charged for 'crimes against peace' and was sentenced to 5½ years in prison of which he served half.

[3] Paul Joseph Goebbels (1897-1945), a German politician, Reich Minister of Propaganda in Nazi Germany (1933-1945) and one of Hitler's closest associates and most devout followers, known for his support of the extermination of the Jews and hatred of capitalism. He had total control over the media, arts and information in Germany.

[4] European Writers' Society.

unfortunate attention elsewhere, and my popularity abroad, such as it was, waned considerably.

I daresay that when I am dead, many people will cite me as a Nazi sympathizer, but all I can say is that the situation was very complex. Since its independence, Finland's sovereignty had been under constant threat from the Soviets, and co-belligerence with Germany was seen as the only way to safeguard it. And Germany came to our aid, generously providing us, not only with troops, but also with food, fuel and armament shipments. Hence, turning down honours from Germany was not the thing to do. Some would even have seen it as unpatriotic. But, at the same time, I considered myself no more a friend of the Nazis than anyone else in Finland.

What I do regret is that I reneged on my promise to help a part-Jewish composer, Günter Raphael, who was under the threat of losing his teaching post in Germany – I chose not to risk Goebbels's disfavour.

But, if, in the future, people draw the conclusion that I was a Nazi sympathizer, they should see what I wrote in my diaries at the time. My views I made quite clear. Whilst I had perhaps been too complacent about the rise of Hitler in the beginning, I did start to feel uneasy and, indeed, did denounce the Nazi policies, adding that my education and culture were ill-suited to those times. Nevertheless, I realize that that will not defend me against my future detractors. Hence, I still have sleepless nights, thinking about the war, the inhumanity of it and what I did and did not do.

*Chapter 27*
# Old Age

I could never have put into words the relief that we all felt that my country had survived the conflict. And I thanked God that I was privileged to be able to walk in the forest every day and hear only the sounds of nature, as opposed to hiding away indoors and listening to the artillery fire, and wondering whether we would live or die.

If it were at all possible, nature had become even more important to me than before. So, nowadays, I went for a walk at least twice a day, and sometimes three times a day.

"Er, that is a, a semi-tone too high!" I said to Santeri when I returned from my morning walk. He was humming a piece by Schubert.

"Was it? I would not know."

"Worry not. Even, even those with perfect pitch can make, um … as much error as that!"

"I am afraid that I do not have perfect pitch."

"But … can you tell me, um … what is between C sharp and D?"

"I am not sure …"

"That is the bullfinch! The curlew, he whistles in A and, and, and then raises it to F. While the nightingale, he sings away in E minor."

"That is extraordinary!"

"What is? That they sing … those notes?"

"Well, yes. And that you have such a good ear!"

"Well, I listen to the birds … a lot. They, they produce the, the best music of all! And, er … it seems to me that, um … all the birds, they are as happy as I am that, that the war is over!"

"I am sure that they are."

"But … I also look at all the colours. In nature. If, if only I did not have these cataracts, I should see them more … clearly."

"Yes, of course. It is a pity …"

"My, my favourite colour is pale green. A certain shade that, that I have only ever seen in the sky. Nowhere else, you see. But, um … mu-musical notes, *they* have colours, too."

"I am afraid that I do not know what you mean. Notes have colours?"

"Ah, but they do! Most people, they do not know that. When, when I hear a symphony, for example, for me, it is … like *ruska-aika*[1]!"

---

[1] Autumn colours.

"Well, that is astonishing! I wish that I had that ability, but I have to be content with just taking pictures of nature and its colours."

"Have you, um, brought your camera with you? We are, after all, here at Ainola, in the, in the middle of this glorious nature.'

"No. I have not."

"But I thought that a, a photographer would have his camera with him … all the time."

"But I am here to work."

"Yes … but you should bring your camera. Look at the trees … so magnificent!"

"Indeed, the trees in Finland are part of who we are."

"Yes, precisely, precisely. I, I could not have put it better myself. When, er, I went to England, I, um, did like the oak trees … and the ash trees … and the bluebells that, that grew amongst them, but –"

"It was not the same thing."

"No. No, it was not the same thing! I, I cannot explain, but you understand me, Santeri. And, um … the older I become, the more I love my own country. You see, I would stay in the, in the forest all day if I did not have other things, er … to deal with. Such as the letters."

"No matter! *I* will help you to deal with them."

"Very good. But first, let us have some coffee and *pulla*!"

I had been meaning to say something to Santeri, and there was no time like the present.

"Ah … about your … notes."

"Yes …?"

"I would like to ask you, er … not to, not to publish anything about me. Before my death. It is just that –"

"Rest assured, I will not do that. But, you *are* a world-renowned composer and, at some point, people will want to read about you. So, who better than I to enlighten them?"

"Hmm … yes … in that case, I shall leave it, um … in, in your capable hands. I know that, er, I can trust you to … give me a fair appraisal."

"That goes without saying!"

"Good ... but, you see, I shall be eighty on my next birthday. And, and I wonder how long, um, you will need to ... keep making notes!"

"Most probably, I shall keep doing that for a very long time!"

"He will see many more midnight suns, believe me! He is as fit as a fiddle!" said Aino, who entered the room, bringing in the day's post.

I turned to Santeri. "Nowadays, the, the changes of season, I have become sensitive to them – well, changes of weather. They seem to, to affect my health."

"Janne has seldom been ill in all the years that we have been together!"

"I, I have walked in the forest – that is why! Man was meant to, um ... be outdoors. It is good for the body and soul!"

"Perhaps, then, we should celebrate your birthday outside this year!"

"And freeze to death! Aino, now you are ..."

"But you just said that man was meant to be outdoors," Aino said, as she left the room. Then, she put her head round the door and added, "It is good for the body and soul!"

Santeri laughed. He then picked up the telegram that we had recently received from Cecil Gray[1], concerning the Eighth Symphony.

"Are you quite sure that you do not want to reply to it?" he said.

"Yes, quite sure. What is there to say? I have, I have already burnt one version. And the other versions, I have destroyed them, also. So, er ... there is little point in, in replying – I have nothing to offer!"

"Very well, we will say no more of the matter."

I could see that he was worried about offending Gray and I wondered whether he would take it upon himself to reply, anyway. I never knew whether he did or not. But I would not have been angry with him if he had; for one cannot condemn sensitivity

---

[1] Cecil Gray (1895-1951), a Scottish music critic and composer. He published a biography of Sibelius in 1931, *Sibelius*.

and diligence.

"What do they want me to ... talk about?"

"It does not say. How do you want me to reply?" said Santeri.

"I suppose that, er ... you have to tell them that, that they can come. Yleisradio[1], I can hardly refuse Yleisradio."

"No, I suppose not."

"But, as you know, I do not like, um ... giv-giving interviews – I never quite know ... what to say."

"You will be all right. You have given so many interviews before. I will let them know that they can come."

"When? When do they want to come?"

"Sometime in December, they say."

In fact, it was just before my eightieth birthday that they came to interview me. I do not remember any more what questions they asked me, with the exception of the last one, which was concerning the advice that I would give to a young composer. This I replied to without a moment's hesitation: 'Never write a superfluous note; for one has to live every note!'

This had been my long-standing formula for composition and it was what I still adhered to. Maybe that was why the Eighth still eluded me; for I did not wish there to be anything in it that was surplus to requirements. In a sense, it had to be a logical progression from the Seventh, in that respect.

Sometimes, I had even thought that perhaps the most logical progression would be silence – the absolute silence in Finnish nature in the middle of winter, so to speak. However, that would have required a statement to the newspapers to the effect that I had made a deliberate decision to follow my twenty-minute Seventh Symphony with a silent one. But then, of course, people would have speculated on what was behind the statement, and I expect that they would have concluded that it was simply a ploy to hide my inability to compose.

But is the silence in Finnish nature in mid winter ever actually

---

[1] The Finnish Broadcasting Company, founded in 1926 and modelled on the BBC, produces and broadcasts TV and radio programmes in Finnish, Swedish and Sami. News bulletins are also broadcast in Russian, English, Romany, Latin and Karelian.

absolute? In fact, it is not. Even then, when you are deep in the forest, several kilometres away from the nearest house, standing quite still, and all the birds have gone to sleep, something, in the distance, can suddenly break the silence. It can be the thud of a lump of snow falling from a branch or the cracking of a frozen branch under the weight of the snow. My final symphony – for in all likelihood, it would be my final one – should reflect this. However, it was not my intention to depict winter only; I wanted the symphony to be the depiction of man alone in the forest in *all* the seasons.

"Alone …," I uttered, and Santeri looked at me with a puzzled expression.


Aino was wrong: I was not as fit as a fiddle, anymore. Just after my eightieth birthday, I was quite ill. I also started coughing blood, but I did not tell Aino; she would only have worried, and why would I have worried her with miserable things? I did tell Santeri, but I made it clear that he was not to divulge the information to Aino.

One morning, Aino brought a huge basket into the bedroom, containing letters, belated birthday greetings and Christmas mail. But I think that she and Santeri soon decided that I was getting too tired to deal with correspondence that day, so they took a pile of letters each and went to the library.

However, I did not like the idea that they were doing the work without me, so, a little while later, I got out of bed, dressed and, picking up the basket, I made my way to the library.

"Janne, what are you doing? You should not be carrying that heavy basket – and you should not be out of bed!"

"I am sure that I can sort through … *some* of these letters. I can, I can always go back to bed, later. If I get tired."

"You *must* keep warm, Janne! I will bring a blanket for you."

Another reason why I had got up was so that I could have a word with the doctor on the telephone. Therefore, I made some excuse to leave the room and I went to the dining room to make the call, hoping that Aino would not hear me. But the doctor said that he could not give a diagnosis without seeing me and that he would come in the afternoon.

When Aino brought him into the bedroom, she looked at me knowingly but did not say anything, before, tactfully, leaving me alone with the doctor. No doubt, she had guessed what I had been doing earlier and would want the doctor to explain my condition to her, and in detail, when he had made his diagnosis.

"You have a disturbance of the circulation of the blood. This is something that can occur in old age, I am afraid. You also have a lung infection – hence, the blood. It could become serious, if left untreated," he said.

"Ahh ... but, um, I wonder can you ... not tell Aino. That, that I have been c-c-coughing blood. I, I do not want her making a fuss, you see."

"But she will ask me, and I am sure – knowing Mrs Sibelius – that she will press for an answer!"

"Then you must tell her that, er ... it, it is nothing serious. And that I shall be well again. Very soon."

"Well, if that is what you wish."

So, the doctor had confirmed it: I was officially in 'old age'. Ironically, in the days before I fell ill, I had been thinking, not for the first time, of writing a requiem in memory of Eugen Schauman. But now I thought that I might, just as well, write a requiem for myself!

Of course, I had not mentioned the idea of a requiem to anybody. Not having produced the Eighth Symphony had already resulted in a stream of pestering letters, and I did not want even more of them, begging me for a requiem – that I might not be able to write, either.

Fortunately, I was distracted from these depressing deliberations by Santeri, who knocked on the bedroom door and asked if I was up to signing a few autographs.

"I might, just possibly ... manage that. As you know, I cannot say no to people if, if they want something from me."

"Well, there is a fine balance between saying yes or no. Sometimes, you just have to say no, for your own good."

"Yes ... I suppose that you are right. But, er ... I feel that, that one should be kind to people. Who-whoever they are. And look for the, um, good qualities in people."

"Of course."

"And ... I suppose that is why, why I was friends with Adolf, Adolf Paul – even, even if he did write books of ... a, a rather dubious nature."

"I daresay that we all have our shortcomings!"

"Indeed … it is, it is the same when, er, say, a musician wants to rearrange one of my pieces … for his own instrument. I, almost always, give my consent."

"Is that wise, do you think?"

"No … no, I suppose not. You see, when, when they have rearranged it, I, er, cannot always approve the publication of it; for, um … it sounds so awful!"

"So what happens then?"

"Well, what happens is that, that I find myself correcting it! Which, which takes up a lot of my time. And, um … the result is, er, there is not much left of the original arrangement!"

"Perhaps you should not undertake such time-consuming tasks."

"I know … but I do not want to dis-dis-discourage people. Especially, when, when they are so determined."

"I always thought that being a composer meant, well, composing! I would never have imagined that there were all kinds of other things involved."

"Ah, well, you would be surprised! Once, a, a Canadian man – a clarinettist, he was – wrote to me, asking why, why he had to stop playing, before the last chord! It was in the Second Symphony."

"Perhaps it was like that in the score?"

"Yes, it was. But I do not know why – you will be astonished, no doubt – but, um … I replied to him! I, I told him that, that if, if, if he *really* wanted to carry on playing, he could play, quietly. For, um … no one would be likely to notice."

"Hah, I wonder if anyone *did* notice."

"Who knows …! So … what do we need to do today?"

"As I said, you just need to sign some autographs. I do not think that we will answer any of the more serious letters today. They can wait until you are feeling better."

I wondered what he meant by 'more serious' letters. In all probability, he was referring to those containing enquiries about the symphony. I knew that he did not want to bother me with those and, having a sixth sense for these things, I suspected that he would reply to them himself, saying that the symphony was 'not quite ready' or something of the sort. Santeri was the kind of man who exuded kindness. I knew that he wished to spare me the indignity and humiliation that he thought answering these letters myself would bring, but he would not have said so. Hence, I decided to change the subject of conversation.

"I noticed – in the newspaper, it was – that, that you have won another, er … pho-photographic competition. Congratulations! That is marvellous!"

"Yes, I did, and thank you. But my achievements are quite modest."

"No! There is an art in, in taking photographs – *I* cannot do it. No, your entry was, um … magnificent! You certainly deserved the first prize!"

## Chapter 28
# Cigars And More Cigars

In the autumn of 1948, Leopold Stokowski sent me some cigars. I often received cigars from people as presents, but no one had ever sent me so many different brands in the same package – there were forty-one different cigars, all of premium quality. Stokowski wanted me to try them and then inform him of my favourite one. This, he said, was so that he could be sure of always sending me my favourite kind.

I later wrote to him, saying that the task gave me immense pleasure, but the competition was intense; for all the cigars were equally intoxicating. I really could not make a definitive choice, but I let him know of my three favourites and I said that any of those would be most welcome in the future.

It was a coincidence, then, that, soon after I had replied to Stokowski, an organisation in America, the National Art Foundation, decided to arrange a collection of cigars for my eighty-third birthday, but I do not think that they realized, at the time, just how big the response would be. Cigars literally poured into Ainola from all over America, and it reached a point where we did not know where to put them all! Some people sent one box only, but others sent several boxes, and some of these boxes contained as many as a hundred cigars!

"Where are we going to put them all?" Aino said, throwing her hands up into the air in mock despair.

"Hmm … I have no idea …"

"I suppose that we could put them in the library cupboards."

"But, er … they would not all fit in there – there are so many!"

"And the 'fox burrow' on the stairs is already full. I wonder if Winston Churchill has so many sent to him."

"Well, I would not be surprised, at all."

"No, there are far too many. I think that we will simply have to pile them up in a corner on the floor somewhere. In the library, perhaps. Some of the boxes, they are so pretty!"

"I will smoke from those … first. Then, then you and the girls, you can have the, the, the boxes. To keep your treasures in. But, er, I have to say that, that there are enough cigars now, um … to last until I die!"

"Heaven forbid! And do you really think that you can smoke all these? And what if they keep on coming?"

"Well … then, then I shall have to give some of them … away."

"Or you could set up a cigar shop!"

"Yes, I could give up music and … become a shop keeper!"

I had just lit up a marvellous Havana cigar and was sitting and talking to Aino, when Santeri came into the library with a pile of letters. He looked at all the boxes on the floor and was speechless.

"Janne has been sent all these from well-wishers in America!"

"Good Heavens! How are you going to smoke all those?"

"Precisely! That is what *we* were thinking!"

"I wonder if people send cigars to Winston Churchill, as well."

"We wondered *that*, too!"

At the mention of Churchill, I was suddenly overcome by an intense wave of sadness. "You see, Santeri, Winston Churchill and I, well … we, we have much more in common … than cigars."

"You have?"

"Yes, he and I both lost a, a precious daughter. It, um, is not something – I mean, I rarely – talk about it – but, er … it is a strange coincidence."

Aino could see that I was getting upset, so, she continued

where I had left off: "Churchill and his wife, Clementine, lost their fourth daughter, Marigold, who was born just after the end of the First World War. Apparently, the poor child caught a cold, or so it was said in the newspapers at the time, and it developed into septicaemia. She died at the age of two. Our third daughter, Kirsti, died of typhus when she was fifteen months old."

"Ooh. I am truly sorry to hear that."

"Janne has never got over it. I am surprised that he mentioned it at all, but I think that he regards you as a member of the family, and that is why he told you."

It was I who had initiated the conversation about Kirsti, but now I wanted to put a stop to all further discussion of her; it was too painful: "Let, let, let us not talk of it, any more, Aino. But, er … what have we got? What letters did we receive today?"

Santeri seemed to understand, and I was grateful for his tact, which he showed by picking up a letter that he thought might prove to be an interesting diversion: "This one has a British stamp on it. I wonder who it is from."

"I hope that, that they are not, um … writing to tell me that, that they, too, are sending cigars!"

"No," Santeri confirmed while continuing to read it, "it is from the Lord Provost of Edinburgh. It seems that you are invited to take part in the Edinburgh Festival next summer."

"I see, er … I am afraid that, that they need to be sent a, a letter of … refusal. A polite one, of course."

"Do you not wish to attend?"

"No … I cannot travel. My doctor, you see. It is my age."

Aino looked at me in surprise: "That is the first time that I have heard you say that you are old!"

"I *am* old! But I do not like it, um, when, when they, the newspapers, mention it! Always! It is not, er … significant; I am still young, in spirit. And my mind, I have not lost my mind. And I can, I can still walk long distances. But … I *will* die before you do, Aino."

"No, Janne, *I* am the one who will die first!"

Of course, I knew why journalists mentioned my age; in their eyes, I was too old to be composing. They had already written me off. But I had not given up yet and I would show them that I could still write relevant music, however 'old' I was.

"Er, have I ever told you, Santeri, about … Manuel García? He was a Spanish … baritone. And, and he, um, also invented the … laryngoscope."

"I do not think so."

"Ah, well, *he* celebrated his, his hundredth birthday in, er … I think that it was 1905, or thereabouts. And, at the celebration party, he showed people that, um … his, his appetite, it was still good. And, and he, also, enjoyed a good brandy! So … you see, compared with him, I am still young!"

"Of course, you are, Janne!"

"Yes, indeed," Santeri agreed.

"But the doctor, I do not understand why, why he forbids me to travel … when I still walk several kilometres, each day. I am, I am probably fitter than, um, many y-y-younger people!"

"Perhaps the doctor just wants to be on the safe side."

"Hmm … perhaps he does."

We continued to go through the letters, mostly the ones concerning public engagements – none of which I was in a position to fulfil – and I was happy to go along with what Santeri suggested in the way of replies. However, I was not fully focused on the correspondence; for my mind was working, yet again, on the elusive Eighth Symphony.

Here I was, I thought, still contemplating another symphony, while my Norwegian counterpart, Edvard Grieg, had chosen to ignore the symphonic form altogether. I had often wondered why he had done that. However, what he had written was some of the most wonderful music, and I admired him greatly. And, like me, he had created something that was representative of the very heart of his country – though, unlike me, he had based much of his music on folk songs.

"Is it, is it not odd that Grieg, that he, um, never wrote a symphony?" I said. "Santeri, you must remind me. Grieg's letter, have I, have I told you about it? I would, um, like to show it to you."

Aino and Santeri exchanged glances: "Janne's mind does tend to wander. You will have to forgive him."

*Chapter 29*

# Uncertainty

The more that I thought about the Eighth Symphony, the more anxious and uncertain I became. Part of me longed to produce a new work, but the other part wondered whether it was a worthwhile endeavour. What could Beethoven have produced after the Ninth that would have lived up to its predecessor? Was I attempting to do something that would tarnish my reputation if it proved to be inferior to the Seventh and, thus, be something that I would live to regret? Besides, there were many new, and much younger, composers on the horizon, so perhaps it was time for me to hand over the baton.

I was thinking along these lines, when the Armenian-born, Canadian photographer Yousuf Karsh – who was known internationally for his portraits, including one of Winston Churchill – approached me with a view to taking some pictures of me. I was not overly fond of having my photograph taken at the best of times, but this request from Karsh made me feel doubly uncomfortable; anyone visiting Ainola these days made a point of asking me about my latest symphony, and I did not want to talk about it.

"Surely, you do not want to give up the unique opportunity of being photographed by a world-famous photographer!" she said. "And what would it say about you if you refused?"

Karsh duly arrived at Ainola in the August of 1949 with two assistants and all manner of photographic apparatus. He was a well-dressed man with dark eyes and dark hair that was receding. He looked a little tired and had bags under his eyes. Nevertheless, he appeared to have abundant energy and, after we had rather hurriedly exchanged greetings, he immediately set to work.

His assistants set about darkening the windows and putting up special lamps in the first room. When they had done this, Karsh began to take photographs of me in various poses. Then we did the same in other rooms, including the library where I sat in the armchair.

I tried not to be too concerned with what he was doing; for I had a tendency to appear somewhat stiff in photographs. Hence, I tried to relax as much as possible, albeit the light from the lamps dazzled me. Eventually, Karsh said that he had managed to get what he wanted and that he had taken the perfect picture – albeit, Aino remarked later that I looked sad in it.

As he packed up his equipment, he told me about when he photographed Churchill.

"He did not like having his photograph taken, either," he said. "And, although Mrs Sibelius warned me that you might be a 'difficult subject' – as she put it – actually, you were quite an easy subject to work with, compared to him!"

"Ahh, I am glad to hear it!"

"I photographed him just after he had addressed the House of Commons in Ottawa. Apparently, he had not been told beforehand that he was about to be photographed and he was very angry. In fact, he looked at my camera as if it were the German army! He said to me, 'Two minutes! You have two minutes, and that is all!'"

"Well, that is not much. Was he, er ... smoking a cigar at the time?"

"Yes, he was! Indeed. But I thought that having a cigar in his mouth was not right for the picture and I asked him to put it down, but he refused!"

"So ... what did you do?"

"I walked up to him and said, 'Forgive me, sir!' Then I took his cigar out of his mouth and clicked the camera remote. And that was it – I had the portrait that I had wanted!"

"Ah, but how did he ... react to that?"

"Huh, you should have seen the look of defiance in his eyes! But then he said to me, 'You could make even a roaring lion stand to be photographed!'"

"Was that a, a compliment?"

"I suppose that it was! And then he said, 'You may take another one!'"

"Another one?"

"Yes. It was a picture where he was smiling, but it was not half as good as the first one!"

Karsh's visit had not been the ordeal that I had expected it to be. Hence, the very next day, I sat at my worktable and wrote some sketches. And, what is more, I found them quite promising. I was aware that the 'promising' sketches which I had written many times before, more often than not, had ended up in the waste paper basket. But these were different – I was sure of it. And even if I did not use them in the Eighth, at least, I could turn them into other pieces.

By the autumn, I began to feel that I was making real progress, which really raised my spirits. So that, one day, when Santeri arrived, I was more eager than usual to assist him.

"The letters. Perhaps today, we, we can go through, um … all the letters," I said.

"You are not usually *so* enthusiastic!"

"Ah, today I am! I told you that, er, I would write one more m-m-major work. Before I die. And, and now I think that that prophecy might be, um … fulfilled!"

"Excellent! That is excellent news!"

"Yes, it is! So … ah, but first, before we start, let me show you the … letter. From Edvard Grieg. The one that, that I was telling you about. If I can find it …"

It took me some time, but I did manage to locate the letter and I handed it to Santeri.

"I am very proud of it. It, er … it means a great deal to me. You see, when, when it was his sixtieth birthday, I sent him my, my best wishes. And … he replied. This is the letter."

"I can see why you would treasure it."

"Yes. Ida Ekman[1], she told me that, that Grieg, um … ad-admired my music! And, according to her, he, um … was very sincere. So, I was very touched by that. And, and that is why I was, er, more than pleased to, to issue a statement, a few years ago, on

---

[1] Ida Paulina Ekman (1875-1942), a Finnish leider, oratorio and opera soprano, whom Sibelius is said to have regarded as his favourite singer of his songs. Her son with Karl Ekman – a pianist, composer, conductor and former student of Ferruccio Busoni–Karl Ekman Jr. (1895-1962) was a noted biographer of Sibelius.

the occasion of … Grieg's centenary.'"

"Ah, I remember us sending that."

"Yes, I admire Grieg very much … and Dvořák. I admire him, too. He was a, a wonderful man. Very kind. Re-remarkable blue eyes. But … he told me that, that he had composed, um, too much music!"

Santeri was intrigued: "How can you compose too much music?"

"You, you can, if … much of it is … rubbish, as in my case –"

"I do not believe that *any* of what you have written is rubbish!"

"No, you are too kind! But certainly none of Dvořák's is! How-however much he has written. But, um … now, what about the letters?"

"We have the usual 'You may be surprised that a total stranger is writing to you' sort of letters. We always get one or two of those!"

"Yes … and I am not at all surprised, any more!"

"This one says, 'I am ten years old and I adore your music.' However, when you read on, it is quite clear that it was written by an adult, who wants an autograph!"

"Ahh … well, I will send an autograph, nonetheless."

"And this one is from a man who says that he thinks that there are two men from whom he will never manage to get an autograph, and they are Josef Stalin and Jean Sibelius!"

"Good Heavens! Am I mentioned, um, in the same sentence as, as Josef Stalin!"

"I am afraid so! And I cannot believe it, the letter is one … two … three … four pages long!"

"Huh, four pages! Then, um, he *deserves* an autograph! It, it, it must have taken him a long time … to write all that. Hmm … I must read it. At some point. And … are there other ones? Are there any of those that, that mention *Finlandia* and *Valse Triste*?"

Santeri laughed. It was a running joke between us that, if these two works – and no others – were mentioned in a letter, we took it as a sign that the sender was not a serious music-lover and he or she only knew these pieces. Nevertheless, I still sent the senders of these letters my autograph; I knew that Toscanini and Strauss sent everybody autographs, and I wanted to do the same.

"Yes, there are one or two of those, and this one here is addressed to 'Jean Sibelius, Europe'!"

"And it arrived, all the same! Hah! And ... where did it come from?"

"America! It starts with 'Your Excellency'! I think that it is from one of those people who will sell the autograph to someone else. Do you remember the man who called you by some title or other? You sent him an autograph and then, a few months later, he wrote again! I happened to recognize his rather flamboyant handwriting and I am quite sure that the autograph was not for himself – he had one already!"

"Well, um ... if, if they make a little money out of it, does it matter ...? But what else do we have?"

"Let me see. There is a letter here from someone who is offering you the opportunity of staying at his luxury villa in America – he has enclosed pictures of it. And he says that there would be no charge."

"Ah ... hmm ... I doubt that, that he is interested in my music. He, he may just want me to visit. So that, er ... he can make other millionaires jealous. Tsk, the Americans! There, there is the constant need to be recognized, in America. Social position, you see."

"I take it that we write a letter of refusal?"

"Yes. Besides, my doctor, he, he has forbidden me to travel. So ... you might cite that as the reason ... why I cannot go."

I had no wish to travel anywhere, in any case. I was quite happy to stay at Ainola, and Aino and I had settled into a pleasant routine that I was reluctant to change. We had recovered the harmony that we had shared when we were young.

Thus, I spent time with Aino, answered letters with Santeri, composed, went for walks and listened to the wireless. It was a quiet life, but I liked it. I did not long for anything more, other than that I would see my daughters and grandchildren more often and that my work on the symphony would bear fruit.

But it did not bear fruit. I did manage to write some shorter pieces, which told me that I still had the ability to create something new. But, when I attempted to work on the symphony, I could sit at my worktable for an hour or two and not produce a single bar of music. I would just stare out of the window, and my mind would drift along with all kinds of thoughts, except those of the symphony. Sometimes, I lit a cigar, thinking that this would aid my concentration. But it did not.

## Chapter 30

# Worries

A letter from the Director of the Sibelius Museum in Turku irked me greatly.

"The museum wants to broadcast a performance of a trio that you composed. It is in honour of your eighty-fifth birthday," said Santeri.

"What trio would that be?"

"Apparently, it is one that you composed in 1888."

"No, no, no! *Perkele*! I cannot understand it! I have, I have already written to him. And told him, very clearly, that, that the pieces which I composed when, er … I was very young, they, they, they should *not* be performed! *Or* published. Not even after my death. They, they are such rubbish! And I do not want them, er … ever to be heard!"

"I wonder why he wants this one to be broadcasted, then."

"I have no idea. I am tempted to – I think that – I ought to telephone him. Right away!"

"Do you think that that is the best way to go about it?"

I hesitated. Santeri usually had good instincts.

"Ah … hmm … perhaps not," I said, knowing what he was thinking. "Yes, on the telephone, he can, er … get round me, easier. A letter is better. With a plain and simple 'no'."

"Will you write it or shall I?"

"I think that, er, I will take care of it … myself."

"Very good. And what shall we do about this letter? It is from one of your publishers."

"They are not, um … pestering me about the symphony, again, are they?"

"I am afraid that they are."

"Well, in that case, I will dictate a letter. So that we can, er … get it out of the way. What about 'Dear Sirs,' er … let me see … um … 'If I can offer … anything … which I know, for certain … that you will accept' –"

"Forgive me, but, perhaps, we would not express it quite like that. It sounds as though you yourself do not have confidence in your own works. And if they think that you do not have confidence, then they might have doubts, also."

"Ah ... hmm ... yes, you are right. I would not like to think that, that they would return a, a composition to me, er ... thinking that, thinking that it was not good enough."

"Of course, not."

"I *am* still working on the symphony. In my head. It is just that, um ... now-nowadays, there is, there is always something else going on. Something important. Or ... something worrying – mostly, the latter. The grandchildren, for example. There is always one of them with a, a high temperature, or something. And ... try as we both might, the letters, they are, um, piling up. And we have visitors."

Santeri smiled sympathetically. "Do not worry about the letters. I suggest that you go and take a nice walk, instead, and leave these letters to me."

Santeri was such a nice man and he was very kind to me in my 'old age'. Also, over the years, we had had many interesting conversations about various composers and their music. Santeri was particularly interested in Robert and Clara Schumann and, in 1952, he published an excellent book about them, entitled *Suuren säveltäjän rakkaus*[1], which was based on their letters to each other.

"It is an *excellent* book!" I told him. "You have, um, done great justice to the Schumanns. But ... Heaven knows what kind of a book you would have, have been able to write, er ... based on, on, on the correspondence between Aino and me! I fear that, that I would have come out of it, um, rather badly. My drinking ... and, and when Aino wrote to me about it, that was not, er .... much of a love story then."

"But all marriages go through difficult times, and it is clear to anyone that you care for each other very much."

"Indeed ... although, um, I have not always deserved Aino."

"Is that how you feel?"

"Yes. But I can truly say that, that she has, um ... always been the, the only one for me."

"Just as Clara was Robert Schumann's only love."

---

[1] *The love of a great composer.*

"Hmm, yes … and Schumann, in my opinion, as a composer, he, he was very under-rated."

"I agree."

"When, when I was young, I, er, used to play a lot of his music, you see. I even played the, the, the second violin in a performance, in Helsinki, of, um … Schumann's E flat quintet – Busoni was the pianist."

"So, you were quite an accomplished violinist."

"Well, I would not go that far. In fact, I believe that, that a lot of composers are, in a way … failed instrument players."

"Failed? Really?"

"Well … yes. Composing, at one stage, takes over, and, and you stop practising. But, er … going back to Schumann, what I admire about him is, is his sense of poetry – although his orchestration was not so … good. However, Mendelssohn, he was marvellous at *everything*! I would say that, um, there are only, only three child prodigies, in, in the history of music. And … Mendelssohn was one of them."

"And the other two?"

"Mozart and Saint-Saëns. Of course, some people, they, they do not rate Mendelssohn and Mozart so highly. But, er … we have to remember that, um, these composers, they, they did not have, at their disposal, the, the, the instruments that we have … today."

"Indeed!"

"There was the article, the English one, on, on Mozart and Saint-Saëns – I once showed it to you. The, the writer attacked their orchestration. But think what, um, they would have achieved if, if they had lived in, in this day and age!"

"Yes, that is an interesting thought!"

We were silent for a few moments, and then Santeri spoke again: "Schumann wrote some beautiful piano music, as did Clara."

"Yes … they did. *My* piano music has fallen into ob-oblivion, but I, um … hope that, someday, it might be, er, as popular as Schumann's! I have sometimes even wondered what, what it would have been like if, if Aino had been a composer …"

"Hmm, would she have been simply a 'fellow composer', or would there have been some rivalry?"

"That is a good question … but, but who would have brought up the children …?"

"You would have needed a nanny."

"Yes … though it, it would not have been ideal. But, er … I would like to think that, that I would have en-encouraged her. To compose. And not have been, um, like Gustaf Mahler. I met him once, in Helsinki. A very nice man, but … *he* did not encourage *his* wife – quite the contrary, from what he said to me."

"What did he say to you?"

"Ah, something like, um … that she should not compose, anything; for … *he* was the composer in the house."

"Not like Schumann, then."

"No, not like Schumann!"

"I must say that Clara was a remarkable woman. A composer and a pianist, as well as a mother to eight children!"

"Yes, indeed … and that comes out, very well, in your book. And … she had a hard cross to bear; her husband ending up in a … lunatic asylum. What must it have been like for her …?"

"Extremely difficult, no doubt."

"Yes … very sad …"

"Indeed …"

"Ah, to change the subject, we, er … must write to America. About the cigars. We have to say that, that there must be no more collections … of cigars. They, um … do keep on coming. Aino, she does not know where to put them all!"

"Hah! Quite so."

"Yes. I, I, I also received some … from Cuba. The other day. From the Ministry of Agriculture. So … we must write to them, also. To thank them."

"We can do that now, if you wish."

"Well … why not? And, er … I can tell them about my uncle, the sea-faring one. He died in Havana! Which is long way … from home. *I* would not like to die abroad, would you?"

"Well … I suppose not."

"But it is highly unlikely that … I will. No. No, I will die here, at Ainola … and be buried here, as well!"

Santeri looked at me as if to say: 'Do we really need to talk about dying now?'

Therefore, I said, "But we will not talk of that now! So, er … what, what sort of amusing letters, um … we have to deal with today."

"Well, I am afraid that there are a few bills to be paid."

"You deal with those. When, um, *I* paid the bills, I was never quite sure whether, whether I had paid them ... or not. Hah, I think that, that I paid twice for things on, er ... more than one occasion!"

"Is that really so?"

"Yes. You see, I have always been hopeless ... with money – ask Aino."

"Ask Aino what?" said a voice, and there was Aino standing at the door.

"I, I was just saying to Santeri that, that I have always been, er ... hopeless with money. And that, if he asked you, you would certainly tell him, um ... *how* hopeless."

Aino smiled. "Well, we have managed and, at least, we have each other."

Santeri looked at me knowingly, as if to say: 'Do you see that she cares for you deeply?'

I knew what he was thinking and I nodded in response.

<br>

*Chapter 31*

# An Undesirable Visitor

It was the night before Christmas Eve, 1952, when we had an unexpected visitor at Ainola. I was eighty-seven at the time.

I remember that it was in 1952; for it was in the same year as the Olympic Games in Helsinki – they were originally supposed to have taken place in 1940, but were cancelled due to World War Two. It was a great honour for Finland to host the Summer Olympics, having been chosen over bids from Amsterdam and five cities in the United States. And we were delighted that the Olympic flame was lit by Olympic winners Paavo Nurmi[1] and

---

[1] Paavo Johannes Nurmi (1897-1973), one of the 'Flying Finns, a Finnish middle- and long-distance runner who still holds the position of the world's most successful Olympic athlete of all time.

Hannes Kolehmainen[1]. These two 'Flying Finns' were national heroes and the perfect ambassadors for our country – at previous Games, Nurmi had won nine gold medals and three silver medals, and Kolehmainen had won four gold medals and one silver medal. Sadly for Kolehmainen, at the 1912 Games, the Russian flag was raised for the members of the Finnish team, and he had said that he almost wished that he had not won!

Of course, they were not running any more, but the Finns still managed to win six gold medals, three silver and thirteen bronze medals at the 1952 Games, meaning that they were ranked eighth – a great achievement for our small nation!

It was very exciting for me to listen to the daily broadcast of the Games on the wireless. And it was not only how the Finns performed that interested me. I recall that our cousins, the Hungarians, did very well, also, winning a large number of medals. And I do not think that there was anyone at the time who was not impressed by the speed of Emil Zatopek from Czechoslovakia, who won gold in the 5,000 metres, the 10,000 metres and the Marathon, the latter being a new event that year.

But, as I said, it was that year that we had an unexpected visitor at Ainola, and he came in the early hours of the morning. I do not know at exactly what time he arrived, but it must have been between four and seven o'clock in the morning; for I went to bed late that night, after 4 a.m., and I awoke at 7 a.m.. When I woke up, I had a strange feeling, sensing that something was amiss, so I got up. I went first to the study and discovered that the drawer of the writing table was open, and 60,000 marks had disappeared.

"Someone, someone has been in the house!" I shouted, waking Aino up.

"Ugh. What? Who has been?" Aino replied, sleepily.

"Someone has been here – an intruder!"

It was alarming that he had been rummaging in the study just meters away from where we were sleeping. And when we went downstairs, we found further evidence of his thieving.

"Not only did he take the money," said Aino, "he drank some

---

[1] Juho Pietari 'Hannes' Kolehmainen (1889-1966), a Finnish middle- and long-distance runner, known as the 'Smiling Hannes' and the first of the 'Flying Finns'. Between 1912 and 1921, he lived and competed in the United States.

cream and took the caviar on his way out!"

"Huh! A burglar with sophisticated taste buds!"

Poor Aino, she was most concerned. "We must call the police immediately! Are you all right, Janne? You look as though you have seen a ghost!"

"Yes. The, the outside doors, they, they, they need to be locked. In summer, they are always left … wide open. But we, um, cannot do that now, can we? They, they need to be locked, for the night. And the windows, they need to be closed downstairs … and in the basement."

The situation was, in fact, worse than we thought; it transpired that our burglar was a murderer, no less, who had escaped from prison! I said to Aino that it was a good thing that I had not woken up earlier and caught him in the act, otherwise, he might have killed us!

Nevertheless, I wanted to make sure that the police did not give out any information about the burglary to the press; I did not want foreign newspapers writing negative articles about life in Finland. After all, a burglary committed by a convicted murderer was unheard of in Finland, so our 'visitor' was not worth making a fuss over.

When Santeri came after Christmas, he enquired about our festivities.

"Eventful – yes! – quite eventful!"

"Did the girls come to visit?"

"Oh, yes. The girls, they came. And, um, we had one extra visitor!"

Santeri hesitated. "You mean, Father Christmas?"

"Well, yes, he *did* come. But I meant … another visitor."

"I am afraid that I cannot guess."

"Well, would you believe it – a *murderer* came! To burgle Ainola!"

"What! Surely not!"

"Yes! He did! Fortunately, the, the culprit, he ran away. With the money! But, um … at least, he did not murder us!"

"Hmm, yes! But when did this happen?"

"The, the night before Christmas Eve. I woke up early and, um … I *knew* that, er, something had happened … while we were asleep – I have this sixth sense, you see."

"Sixth sense?"

"Er ... yes! There are other instances when, when I have been in danger and ... I have escaped harm."

"Ahh? Have you? When?"

"Yes. In New York, for example. Have I, have I ever told you that story? Perhaps ... I have. You see, when, when we get old, we, um, start repeating the same, old stories!"

Santeri smiled and said, "I cannot say that you do that."

But I think that he was just being polite. Why would I have been any different to other old people? But, as I could not say, for sure, whether he had heard it before and I really wanted to recall it, I continued my story:

"This adventure – if you can call it that – it, it happened in New York – a long time ago. There was a, a taxi driver in, er ... where they usually are. And ... I wanted to go to a restaurant. So, um, I asked him to take me to one. But – and I do not know why – but he, he took me into a, a dark and ... murky-looking, run-down area. And he stopped the car in front of a ... bar – a squalid one, in my opinion. So, naturally, I was a bit hesitant. But ... I got out of the car, anyway. And there were steep steps – I remember the steps. Going down. Very steep. Leading down to the establishment. And it was halfway down, when, when I had a, a most unpleasant feeling ... about the situation. A man – to me, he looked like a gangster – stood there, as if ... waiting for me. I thought, 'This is a trap!' So, I, um, turned on my heel and ... *ran* back up the steps. And I ran away from that place as fast as, as, as my legs would carry me!"

"That must have been scary! I wonder who the man was."

"I have no idea. And, and I did not wish to ... stay and find out! Then, er ... there was a similar incident, in Berlin."

"You were in another dangerous situation?"

"Yes, I was. It was a ... restaurant. In, in the outskirts of Berlin. I had just ordered my meal when, um ... someone, a complete stranger, passed me and said to me, er ... quietly, that, that, foreigners, they can get drugged and robbed in that place. So, I, um ... pretended to go to the lavatory but I picked up my coat and ... left!"

"Good Heavens! You have been very lucky twice. No, three times."

"No, *four* times! And, and this is the scariest one of all. Ah ... it must be over thirty years ago that, that I met a, a famous Finnish airman, Major Väinö Mikkola. He, he was going to Italy, with two young officers, to fetch two … Savoia planes, um, for the Finnish armed forces. So, Mikkola said to me: 'You should come with us. You would enjoy a spectacular flight across the Alps!' Well, I was quite tempted. Anyhow, for some reason, or other – I cannot remember now – I was not able to go on the flight. And, and it was a good thing, um … that I did not go."

"Ahh, why was that?"

"It, it was terrible; both planes crashed! In the Alps. And, and all the airmen, they died! The, the, the planes exploded!"

"Exploded? That *is* terrible … why was that?"

"No one knew. Although, um, there was talk – of sabotage. But … nothing was proven. A mystery, the whole thing is a mystery."

"You certainly do seem to keep out of harm's way!"

"Yes! Coincidence …? Good luck …? I do not know. I have no idea how to, er … explain it. But … it is as if, um, there is some, some greater power. Protecting me."

"God is protecting you?"

"Who knows … you see, I am not a believer in the way that, that my mother was. But, er … when I see the sun, after a long period of rain, or … when I witness the harmony in nature, that is, um, what I call God. I suppose that God, He reveals himself to me, er, most clearly, through … my music. I think that, that Christ must have been a good man!"

"He undoubtedly did good works."

"Yes. But … to say that He was, um, a good *man*, I would never have said that in, in front of my mother!"

"Why not?"

"That, Santeri, would have meant that, um, I was denying the, the, the divinity of Christ. And, and there could be nothing worse than that, in my mother's eyes! And she often talked about the, um … Second Coming of Christ. But, er, I do not think that, that He should come a second time; they would only crucify Him, again!"

Santeri nodded. "Yes … they undoubtedly would!"

"Religion, Santeri, it is something that, that I have often … thought about. But I am not, er … the kind of person who would go to church. I would not feel comfortable about, um … showing my devotion … in public. It is a private matter. And … if, if that is not acceptable to God, then, er … why did He make me, um, such as I am?"

## Chapter 32

# Slowing Down

Now that I was almost ninety, I was doing a lot of thinking – and hardly any composing. The *desire* to compose was still with me, but the *compulsion* was not. Therefore, I was spending much of my time either reminiscing about the past or reflecting on things that I had not had the time to reflect on in my busy youth. Even when I was listening to the wireless in the evenings, I would find my mind wandering – I would relive incidents and long-forgotten experiences, and recall conversations from years gone by.

"I am officially … old," I said to Aino one day.

"And how did you reach that conclusion, Janne?"

"Well … whatever Santeri says, I think that, er … I, I do retell the, the, the same stories, again and again. That is, um, what *old* people do!"

"Well, none of us will remain young for ever!"

"Hmm, I have been thinking that, er … it is a pity that, that we do not think more … about things … when we are young."

"What sort of things?"

"All sorts of things."

"Such as?"

"Er … whether we have done the … right thing."

"But none of us does the right thing all of the time!"

"Yes, but, um, *I* have made so many … mistakes – more than most people! You see, nowadays, I ma-ma-manage fine, without, um, even a brandy, after dinner. But … there was a time … and, and it pains me to think of, of all that time that I … wasted. And which I cannot get back!"

"But we are happy now!"

"Yes, we *are*. But … how much time do we have left …?"

"No one knows how much time they have left. We must take one day at a time and make the most of it."

"Yes ... I suppose so. But, you know, Aino, that, um ... I could not have done any of it – the music – without you."

She laughed. "Is that so?"

"Yes, it *is* so. And ... I must tell you that, that, when, when I die, I want to be buried here, at Ainola. And, and I want, um, you to be buried at my side. For, er ... it is, it is at my side that, um, you have always belonged!"


"Last night, I heard *Finlandia*, on the wireless. But, er ... I could also hear, um, Beethoven's *Egmont Overture!*"

Aino and Santeri both stared at me, before saying, in unison, "What do you mean?"

"I, er ... have not noticed it before, but, um ... *Finlandia*, the, the, the beginning of it, reminds me of the ... *Egmont*."

"But they are not the same, Janne."

"Well ... similar."

Santeri looked at me questioningly. "It would be difficult, I suppose, *not* to be influenced by someone as great as Beethoven, however unintentionally."

"Yes. We, we modern composers, we would not be, um ... whe-where we are ... without our forebears."

"And, Janne, you *love* Mozart!"

Santeri's eyes lit up. "So do I."

"Whereas, I *respect* Beethoven," I said.

"But I love Brahms, although Janne does not *quite* understand that."

I looked at Santeri. "In, in my view, Brahms, he is, um ... an epigone of Beethoven – although, er ... Brahms's music is heavier. And ... o-o-overly emotional, perhaps. But, but I suppose that one can say, um, that, that he became clearer ... in his old age."

"Oh, Janne! Whatever do you mean by that? Are you saying that his earlier works were not good?"

"My, my wife, she is a romantic, Santeri – that is all that ... I am saying."

Brahms had turned me down in Vienna, all those years ago, when I had wanted him to teach me. That was why I was reluctant to sing his praises now – I did admire Brahms's music, but I did not want to admit to it. In fact, his use of the brass section of the orchestra had influenced my own writing quite considerably.

"Brahms, he, and many other composers, they, they died relatively young. So, they did not have, um … the, the, the pressure on them, um, to compose, in later life – the pressure that, that I have had. Although, I have all but … given up now."

"Do not pay any attention to him, Santeri. He will change his mind about it tomorrow!"

"But, but Bruckner, he was an exception. He, um, started composing his Ninth Symphony in … in his sixties! *And* he struggled … in the, in the same way as, um … I have done. He, he worked on his Ninth for years and years and, er … he *never* managed to finish it."

Santeri leaned forward in his chair. He was clearly interested in what I had to say about Bruckner.

"His symphonies, they are … poetry – yes, Santeri – poetry!"

"But I do not think that everyone has thought so."

"No … I, I cannot understand why he is so, um, maligned. Perhaps it is on, on, on account of his compositions, er … being so original, and they do not like, um … his sudden shifts of tempo. And key. Apparently, people, they left the concert hall in, in the middle of the première of his … Third Symphony. Huh, what a … distressing, and hu-hu-humiliating, state of affairs that must have been!"

Aino and Santeri both nodded.

"But his music, um, such striking ideas … about structure, and harmony. And orchestration. There is hardly a bar, in, in his music, that … sounds like any other composer – it is music of, of, of great beauty! But … as I said, he struggled. He, um … rewrote his Third as often as, as I rewrote my Fifth! Nevertheless, he, er, believed in his vocation, I suppose."

"As you yourself have done, Janne!"

"Well … yes. *I* continued writing – for … I needed to say more – in, in a more compressed form. But *Bruckner*, I, I cannot, um, e-e-express exactly why his music … speaks to me. In, in the way that it does. The sudden shifts in mood … the darkness … and light – that is what it is."

Aino and Santeri evidently saw that speaking of Bruckner was important to me and they, tactfully, remained silent.

"His, his music is, er … intensely spiritual. You see, he never married. So the, the most important relationship, um, that, that he had, in his life, was … the one with God – one can truly feel it, in his music. One of the, um, loveliest codas, in, in my opinion, ever written, can be found, er, in the Adagio of … his Sixth Symphony. In fact, I once had, um, tears in my eyes when, when I sat in the library, listening to it … on the wireless. Perhaps, one day, er, people will understand his … genius."

"Janne has always been very sensitive and quite often has tears in his eyes when he is listening to music."

"We, we composers, we are *all* sensitive. If, if we were not, we would not be composers!"

Santeri looked thoughtful. "Perhaps *I* should listen to Bruckner!"

"Indeed, you should! All his symphonies, they are a … journey. Towards something. In, in that sense, they, um, set the, the, the listener … a challenge. And you will be impressed by the, the enormous breadth of all the phrases … and the great, sprawling forms. The melodies, they, um, go on for ever. And, and what is wonderful is that when, er … when the phrases finish, often there is a pause, for the music to … breathe."

"I see. So, what would you recommend me to start with?"

"Well, er … I would start with the Fourth. There are wonderful, enormous vistas, in the Fourth. Romantic harmonies … with classical rhythms. It is majestic and grand. And your spirit, when, when you hear the Finale, it will soar!"

"It sounds impressive! It seems that I am destined to like Austrian composers."

"I am sure that, um … you will thoroughly appreciate Bruckner. There is a lot of, of the feeling of the … folk music of Austria, in his music. But, but that is not what his music is … all about. It, it, it is about, about the clashes of elemental forces – like my own music is."

I noticed that Aino got up and went to fetch some coffee, and I could not make my mind up whether she had intended to fetch the coffee anyway or whether something that had been said had aroused unpleasant memories for her. Indeed, the clashes of elemental forces were prominent in my music, but so were the clashes in my personal life. During my most productive years, we had not enjoyed a harmonious marriage. Nowadays, she no longer alluded to the difficult times, but I still wondered whether there was something beneath the surface, something that she fought hard to control so as not to disturb the new-found contentment of these later years.

However, she returned to the room with such a broad smile on her face that I immediately put all my doubts to rest. In spite of everything, she had stood by me, and there was no greater confirmation of her love than that smile.

No, I did not doubt my wife's affections, but what I had begun to doubt was the quality of the music that I had composed. Now that I had given up the idea of ever completing the Eighth Symphony, I started to go over all the music that I had composed. And it made me anxious – to the point where it tormented me at night when I was trying to sleep.

Perhaps it was one of the disadvantages of growing old; all our achievements suddenly become questionable and prey on our minds, so that we wonder whether we have left anything behind that has any real worth.

I had also begun to ponder the question of how long my music would live on, after I was dead. I had no illusions about my indispensability and I knew of many – so far, unrecognized – composers who would rise to prominence and be more than adequate replacements for me. I had never doubted their integrity for one moment and I greatly admired their music. In fact, some of them had sent me their scores, and I had recognized in them the flowering of musical genius.

Where, I had often asked myself, would the musicologists of the future place my music? And how would my symphonies ultimately be rated? After all, they were the works for which I had sacrificed so much, and yet, up to this point, the reaction to them had not always been so positive.

I hoped that time would rectify this and that, in the future, people would be less concerned with their unusual form and more concerned with listening to their content. Then, they would be better able to appreciate that I had attempted to create art, as defined by Tolstoy; writing about emotions that the listeners of my music and I had in common.

Beethoven, too, had made many sacrifices for his art, which was why I was troubled by some modernists' lack of appreciation for his greatness. Beethoven's works had certain failings, but they *lived*, and the moral depth of his work was beyond compare. In fact, it was owing to the fact that I had felt so strongly about his music that I had asked Santeri to reply to the letter from an English editor who had wanted me to write a critique of Beethoven for some sort of symposium. I told Santeri that Wilhelm Furtwängler[1] had written an article in which he had expressed exactly what I would have said about Beethoven. So, Santeri just sent Furtwängler's article to the editor in question; for, luckily, I had cut it out of the newspaper and kept it.

I hardly recognized myself nowadays when I looked in the mirror. Aino said that I was handsome in my youth, but now I was much fatter, and bald, and the skin over my eyes and under my chin was sagging. I had also developed the protruding lower lip that is typical of heavy drinkers.

Aino had aged much more gracefully than I had. In my eyes, she did not look much different to the girl that I fell in love with – apart from the fact that her long, dark hair was now grey. She still dressed prettily and had that same gentle look in her eyes that had beguiled me all those years ago. If I had precious little else in my life now, at least, I had Aino.

But how much longer did we have left to live? Most probably, I would be the first to die; for I was older than she was and, in truth, I was beginning to sense that I did not have many more years in front of me. I was beginning to get fragile and, indeed, I was now sleeping downstairs; for I found it too difficult to climb up to the upstairs bedroom.

In spite of that, when I got up in the morning, I shaved – albeit with difficulty on account of my trembling hands – and I put on my suit and tie, and leather boots. I needed to look my best in case we had unexpected visitors, although, nowadays, there were not quite so many of them as there used to be. But, of course, on special occasions, we had a full house, and there was a

---

[1] Wilhelm Furtwängler (1886-1954), a German conductor and composer, widely considered to be the greatest symphonic and operatic conductor of the 20th century. He favoured a weighty, less rhythmically strict, more bass-orientated orchestral sound with a more conspicuous use of tempo inflections than was on the printed score.

lot of hustle and bustle.

Then, before I knew it, it was my ninetieth birthday. When I woke up in the morning, my bedroom was full of the intoxicating scent of flowers. In fact, large bouquets of all kinds of flowers had been arriving at Ainola for days, and we were running out of places to put them. The scent in my room was so intense that it took me back in time to when I was a boy; it was as if I was in the flower shop where I often went with my mother.

That morning, I was the first one to rise, as I always was. Some members of the family had arrived the previous day for my birthday celebrations, but they were still in bed, as was Aino. When she came downstairs, she gave me a big birthday kiss.

"Yes, I am ninety now! Not much longer to go –"

"We will not have any of that kind of talk today! Ninety is a big milestone, and we will celebrate it with joy!"

I leaned over and kissed her forehead. "Every day is a, a celebration when, um … I can spend it with you!"

"Oh, Janne! You are getting more and more charming!"

"Yes, perhaps I am! But … I, er … hope that, that we will not have … *too* many visitors, today. I am too old now to, to, to spend hours … talking to people. And, um … I would not like to be a, a disappointment … to any visitors."

"That is why I have specifically arranged it so that we have a quiet day, just for the family. Of course, if people arrive here with cards and presents, we will not turn them away, but I will tell them politely that you cannot cope with too many visitors – I am sure that they will understand."

"But, but I am not complaining. Every day, I count my … ble-ble-blessings. And congratulate myself on, um … having married someone like you. I, I doubt that, um … I would have lived this long, without you. By my side."

"Well, I do not know about that … but what would you like to do today?"

"Er … I, I might venture out. For a short walk … later. With the grandchildren."

"And Hellu is cooking something nice for your birthday lunch."

"Hopefully, she is, she is not going to … any trouble."

"I am sure that she does not mind. Shall we have some breakfast now? What would you like to have?"

"I think that, um … I will have my usual – porridge with brown sugar. Perhaps, perhaps that is the, the secret of my … long life!"

Aino laughed. "In that case, you had better *continue* with the porridge!"

While we were having breakfast, the rest of the family began to wake up and, before long, the entire family had assembled at the breakfast table. There they were – Eva, Ruth, Katarina, Margareta and Heidi, with their husbands and my grandchildren – all seated around the table, ready to celebrate my special day.

Their smiling faces and effusive congratulations touched me to the bottom of my heart, so that I felt a tear roll down my cheek – which I hurriedly wiped away. I felt happy *and* sad at the same time; happy that we were all together, but sad at the realization that there would not be many more occasions like this one.

I was also sad for another reason. On occasions like this, I always felt that there was someone missing – and that someone was Kirsti. But I never said anything to anyone – for fear of appearing maudlin, and I did not want the other girls to feel that they were not enough for me – but I mourned little Kirsti, nonetheless, and always said a silent prayer for her.

"Well, who would have, um … imagined that, that Pappa[1] would live … this long?" I said.

"Long? What is the young man saying?" said my son-in-law Aulis, to everybody's great amusement.

"Well … but … at least, I am in spirit!"

"Yes, indeed you are, Janne!" said Aino.

"Yes. But … if getting old is worth celebrating, um … I wonder whether, whether there will be … a cake, later?" I said.

Aino nodded. "Yes, we will be having a large layer cake with cloudberries and cream, and Hellu has also made some *rahkapiirakka*[2] and *mustikkapiirakka*[3]."

"Mmm! Enough for, for all of us, I hope, and, um … perhaps some left over!"

"There will be enough for you to feast on for days!"

"There are so many telegrams," said Nipsu, "and they are still

---

[1] Grandad.

[2] Sweet curd cheese pie.

[3] Blueberry pie.

coming! There must be thousands of them by now!"

What she said was true; congratulatory telegrams had been arriving at Ainola for days and showed no sign of stopping – messages came from people such as Sir Thomas Beecham, Eugene Ormandy, King Frederick of Denmark and President Heuss. But most of the telegrams came from the United States. I also received a lot of claret, my favourite wine, from France. That was in addition to all the letters and parcels from people all over the world. Even Winston Churchill sent me a box of Havana cigars – of course, cigars were something that I received in abundance, again – and Toscanini sent me his recordings of my music.

Furthermore, there were wonderful tributes from Vaughan Williams and President Paasikivi. Vaughan Williams said that I was truly original and that he did not count as civilised those mid-Europeans who ignored me. He also said that great music was written, he believed, not by breaking the tradition, but by adding to it, and, in that sense, I had shown that the new thought that could be discovered in the old material was inexhaustible. I was grateful for his words and very pleased that he had understood what my music was all about.

In a wireless broadcast, Paasikivi said that my music – inspired by the ancient Finnish people and the rugged beauty of Finland – would live for ever. I certainly hope that it will.

"I think that the whole world is celebrating with us," said Heidi.

Indeed, there were many concerts devoted to my music all over the world, from Helsinki to New York, from London to Shanghai. Many of the concerts were broadcast on the wireless throughout the course of the day, including one conducted by my friend Sir Thomas Beecham from the Royal Festival Hall in London. This was quite a long concert, and I was particularly pleased that the Fourth Symphony was played, as well as some of my lighter pieces. The concert also included the British and Finnish national anthems and an address by Sir Thomas.

Special arrangements had been made for me to hear the concert; it was beamed on an especially powerful signal and relayed to me at Järvenpää. But it was a great pity that, as Aino told me later, I had fallen asleep while listening to it!

## Chapter 33

# The Twinflower

For our school botany project, we had to collect a certain number of plants during our summer holidays. For some, this was a real ordeal but, for me, it was a great pleasure, and I happily spent hours in forests and meadows looking for good specimens. These I took home and the first thing that I did was to put them between the pages of books to press them. When they were dry, I then mounted each one on a large piece of paper and wrote its Latin name and a brief description of it underneath.

This taught me a lot about plants. And there was one plant, in particular, that I really liked – the twinflower. I thought that it was the most delicate flower imaginable. Carl Linnaeus[1] named it *Linnæa*[2]. It became his favourite flower after he had been to Lapland, where it grew in profusion, and he said that it was as close to perfection as a flower could be.

A member of the honeysuckle family, this evergreen plant, with rounded, slightly oval, leaves, is a Finnish treasure. It is found in shady areas of old fir forests where the floor is mossy. There it stands tall, often reaching two meters or more in height.

The paired ponderous, bell-shaped flowers with their five-lobed, pale pink corolla were so fragile-looking that, as a boy, I was mystified that such a diminutive flower could produce so much scent. I would describe its scent as sweet and light, not quite that of fir, and lighter than that of a rose, more reminiscent, perhaps, of the smell of a butterfly orchid or lilac.

Unfortunately, twinflowers only flower for a short time, in June and July, and my mother told me that they did not last long as cut flowers, which is why, she said, it was better to leave them

---

[1] Carl Linnaeus (later ennobled as Carl von Linné) (1707-1778), a Swedish botanist, physician and zoologist who devised the formal two-part naming system we use to classify all life forms.

[2] *Linnæa borealis* in Linnaeus's later classification.

in the forest.

Whenever I close my eyes and picture these wonderful flowers, I can smell their heavenly perfume, and I am reminded of Eino Leino's poem, *Nocturne*:

'…

I do not laugh or grieve, or sigh;
the forest's darkness breathes nearby,
the red of clouds where day sinks deep,
the blue of windy hills asleep,
the twinflower's scent, the water's shade –
of these my heart's own song is made
…'[1]

I enjoyed reading Eino Leino's poetry when I was young; for he expressed perfectly what I felt in my heart about nature – and what many of us Finns would never have been able to express ourselves. Nature and its effect on people is something that most, if not all, Finns understand. If you were to ask a Finn what his three favourite things were, undoubtedly, one thing that he would mention would be 'untouched nature'.

Now that I was not busy composing any more, I had plenty of time to enjoy nature. Even if I did not venture very far outside – particularly in the winter, that was the case – I spent quite a lot of time each day looking out of the window and enjoying what I could see from there.

But I had grown so frail of late that I was very different to the man that I used to be. Not only were my eyes failing me, and my hands shaking, but I was also growing quite breathless when I exerted myself. Climbing the stairs to the upper floor of the house was becoming quite a challenge; I had the will to climb the stairs, but my legs had difficulty in carrying me. This was a typical sign of old age, I thought; the mind insisted on making decisions that the body could not agree with. And so, I saw myself as being as fragile as the twinflower, and the brevity of its flowering was akin to the time that I had left.

I had lived on earth for ninety years, and so much had happened in that time – both to me personally and to my country. It seemed like light years away when I was a boy, collecting flowers, and I hardly remembered my mother and father any

---

[1] From a translation by Keith Bosley.

more. My father was but a smell – the smell of tobacco – and, as for my mother, she was even less tangible. More tangible were the memories of the food that she prepared. For instance, I remember running home hungry in the summertime to have a bowl of *talkkuna*. I really enjoyed it, as I still do. And it never ceases to amaze me how something so delicious can be made of leftover grains, but when the grains are roasted in the oven with peas and turned into flour, and salt added, it produces something that, to me, is food heaven-sent. It is, to my mind, the quintessential summer food, and there is nothing like it when a little bit of sugar is added and it is mixed with cold *piimä*.

My mother sometimes made *uunijuusto*[1] for which my brother, sister and I had a great passion. We did not get it very often but, when we did, we enjoyed it all the more. Again, the smell of it coming from the oven was one of those things that stayed with me over the years and, indeed, whenever I think back to my childhood and youth, it is the smells and sounds that come back to me above everything else.

And when I thought about my years at the Institute, I remembered the music, and the laughter and the singing, and the smell of wine at Busoni's parties. Now, sadly, Busoni and so many of my other friends had long passed away.

However, I clung on to the memories, vague as they were; for I now spent my days looking backward rather than forward – there was little else that could happen to me from now on. Things were happening to other people in other places – but not to me.

And I sometimes wondered why people sent me beautiful things when I had little time left to enjoy them. And yet, the gifts kept on coming.

There was the German lady, for example, who sent me, without fail, a wooden figure of an orchestral musician every time that I celebrated a birthday. The very first one was of the leader of the first violins and that was followed by a cellist and a trumpeter. Then, one player or sometimes two arrived on each birthday, and I placed them on the window ledge in the library with the others.

Eventually, I had collected an entire orchestra and, when she sent the last figure, which was the harpist, I wrote to her to thank her – as I always did – saying that the orchestra was now able to

---

[1] Oven-cooked dish made of bovine colostrum. It has curd cheese-like consistency.

play any symphony!

She was not the only person to show such kindness and generosity towards me; there were many others. And I had always considered it a matter of common courtesy to thank them, knowing that my letter would mean a lot to them. Every Christmas, for instance, a lady from America sent me a cake, and Santeri and I made sure that she received a letter of thanks for her trouble; for her cakes not only looked good but they tasted delicious.

I was grateful for these gifts – of course I was – but I sometimes thought that, instead of sending cakes to me, the American lady should have given them to poor people who were in greater need than I was. It was wrong, in my view, that there were people in the world who had so little. But that was the way it had always been: some people lived well, while others did not. This would not change.

However, many other things had changed in my lifetime. I had lived through two World Wars and a civil war in my own country, and I had seen seven Finnish presidents in office so far: Ståhlberg, the very first president, Relander, Svinhufvud, Kallio, Ryti, Mannerheim, Paasikivi and now Kekkonen. But how long would Kekkonen be in office[1], and who would succeed him? And what would the future hold for Finland?

In Russia, there had been three tsars, after which there had been four secretaries of the Soviet Union, the latest being Krushchev, who had been elected in March 1953.

As regards our neighbour Sweden, there had been ten prime ministers under the United Kingdom of Norway and Sweden, Boström having served two terms, and twenty-one prime ministers under the Kingdom of Sweden, most of them having served very short terms – under a year – although Hansson served for no less than ten years and eighty days!

There had also been numerous different leaders in other parts of the world. I had lived through the presidencies of Roosevelt –

---

[1] Urho Kaleva Kekkonen (1900-1986) became the longest-serving president in Finland, holding the office for 26 years. Under his autocratic leadership, Finland prospered, and he became almost a cult figure who is revered even today by many Finns. However, Anatoli Golitsyn, a former KGB Major, claims that, since 1947, Kekkonen was a Soviet agent, codenamed 'Timo', a view now widely accepted by most historians.

Theodore Roosevelt – Taft, Wilson, Harding, Coolidge, Hoover, another Roosevelt – Franklin D. – and Truman, and now Eisenhower was in office, having been elected in January 1953.

There had been quite a few British prime ministers in my lifetime, as well. In fact, there had been so many that I could not remember them all, and some of them had been prime minister more than once, including Churchill. The latest one was Sir Anthony Eden, but who knew for how long?

When I thought about the fact that I had lived long enough to witness all these men coming and going, it made me feel very old indeed.

Sometimes, when I sat in my armchair in the corner of the library, I reflected on how much life had changed, and I amused myself by making mental lists of things, such as, all the inventions that had been patented since I was a boy.

Our lives had been transformed by such things as the typewriter, the telephone, the microphone and the aeroplane, and advances in the field of medicine meant that we now had the X-ray, a vaccine for polio and a wonderful thing called penicillin. Our lives were easier now, we had more freedom and we were destined to live longer when many serious diseases were either preventable or curable. Man's ingenuity never ceased to amaze me. I was but a humble musician, but there had been those who had been able to give so much more to the world than I had.

But, in spite of all the progress, were people any happier now? I did not think so.

I have learnt that man's happiness does not stem from material things alone. He needs to belong somewhere – I myself have always belonged at Ainola. And to feed his soul, he needs such things as poetry and music. Therefore, perhaps even I have had something to offer for man's survival in the world.

However, ultimately – and this I sincerely believe – to be happy, man needs to be at one with nature. Despite Turgenev's pessimistic view that nature is indifferent to man's fate, which I partially agree with, nature offers a sanctuary where the mind comes to rest.

Nature is also an inspirational world, full of wonder and colour, and awe-inspiring beauty. Where would *I* have been without the whispering silver birches, the fragrant, towering pine trees that stood as solid as rocks and the lakes that glistened in the summer sun and became dazzling ice rinks in the winter?

How would I have survived the cruel arrows of disaster and misfortune had I not been able to follow the movements of the birds in the forest or to marvel at the majestic beauty of an elk trotting through a glade?

I only hope that I will see such images flashing before my eyes as I leave this life for the next one.

*Chapter 34*

# Another Birthday

Now that Aino and I were growing old, each birthday that we celebrated had much more significance than the ones of our youth; so many of our friends and acquaintances had passed away that we were grateful for each successive year.

We lived quietly and sedately and, for my part at least, happily. Gone were the petty arguments that tormented our daily existence when we were young and they had been replaced by contentment, jollity and a feeling that, at last, we sailed on a calm sea.

Our days revolved around meal times, and, after lunch, we always had an afternoon nap, which we found very agreeable. When we woke up, we had coffee and *pulla*, and we both thought that this was the best moment of the day. We had fun reminiscing about the past, and recalled the many people who had come into and out of our lives, including some of the more 'unusual' characters – Axel Carpelan being one of them.

By this time, we were both becoming fragile but, in the main, we were still hearty and healthy. We lived each day without any great expectations and were satisfied with what we had, which was each other.

Sometimes, I did not know what day it was, but that was not on account of me losing my faculties, it was merely a reflection of all the days becoming as one. When people are at home day after day with no engagements to go to, it does not actually matter what day it is.

Like many elderly people, we rose early — I rose even earlier than Aino, sometimes as early as 4 a.m.. I would go into the kitchen, get myself a drink and then potter around the house. In the summertime, I would venture into the garden but, in the winter, I would have to be content with observing through the window what was going on outside.

I enjoyed the stillness of early morning, before the world woke up, and I would imagine how, in a few hours' time, the daily routine of people in the capital would begin.

Helsinki, the city where my musical life had taken shape, now seemed a million miles away. But, in my absence, it lived and thrived. While my immediate successor would be Rautavaara[1], the Conservatoire was full of aspiring musicians and composers, some of whom, one day, would write masterpieces. Following their own paths, they would take Finnish music into new directions.


It was Aino's eighty-fifth birthday. This was worthy of a special celebration, and I dearly wished that she would have a day to remember. Hence, I planned to surprise her; I arranged for twenty red roses to be delivered to Ainola early in the morning, before Aino was awake, and I had decided that I would take them upstairs to her bedroom. I had not climbed the stairs to the upper floor of the house for quite some time, owing to my impaired mobility, so it was quite a considerable undertaking and required a great deal of effort on my part. However, I was determined to meet the challenge that I had set myself and I resolved that, even if it took me all morning to do it, I would climb those stairs!

Hence, holding on to the rail with one hand and tightly gripping the bouquet of flowers with the other hand, for fear that I would drop them, I began my slow and careful climb up the stairs. And I managed to reach the top. I rested for a short while to get my breath back and then continued to Aino's bedroom.

---

[1] Einojuhani Rautavaara (b. 1929), a Finnish composer of contemporary classical music who is regarded as one of the most notable composers after Sibelius. His prolific output includes eight symphonies, 14 concertos and several biographical operas, e.g. on Vincent van Gogh, Aleksis Kivi and Rasputin.

But, when I knocked on the door, there was no response, so I knocked again, and a sleepy voice asked who was there.

"Me!" I said.

"Is it you, Janne? Surely, it cannot be you!"

"It, it *is* me! Can I ... come in?"

"But of course!"

I opened the door and walked over to Aino. She was wearing a flowery nightdress, and her hair was a little dishevelled after sleeping, but she looked so pretty in the morning light.

"Happy eighty-fifth ... birthday! These, these roses ... they, they are for you."

"For me? Oh, Janne, how wonderful! What a nice surprise! You remembered!"

"Have I, um ... e-ever forgotten?"

"No, I do not believe that you have."

"No, the, the, the tenth of August, it, it is a date that ... is engraved on my memory! I may have forgotten, um, ma-many things, but, um ... *that* I will never forget."

"Ahh, but how did you manage to climb up all those stairs?"

"Well, my dear ... it is ... one, one of life's little miracles!"

"And how long did it take you?" she said, suppressing her laughter.

"Quite a long time – yes! – quite a ... considerable period of time! Although my mind, it, it is still ... vi-vigorous, my body, it is, well ... deteriorating! But, but to see your happy face ... and your smile, at the unexpected, um ... it, it was worth it!"

"But you might have fallen!"

"But ... I did not."

Aino smelled the roses and sighed with pleasure. "They have such a delicate perfume! And they are at their most perfect – not in bud, but not in full bloom, either."

"As, as perfect as, um ... you are, my dear! As you have ... always been."

"Janne Sibelius, you are an old fool!"

"No, no! I am, er ... romantic, by nature – I was, I was brought up on ... Tchaikovsky! Therefore, I come to, um ... propose to you a, a second time ... if I may."

Aino laughed. "I never regretted my first answer!"

"Well, that is a ... relief! And ... there might be some more, um, surprises ... for you, today."

"I do not think that I need any more surprises after this!"

"Nevertheless, there ... shall be some!"

"Oh, this is quite exciting!"

"Well, er ... it should be! On your birthday."

"I think that perhaps I will get up now. Have you had any breakfast yet?"

"No, I was waiting for you."

"Waiting for me? You poor thing, you must be hungry. Let us go and have breakfast together!"

"If, if I am able to ... get down the stairs!"

"Now you have me to help you!"

"Indeed ... as I, as I have always had, and, um ... for which I am, eternally, grateful."

And so, Aino and I made our way down the stairs and into the dining room. And that was when Aino got her next surprise.

"Happy Birthday!" was what greeted her, and there, seated around the dining room table, was our entire brood with their spouses and our grandchildren.

"Eva and Heidi, they, um ... came late ... last night. After you had gone to bed. And, and the others ... not long ago!"

"Oh, how wonderful! This is *such* a wonderful birthday!"

"And, and the weather, it, um ... is going to be good! So, perhaps, we, we will have lunch ... outside. And afternoon coffee, also – coffee, it always tastes better outside!

"It does! Yes, let us do that."

"But, um, shall we first ... have breakfast ... and then see w-w-what presents we can find?"

"But I do not need any presents! To have you all here is a present enough!"

"Ah, wait until, um ... you see what I have for you!"

After breakfast, with all the family exchanging news and gossip, I handed Aino a small box wrapped up in blue crêpe paper. Everyone stopped talking; they waited eagerly to see what was in the box.

"Of course, I, um ... did not choose it ... myself. I, I sent word to the, to the shop, um ... about what you would like. And, er ... I think that, that they made a very wise choice ... on my behalf."

"Oh Janne, it is one of the most beautiful things that you have ever given to me!"

"I thought that, um, you would like it ..."

"What is it, Mummy?" said Katarina.

Aino handed over the box to her. "Oh, it is the most beautiful necklace! It must have cost a fortune!"

"Well, the cost, um ... it, it is immaterial when ... it is for a, a fine lady, like your mother!"


## Chapter 35

# A Long Hot Summer


It was a very long, hot summer this year – one of the hottest that I can remember. And it was not only hot in the daytime, it was also stifling at night, making it difficult for us to sleep.

When it is very hot, it is tiring for old people, and we were forced to take things easy. During the hottest time of the day, we might even have gone down to the lake, hoping to catch a little breeze, and settle down in our deckchairs, in the shade, and either read or just let the day go by. Invariably, we just dozed off. Although the hot weather was tiring, we enjoyed all the sunlight that we had so little of in the winter.

In the evenings, when it was slightly cooler, we felt a little more energetic, so while I sorted out my papers, for instance, Aino liked to potter in the garden. Although her rheumatoid arthritis prevented her from doing much, she still wanted to look after the garden that she had cherished for so many years. Later in the evening, she would sometimes sew or knit socks. A little activity, such as gardening or knitting, she said, was good for her arthritis, as was the warm weather.

But now that autumn has come, and it often rains, we have to spend a lot of time indoors. Therefore, we read and listen to the wireless more than we did in the summertime. Santeri still comes regularly, but we do not have many other visitors, compared to the number of people that we used to entertain. Besides, if the weather is bad, even fewer people come. However, that is just as well; for we are quite content when there is just the two of us. And that leaves us time to reminisce about the old days!

Both Aino and I now have the habit of telling the same story twice – or sometimes even more than twice – but that does not matter to us; for we like to hear the other one recalling all the details of what happened and who said what. And it is remarkable how much we remember from long ago – Aino, in particular, has the unique capacity to remember whole conversations that took place many years ago – and, yet, we often do not remember what it was that we did yesterday! And it has happened more than once that Aino mentions the lunch that we ate not so many hours ago, and I cannot recall what we had, however hard I try.

But we laugh about these moments of forgetfulness, knowing that there are many more to come and that there is nothing we can do about it. In fact, we laugh a lot nowadays – perhaps it is true that we mellow as we age – and nothing seems to disturb us in the same way as it might have done when we were young. Also, we know that we will not live for ever, so why would we spend the time that we have left worrying about trivial things? Hence, we take one day at a time and enjoy life as much as we can.

But we are not only reminiscing between the two of us; we like to tell our grandchildren, and also Santeri, our stories which they seem to find interesting and amusing.

Our Christmases provide many stories; for example, how the family used to gather around the piano to sing when I played Christmas songs – I had even written some of them myself, such as *En etsi valtaa, loistoa*[1] and *On hanget korkeat nietokset*[2].

And how difficult it always was to get the children to go to bed on the night before Christmas Eve, and how we told them that *Joulupukki* only brought presents to *good* children and smacked the bottoms of the naughty ones with a twig. Luckily, none of our children were ever really naughty. And they delighted in telling us that, adding that *surely Joulupukki* would bring presents, as he had

---

[1] Named after the first line: 'I seek no gold or majesty' (from English revised translation of the lyrics by Alexandra Glynn). One of the most popular Christmas songs in Finland.

[2] 2 Named after the first line that translates as: 'Abundant snow in deep drifts'. A popular Christmas song in Finland.

done so *every* Christmas! But they did worry about whether the presents would be labelled clearly; for there were so many of us that they might get mixed up! But when *Joulupukki* handed out the presents on Christmas Eve, he never made a mistake; everyone got the right presents.

And imagine the chaos that ensued when the girls began opening their presents – there were boxes and wrapping papers all over the floor. But it was a wonderful kind of chaos, which we would not have exchanged for the world.

However, one Christmas, there was chaos of another kind when the candles caused the Christmas tree to catch fire, and we were all rushing to fetch buckets of water to put the fire out!

And it was that same Christmas that Aino received a beautiful Christmas card which the sender had forgotten to sign! Unfortunately, Aino did not recognize the handwriting on the envelope, and we were puzzled as to who the sender was – it was obviously someone who was a little absent-minded. We checked the postmark to see where the card had come from, and that told us that it was from someone local, but Aino still could not work out who it was.

She then decided to look in the cupboards for some old Christmas cards and, sure enough, she found one signed in the same handwriting on it as the address on the mystery card. The identity of the sender was, finally, solved!

Easter was another colourful celebration in our household, with many traditions. The children spent a long time making a *pääsiäisvarpu*[1] – or, rather, several of them – and then, on Palm Sunday, they recited the Easter rhyme to relatives and exchanged each *pääsiäisvarpu* for chocolate treats. And, on Easter Day morning, they woke up to find that the Easter Cockerel had been to lay chocolate eggs under their pillows. Surprisingly, none of them ever questioned the idea that a cockerel laid eggs! But neither did I when I was a child; for when we are children, we believe whatever we are told, however impossible it is. We also believed that, at Easter, witches – flying on broomsticks with their black cats and coffee pans – came to steal wool from the sheep in the farmers' barns!

---

[1] A colourfully-decorated catkin twig.

We also like to reminisce about our own childhoods and, particularly, how exciting it always was when summer came. I especially remember when my brother, sister and I went to stay with my aunt in Loviisa, and we had nothing to do all day but play and swim!

Sometimes, we took out the rowing boat and laid down in it, with our arms stretched over the edges. We were so relaxed, enjoying the feeling of the hot sun on our skin. The little trickling noises that our fingers made in the water were the only sounds that we could hear in the stillness of the day. When the boat slowly drifted along the shoreline, we would look up at the pine trees and marvel at how straight their trunks were, reaching far up to the sky.

I often say to Aino that I would so much like to be able to go back in time and relive one such day. It would be like returning to paradise! They were wonderful, carefree days, when anything was possible, and there were magical lands beyond the horizon.

And if only I could turn back the clock and see my mother and father one last time.

When I think of my mother, I wonder whether she was happy, and I find myself concluding that she was not. I am sure that she found it difficult to live with my father, who was, by all accounts, a heavy drinker who was hopeless with money. Unfortunately, I became the same, and it makes me sad to think of this, knowing that Aino would have had an easier life if she had been married to someone else, and not to me.

But I have to console myself by thinking that I must have *some* redeeming qualities; for how else would Aino have continued to love me? In spite of my shortcomings, I believe that Aino has taken comfort in knowing that I have always loved her, and only her. I know of many a man who has left his wife for another woman, but I have never been tempted to do that. Indeed, I have never even contemplated it.

I thank God a million times a day that I have had the honour of sharing my life with Aino. Not only has she been an exemplary wife but she has also been a wonderful mother to our children, who all adore her, as do our grandchildren.

But how strange it sometimes feels to talk of us having grandchildren when it does not seem long since our own children were small. Yet, all our girls, our babies, are grown up and have children of their own.

In many ways, now that there is just the two of us, it is good that I no longer have the compulsion to compose; for, if I was locked up in my study all day, she would feel lonely. Besides, I delight in her; for she has a quick mind and a playful sense of humour – as well as still being, in my eyes, the prettiest girl in Finland.

And there are still plenty of things for us to enjoy. Simple things, like watching the clouds drift by in the changing colours of the sky or following the colourful autumn leaves as they flutter through the air, can be most pleasurable. Aino often says that, if you look closely, there are many more different colours in the sky than you first think – coming from an artistic family, she notices such things. She also often comments on how beautiful the branches of the birch trees look against the sky and how delicate their branches are.

We also spend a lot of time watching the birds in the garden. For some reason, the birds have been singing more this year than I have ever heard them sing before, but perhaps it is my imagination. I think that, of all God's creatures, I still love the birds the most. Maybe the reason for this is that they appear so vulnerable – I do not know. I often think that their legs are so tiny that it is amazing that they can carry their weight.

And what makes a bird suddenly fly off into the distance; does it have an express intention, or does it simply tire of being in one place for too long? And how many times does a single bird take off and land each day? These are the things that I often ponder.

I love all birds, but I do have a particular fondness for the swans and cranes. In fact, today, I saw a large formation of cranes flying very low over the house. I heard them coming – for they were extremely noisy – and Aino and I managed to get out onto the veranda in time to see them. It was a magnificent sight.

"There! There they are, um ... the, the birds of my youth!" I said.

"Mmm, the autumn is over ... they are flying south," Aino replied.

Then, we saw how one crane detached itself from its fellow travellers and circled the house. But as soon as it had done that, it rejoined the other birds, and they all disappeared into the blue horizon.

"It is sad to see them go," Aino continued, wiping away a tear.
"Yes …," I said, putting my arm around her, "it is …"


The End


# Postscript

Two days after he stood with Aino on the veranda at Ainola, watching the cranes fly south, Jean Sibelius died of a brain haemorrhage, at the age of ninety-two. He collapsed while having breakfast and died at nine o'clock in the evening on Friday 20 September 1957. Four days later, his obituary contained the line: 'Music is made from sorrow.' It is believed that this was at the request of the composer himself.

A private memorial service was held at Ainola, on Sunday 29 September, during which Jussi Jalas played *The Song of My Heart* and music, depicting Prospero, from *The Tempest*.

After the ceremony, the composer's body was transported to Helsinki by motor hearse. Musicians from the Helsinki Philharmonic Orchestra and the Radio Symphony Orchestra acted as pallbearers and carried the coffin into Helsinki Cathedral, where Tapani Valsta played music by J. S. Bach on the organ. The cathedral then remained open for people to pay their last respects to the dead composer, his body being guarded by students.

The next morning, over one hundred wreaths were laid at Sibelius's coffin by Finnish and foreign government officials and representatives of various organisations. The last two wreaths were laid by President Kekkonen and one of Sibelius's grandsons, on behalf of Aino Sibelius. The ribbon on Aino's wreath bore the words: 'Thanking you for a life blessed by your great art. Your own wife.' The music played during the service consisted of two hymns by the composer, *The Swan of Tuonela*, *Il tempo largo* from the

Fourth Symphony, *In Memoriam* and three sections from the music for *The Tempest*. As the coffin was carried back to the hearse, it was accompanied by *Marche funebre*. Thousands of people lined the streets to watch the long funeral procession to Ainola where the composer was buried in a private ceremony.

Aino Sibelius continued to live at Ainola after her husband's death, spending her time sorting out family papers and helping Santeri Levas and Erik W. Tawaststjerna, who were both writing biographies about the late composer. Sibelius's daughters took it in turns to visit Ainola so that their mother did not have to be alone. Aino died on 8 June 1969 – two months short of her ninety-eighth birthday – and was buried alongside her husband, her name being inscribed on his memorial stone.

In 1972, Sibelius's daughters, Eva, Ruth, Katarina, Margareta and Heidi, sold Ainola to the Finnish state, and it was subsequently opened to the public as a museum in 1974.

Eva (b. 1893) took charge of the family's affairs after her father's death. She and her husband, Arvi Paloheimo (1888-1940), M.A. (Law), a businessman, had a daughter, Marjatta Kirves (b. 1915-2013) and two sons: Janne (1922-1989), B.Sc.(Econ.), an adviser on real estate; and Martti (1917-1987), M.A. (Law), a bank manager. Eva died in 1978, at the age of 85.

Ruth (b. 1894), an actress at the Finnish National Theatre, was married to Jussi Snellman (1879-1969), an actor at the same theatre. They had two children: Erkki Virkkunen(1917-2013), M.A. (Law), a bank manager; and Laura Enckell (b.1919). In 1951, Ruth was awarded the Pro-Finnish medal for acting and, in 1963, she received the Jussi-Prize for the best female lead for her role in the film *Ihana Seikkailu*. She died in 1976, at the age of 82.

Katarina Elisabeth ('Nipsu') (b. 1903) and her husband, Eero

Ilves (1887-1953), a bank manager, had two children: a son, Jan (b.1927), B.Sc. (Econ.), a pianist; and a daughter, Merike (1925-2006), a TV journalist. Katarina died in 1984, at the age of 81.

Jeanne Margareta (b. 1908), M.A., married Jussi Blomstedt (who later changed his name to Jalas) (1908-1985), a teacher and a prominent conductor. An author and translator of books, including titles on Sibelius, she was the only one of the composer's daughters to have a university degree. She and her husband had three sons and two daughters: Risto (1929-1956), M.A. (Law); Paul (1937-1941); Tapio (1941-1993), a flautist and lecturer; Aino Porra (b.1946), an oboist; and Satu Risito (b.1943), a violinist. Margareta died in 1988, at the age of 80.

Heidi Kristina (b. 1911) became a renowned ceramic artist, and her work can still be seen at the Ainola Museum. Her husband, Aulis Blomstedt (1906-1979), an architect and a professor, designed an extra building for the museum in the 1970s. This building is now the museum's café (Café Aulis). Heidi and her husband had four sons: Juhana (1937-2010), a painter and a professor; Petri (1941-1998), an architect; Anssi (b.1945), a film director; and Severi (b.1946), an architect who designed the renovation of Ainola in the 1980s. Heidi died in 1982, at the age of 71.

Benno Aleksander ('Santeri') Levas (born Lehmann) (b. 1899), M.A., published seventeen books, including several titles on Sibelius. He was also known internationally for his photography and he was the chairman of the Finnish Photographic Society, an honorary member of Fédération Internationale de l'Art Photographique and an Associate of the Royal Photographic Society. Levas died in 1987.

# Sibelius's music

Sibelius's music is seen as the very embodiment of his native country, growing organically from the Finnish lakes and forests. Although he was, and still is, well known for his tone poems, as well as nationalistic works such as *Finlandia*, Sibelius regarded himself first and foremost as a symphonist, and many musicologists consider him the most important symphonist since Beethoven.

Each of Sibelius's symphonies marked a new structural development, culminating in the single-movement Seventh, which was an intense condensation of musical expression distilled into twenty minutes.

Like Beethoven, Sibelius set a challenge for future composers, and Finnish composers, in particular, have been faced with the dilemma of either following in his musical footsteps and seeking inspiration from Russian composers, such as Prokofiev and Shostakovitch, or allying themselves with more avant-garde composers, like Stravinsky, Schoenberg and Webern.

In recent years, his music has seen a huge revival, thanks to the many eminent Finnish conductors holding posts abroad who have championed his music and reinterpreted his scores. Whilst his music continues to be popular, not only in Finland, but also in England and the United States of America – as it was in his own time – it is regaining favour in many other parts of the world. His most popular pieces are *Finlandia*, *The Karelia Suite*, *Valse Triste* and the Second and Fifth Symphonies, although the more enigmatic Fourth and Sixth Symphonies are proving more and more popular.

The use of Sibelius's music in films and TV programmes has been widespread – there are over 120 credits to his music, examples of which range from the early *Leaves out of the Book of Satan* (Denmark, 1920, *Finlandia*), *The Jazz Singer* (USA, 1927, *Pélleas och Mélisande: Mélisande*) and *Death Takes a Holiday* (USA, 1934, *Valse Triste*) through *The Unknown Solder* (Finland, 1955, *Finlandia*), *Salomé* (Italy, 1972, *Valse Triste*) and *Monty Python's Flying Circus* (UK, 1974, *Finlandia*) to *Die Hard 2* (USA, 1990, *Finlandia*),

*Radioland Murders* (USA, 1994, *Valse Triste*), *Paragraph 195* (Germany, 2002, *Symphony No.5*), *Kinsay* (USA, 2004, *Violin Concerto in D Minor*), *The Mentalist* (USA, 2011, *The Karelia Suite*) and *Grace of Monaco* (UK, 2014, *Valse Triste*).

Finlandia has also lent itself to various modern renditions, such as those by The Finnish symphonic metal band Nightwish and The Finnish thrash metal band Stone. What would Sibelius have thought about a cover version of *Finlandia* by Nightwish, featuring a solo for uilleann pipes (Irish bagpipes) – the band used *Finlandia* as an intro to their live concerts, such as those in the Imaginaerum World Tour – or Stone opening their album *No Anaesthesia!* with a metal rendition of *Finlandia*?

And what do Sibelius and James Bond have in common? Tom Service of *The Guardian* posted a blog on the Internet on Wednesday 15 September 2010 in which he suggested that composer Monty Norman, who wrote the famous James Bond theme, might have been a secret Sibelius fan. Referring to the little-known work entitled *Cassazione*, written by Sibelius in 1904, Service wrote: 'It starts with a typical Sibelian shimmer of strings playing a tremolo. And the music they perform is the riff from the James Bond theme.' Monty Norman, he said, transposed the original Sibelius up a major third, but the two tunes share a symmetrical semitonal ascent and descent up a major second in equal note values, and they are played at approximately the same speed.

Following the success of *Finlandia* as a full-length tone poem, Sibelius also published the 'Finlandia Hymn'. Its original Finnish lyrics were by opera singer Wäinö Sola, but the version that is heard today, first performed in 1941, has lyrics by Veikko Koskenniemi.

Other songs to the tune of *Finlandia* include *Gweddi dros Gymru* (*A Prayer for Wales*), several *alma maters* of universities, such as St. Ambrosia, Iowa and Capital, Ohio, *Land of the Rising Sun* (the national anthem of the short-lived African State of Biafra) and a number of Christian hymns, namely: *Be Still, My Soul*; *I Sought The Lord*; *We Rest On Thee*; *A Christian Home*; *This Is My Song*; and *I Then Shall Live*.

\* \* \*

For a long time, it was not known for sure whether Sibelius had ever written a complete score for the Eighth Symphony, but there was much speculation on the matter. Finally, years after the composer's death, his relatives handed over manuscripts to the University of Helsinki, amongst which were sketches for what appeared to be the Eighth Symphony. It is now being debated as to whether an attempt should be made to reconstruct the symphony, or whether his desire to leave it unpublished should be respected, and his legacy left as it is.

## About the author

Caroline J Sinclair, a graduate in modern languages, is an Oxford-based author who has a keen interest in classical music. She has done extensive research into Sibelius's life and music, including sourcing information from his letters and diaries, enabling her to keep the story historically authentic and factually correct. Furthermore, having once lived in Finland, she is familiar with the Finnish language, culture and customs. Her first novel was on the life of Ludwig van Beethoven, and she is currently working on the third book in this series of famous composers' memoirs.

## Main sources

Barnett, A. (2010) *Sibelius*, New Haven, Yale University Press.

Goss, G. D. (2010) *Sibelius: A Composer's Life and the Awakening of Finland*, Chicago, The University of Chicago Press.

Gray, C. (1934) *Sibelius*, London, Oxford University Press.

Grimley, D. M. (2011) *Jean Sibelius and His World*, Princeton, Princeton University Press.

Levas, S. (1972) *Sibelius – a personal portrait*, London, JM Dent & Sons Ltd.

Mäkelä, T. (2011) *Jean Sibelius*, Suffolk, The Boydell Press.

Rickards, G. (1997) *Jean Sibelius*, London, Phaidon Press Ltd. (Used with discretion due to its factual errors)

Tawastjerna, E. (2008) *Sibelius* Vol I-III, London, Faber and Faber.

https://en.wikipedia.org/

https://fi.wikipedia.org/

sib.fi/

www.ainola.fi/

www.edu.vantaa.fi/

www.heikel.com/

www.sibelius.fi/